Praise for *Emis*

"A wonderful journey away from t... start to this intriguing series."

—*RT Book Reviews*, 4 stars

"Readers of inspirational fantasy will enjoy [Bunn's] foray into a new genre."

—*Publishers Weekly*

"A superbly crafted fantasy adventure novel that engages the reader's total and rewarded attention from beginning to end. Very highly recommended."

—*Midwest Book Review*

"A thrilling new journey in the realm of fantasy and science fiction. Filled with action, romance, and subtle humor, this is the beginning of a promising new series."

—*LifeIsStory.com*, 5 stars

"Locke is a master wordsmith, weaving lyrical prose, fully fleshed characters, and a consuming plot into a tale that is beautiful and epic."

—*BuddyHollywood.com*

"Moves like a contemporary thriller but harkens back to the enduring genre of classic fantasy."

—*FamilyFiction.com*

"Thomas Locke transported me into this wonderful, dangerous world . . . An amazing fantasy novel."

—*Fresh Fiction*

Praise for *Trial Run*

"*Trial Run* is wonderfully told: a swift, engaging story that shows a large understanding of the human condition, our essential frailty, our drivenness, our need for connection. As three stories collide, Locke brings into play some key questions that face each of us as human beings: Do we know what is really going on? If we don't, can it destroy us? This is artful writing, full of suspense."

—**Jay Parini**, *New York Times* bestselling author
of *The Last Station*

"Readers will love this storyline . . . A true psychological thriller that cannot be put down . . . An awesome jaunt into a world that may be closer than we think."

—*Suspense Magazine*

"A thrilling cocktail of science, technology, and danger elegantly served at breakneck speed. Intoxicating and seriously addictive as only Thomas Locke can deliver."

—**Tosca Lee**, *New York Times* bestselling author
of *Forbidden*

"High tech mixed with intelligence gathering, combined with a fast-paced story and evocative writing. *Trial Run* grabs readers from the first page. Locke weaves words to create masterfully evocative descriptions, scenes, and characters. The science is presented in a Crichton-esque manner, compelling readers to believe that not only can it be true for some future date, but it is probably being used in some secret laboratory right now. *Trial Run* will make a great last-of-summer read. Once you start, you won't want to put it down."

—**BuddyHollywood.com**

"Thomas Locke masterfully keeps the suspense level taut throughout the book. It is a rare author who can create such dramatic tension in a storyline that contains areas of technical discussion, like quantum computing, while still maintaining a character-driven plot. A fast-paced, constantly unfolding mystery with well-developed characters, *Trial Run* promises to begin a strong new series that manages to transcend the bounds of science fiction writing."

—*The Manhattan Book Review*

MERCHANT
of ALYSS

Books by Thomas Locke

MERCHANT
of ALYSS

THOMAS
LOCKE

Revell

a division of Baker Publishing Group
Grand Rapids, Michigan

© 2016 by T. Davis Bunn

Published by Revell
a division of Baker Publishing Group
P.O. Box 6287, Grand Rapids, MI 49516-6287
www.revellbooks.com

Printed in the United States of America

Library of Congress Cataloging-in-Publication Data
Locke, Thomas, 1952–
    Merchant of alyss / Thomas Locke.
        pages ; cm. — (Legends of the realm ; #2)
    ISBN 978-0-8007-2386-6 (pbk.)
    ISBN 978-0-8007-2448-1 (cloth)
    1. Magic—Fiction. I. Title.
PS3552.U4718M46 2016
813′.54—dc23   2015027194

16   17   18   19   20   21   22   7   6   5   4   3   2   1

This book is dedicated to

Phyllis Tickle

Wise Counselor, Dear Friend

ETHRIN
LYSTRA
BADLANDS RANGE
EMPORIS
GREAT DESERT
ELLISMERE VALE
ROTHMORE VALE
FALMOUTH PORT

OLOM
HILLS of ALYSS
ALYSS
YELLOW REALM
EASTERN SEA
THE REALM

1

Falmouth Port was gripped by a late winter storm. Upon the battlements, the cold bit like nature's acid. The broad stone passage that rimmed the city wall was made treacherous by fresh ice. The soldiers on duty endured long hours and searched silent roads. The avenue leading from Falmouth's main gate to the northern highway was empty. The wind seemed determined to drive the sleet straight through the night watch. After every circuit, they slipped inside the tower room for a mug of brew heated on their central fire. Which meant only one soldier noticed the solitary man that hour before dawn. At least, when the night was over and the guard was forced to endure the earl's harsh questions, he was fairly certain the lone traveler had been a man.

The stranger halted by the blacksmith stables. His back was to the distant vales and the lonely route leading to Emporis, the city at the edge of the known world. His cloak shivered and rippled, but otherwise the tempest did not touch him. He seemed to study the gates and towers intensely, though the lone soldier could not be certain, for the traveler's face remained hidden beneath a cowl.

The soldier's unease mounted and twice he called for his mates, but the wind clawed the words away. The guard was young and courageous and known for his artistry with blade and bow. But the longer he stood there, the more his belly was gnawed by something he could not name. He gripped his sword's pommel and forced himself not to flee.

Finally the cloaked figure broke off his inspection and turned down a side lane. The soldier felt his chest unlock. He watched the empty road for a time, until his best mate clapped him on the shoulder and told him to go warm himself by the fire. But the young soldier knew he was obliged to take a dreaded move.

Gingerly he descended the icy stairs and pounded upon the door at the tower's base. "Officer of the watch!" He heard nothing in response save the wind's constant howl, so he pushed open the door and entered the tower's lower chamber. "Begging your pardon, my lady."

Captain Meda had been knighted by the earl following the Battle of Emporis. She had a well-earned reputation as a fierce brawler with a fiery temper. She was sprawled on the cot, her weapons heaped upon the watch table. All but the long knife in her hand. "What is it?"

"Thought I saw something, ma'am."

"Either you saw or you didn't. That's your duty. Not to think. Try again."

"A lone stranger. He stood at the point where the Emporis road meets the smithy's stables. Watched us for a good long time."

Meda swung her feet to the floor. "Is he there now?"

"No, my lady. He turned away." He fidgeted, fearing a good old lashing for what sounded feeble now, here in the warmth and safety of the officer's ready room.

But Meda seemed to find nothing amiss in his report. "No one else noticed?"

"I was the lone guard by the west tower. The gate is sealed, and the storm . . ." He shrugged. "Perhaps it was nothing, Captain."

"Your name. Corporal Alembord, is it not? Recently arrived from . . ."

"Havering. Yes, ma'am. With the last ship."

"Just in time for winter." She offered a tight smile, meant to reassure. "Now tell me why you felt this deserved my attention."

"Something about the man made me clench up tight as a fist. And . . ."

"Go on, Corporal. Speak your mind."

"The cloak he wore wasn't touched by the wind. He stood facing straight into the storm, but the cowl that covered his head . . ."

Alembord halted as the captain leapt from the bed. The snarl on her face caused him to take an involuntary step backwards, ramming into the door.

Meda demanded, "What was the cloak's color?"

"Couldn't say, Captain. Not in this storm. The torches

lining the road were all doused. All I could see was his silhouette."

She reached for the scabbard and belted it to her waist. "Where did he go?"

"Down the side lane." This time, when the snarl reappeared, he knew he was right to have come. "Toward the emissary's home."

"Twenty men, Corporal. Armed and in the forecourt. Three minutes." She flung open the door. "Who is the wizard on duty?"

"Wizard? Ma'am, we're ordered to have nothing to do with that lot down in the palace cellars—"

His words were cut off by a blast that dwarfed the storm and shook the palace. Alembord and the captain were both flung onto the flagstones.

Meda scrambled to her feet and leapt through the door. "Alarm! Sound the alarm!"

Alembord forced his limbs to obey his addled brain. He struggled into the palace forecourt and used his sword's pommel to pound the brass gong. Another blast ripped the darkness, illuminating the troops who scrambled and slithered across the icy stones. Alembord managed to hold to his feet, though he quailed at the sight of sleet turned to flying rubies by the illumination. He rang the alarm as lightning flashed red as the dawn he feared would never come.

❖

The road leading to the forest was empty, which was hardly a surprise, for it meandered past frozen corrals and empty stables and unoccupied hovels. When the crimson mage of Emporis had been defeated a year and a half earlier, the wild border clans had returned to their valley fiefdoms, but only after swearing fealty to Bayard, Earl of Oberon and Lord of Falmouth Port. Some claimed Bayard was also the rightful king of all the realm. But they did so softly, even here in the heart of Oberon's land, for throughout the rest of the human realm such words carried a death sentence.

The traveler stopped a second time where the emissary's grove met the lane. This would hardly be cause for notice, were it not for the hour and the storm. All the city's dwellers paused here from time to time. Many made it a destination when courting or simply filling an idle hour. Legends were recounted here, about green-skinned people that emerged from the forest and secretly planted the trees. About battles that ravaged the land with forces not seen for over a thousand years. About the man who dwelled in the unseen house within the supernatural glade. None denied the fact that magic had been applied, even though the obscure sciences were officially forbidden throughout the realm. But here, in this place, the power of enchantment rose in silent defiance to all such human laws.

Between the emissary's grove and the western forest stretched a vast expanse of stumps and knee-high new growth. Over the previous decade, the woodland had been cut back three hundred paces by the refugees. Clansmen who had managed to escape the crimson rider's wrath had cut the forest to erect crude huts. The emissary's grove had been planted just seventeen months earlier, the same season when the badland refugees returned to their vales and sought to rebuild their lives. Yet the glade that began where the traveler stood was already taller than the city gates, with trunks thick as a warrior's girth. Some who stopped here claimed they could actually hear the trees grow. On this night, however, the only sounds were the shrieking wind, a distant shutter pounding against an empty window, and ice cracking on tree limbs as they danced.

A narrow lane of white stones weaved through the emissary's grove. The stones were another marvel, as none had ever seen the like before. Some claimed they were a gift from the Ashanta, a telepathic race few had ever glimpsed. The Ashanta were said to fashion their fabled cities from these very same stones, which led to much conjecture over what this meant, being laid as a path through a glade all knew to be enchanted. The softly glowing lane curved twice as it passed through the trees, so that the emissary's home and its surrounding gardens remained unseen.

The stranger stood there for a time, long enough for anyone else to freeze solid. Yet he seemed as untouched by the tempest as the emissary's glade. The tall trees blocking the stranger from the home moved less than the traveler's cloak. Were it possible, it might have seemed that the trees watched him intently. Waiting to see what he might do next.

The traveler started forward.

Instantly the trees bowed inward, lacing their branches together.

The traveler backed away. The trees now blocked the lane with a shield of bare winter limbs, woven tight as a wicker wall.

The traveler snarled a curse and opened his cloak. Attached to his belt in the same manner that another might carry a sword was a wand carved with a multitude of symbols and topped by a glass orb the size of a thumbnail.

The wizard raised the wand above his head, aimed the tiny orb at the glade, and droned a few words, enough to light the orb and the woven limbs with a crimson fire.

The branches trembled as the force sought to wrench them apart. But the trees revealed their own power as they resisted the command and the blast and the shaking of the earth. Instead, when the tremors and the fierce red lightning ended, the remaining trees drew together more tightly still.

The wizard roared a spell with such fury his words emerged in a writhing spew of fire. The verbal onslaught joined with the orb, which burned now with a blinding ruby light. The power crackled and hissed through the air before blasting into the grove. The earth shook more violently still with the second spell's power.

The first line of trees was demolished. The sleet was tainted by the bitter taste of magical ash. Not even the stumps remained. The nearest empty hovels were also flattened by the backlash.

But beyond this new destruction, the trees appeared more tightly woven than before. Thirty paces deep the grove stretched, every tree now a living guardian. Intent upon sacrificing life for duty.

Again the wizard raged his volcanic spell. Again the lightning blasted. Another line of trees was reduced to flames that hissed and vanished.

The wizard started to unleash another detonation. Then he realized that the glade was now on the move.

Trees to his left and right ripped their roots free of the frozen earth. They moved with the sullen grace of Ancients. The earth shivered from the impact of their gnarled limbs striking the frozen ground. They encircled the spot where the traveler stood, closing off his escape.

Then they started in. Now they were the ones on attack.

The wizard lifted his wand high over his head. He shouted words not heard in a thousand years. The tempest plucked at him, shredding the cloak and then the mage into a million crimson flecks.

The wizard and his wand were gone. The sentinel trees swatted at the swirling mist, but they might as well have sought to halt the sleet.

The trees remained as they were for a time. But when shouts arose from where the forest lane joined the highway, they clumped and they marched and they rejoined the glade.

When the first grey glimmer of daylight forced its way through the tempest, the human soldiers and palace courtiers who gathered by the emissary's white-stone lane could find no sign of anything amiss. Even the ash was gone.

2

Two days later, there was nothing to show for the ferocious spring storm save puddles. Hyam and his wife walked beneath a benevolent sky. The light was still strengthening, and the morning was already springtime warm. The trees dripped a noisy pattern as the couple left the glade and turned toward the port.

At the main route leading to the city gates, they joined an impatient throng. Farmers and merchants jostled and cried and shoved, as was always the case on market days. Joelle spoke with a farmer who supplied them with cheese, while his wife and daughters shooed a flock of squawking geese. The prime spots around the city's main squares would be taken within the hour.

Ahead of them, the city rose like the onyx crown of some forbidden warrior race. Falmouth was fashioned from the black rocks upon which it stood. Where some might find the unbroken dark stone forbidding, Hyam thought it held a timeless grace. Within the outer walls ran narrow lanes that were home to a quarter-million souls. At the city's heart rose the inner keep, rimmed by broad plazas and fountains, where stood the homes of courtiers and the richest merchants. Within the ancient second wall stood the palace.

The earl's residence sprouted eleven towers. Since the Battle of Emporis, they were crowned by the banners of those first badland clans who had come to the aid of the Oberons. All of these clan names were officially banned by the king who now possessed the throne in Port Royal. But what the king felt about the earl's defiance no one knew, for the ruler had not been seen since the crimson foe's defeat. Today the standards hung limp and easy in the windless dawn, as though promising a calm to all who dared call Falmouth home.

Hyam's wife saluted the guards on duty by the moat bridge. Joelle trained with sword and knife as often as her magical duties permitted. She liked the company of soldiers, particularly the women who had flocked to the earl's banner. The king in Port Royal had forbidden all female soldiers from serving within the realm's borders. The Earl of Oberon defied this ban as well. He regularly sent word throughout the realm that all troops who sought to serve beneath the ancient banners were welcome, men and women alike. Bayard's current mission was being led by Edlyn, Mistress of the hidden orb. Trace had reluctantly accepted the position of Master Wizard until her return. He daily accused the absent mage of tricking him into a role he was born to loathe.

Joelle was happiest on the days she could slip away from the stone-lined caverns where the magicians practiced their arts, and join the earl's company in the brash and noisy training ground. They knew her abilities and her role in the Battle of Emporis. They made her welcome. This brought her untold joy. Before her arrival in Falmouth, Joelle had never belonged anywhere.

Captain Meda lolled by the outer moat, a position she had maintained for most of her duty hours since the assault on the glade. Her shield and battle sword leaned against the bridge support. Few women felt comfortable wielding a full-sized blade. But Meda was as seasoned as she was tough, one of the first officers hired by Hyam, and a veteran of many battles. She studied the passing crowds with a gaze seamed by years of sun and harsh climes.

Meda greeted the couple with, "Where is Dama?"

"Guarding the house," Hyam said.

"You should let her accompany you," Meda said, her eyes never still. "I've never known a better beast for sniffing out danger."

Hyam indicated a trio of lowing calves being forced through the gates. "A wolfhound has no place in Falmouth on market days."

"Any sign of your attacker?" Meda asked.

"None." Hyam did not say what he thought, which was, his first alert of the assault had been Meda pounding on their front door.

Joelle replied, "The Elves claim the enemy hasn't returned."

Hyam stared at his wife. "When was this?"

"At dusk yesterday, and again before today's dawn. Three times they sang to the trees that bordered the lane. They searched the ground for signs." Joelle touched the sword's hilt rising above her right shoulder. "They urged me to carry the Milantian blade."

Hyam asked, "Why am I only hearing about this now?"

"How often have you avoided any mention I make of the Elves or their requests for us to join them? They have waited seventeen months, and still you will not agree to a feast day. I am tired of making excuses for why you will not accept their invitation."

"I should be told of such events," Hyam replied.

Joelle rolled her eyes and tugged on his hand. "I'm already late."

They did not speak again until they arrived at the inner keep's main portal. Hyam knew Joelle was readying herself for an argument, so he merely asked, "Shall I meet you tonight at dusk?"

"I may be late, and you shall not walk back alone."

"We've been through this already."

"But you did not agree." When he tried to turn away, her voice grew sharp. "Hyam!"

"Yes. All right. I'll wait for you."

"And you must let me tell the Elves you will come."

"Soon," he promised.

"Today!"

Hyam turned away. He waited until a turning hid him from view, and then he scratched the scars that ran from his right wrist to his breastbone. The physical wounds had healed well enough, but defeating the crimson mage had seared away Hyam's arcane talents and shattered his orb of power. The losses left him bereft in a manner that none could see and only a handful even comprehend.

To the citizens of Falmouth, Hyam was the reason why they lived and walked in safety. He now served as adviser to the earl, though he seldom attended the council meetings and never spoke when he did. He was the subject of minstrel tunes, his triumph carried in secret songs that were played throughout the realm. Hyam never discussed how much he ached for what he had lost. But Joelle knew he seldom slept well. She sensed his yearning for powers he would never know again. And she thanked him in her own silent way for how he struggled to look beyond his loss and be happy with what was still his to claim.

❖

It came to Hyam like a scent carried on a war-torn wind. But there was no hint of breeze within the city walls. Nor did he actually smell anything. But he knew it nonetheless, the electric potency of a spell not yet cast. He had almost forgotten how tantalizing the flavor really was.

He ran, stalking the scent like a ravenous wolf.

The crowds thinned as he rounded the keep's eastern side. The squares were smaller here, but also more elegant. Scattered about these neighborhoods were parks ringed with fruit trees and spacious manors. To his astonishment, the magical lure drew him to the house where he had been working for over a year.

Fronting a tree-lined park rose a square residence constructed from the dark Falmouth stone and adorned with the Oberon crest. This home held a warmth and peace that had always appealed to Hyam. Even now, when his belly quivered with a ravenous longing. Hyam pushed through the front portal and shouted, "Timmins!"

The maid bustled in from the kitchen, wiping her hands upon a flour-spackled apron. "They're all in the rear yard, your lordship. Every one of them dropped tools and quill the instant the colonel arrived."

Hyam raced down the flagstone hall, past the four grand chambers that served duty as chartroom, record room, and two libraries. Normally a city's keeper of records would hardly occupy such a villa. But Falmouth's chief scribe was also the earl's older cousin. The two had been friends since childhood. Bayard, Earl of Oberon, was a fighter and keen strategist who treated history as a road map to his next victory. Timmins was a scholar by choice and temperament.

Hyam slammed through the rear portal to find the scribe and three offspring and six apprentices clustered about a dusty wagon, joined by Timmins's thickset wife and a dozen grinning soldiers.

The scribe cried, "There you are at last. I've searched everywhere!"

"You haven't done anything of the sort," his daughter Shona chided. "Good morning, Hyam. How is Joelle?"

"Fine, she's fine." He nodded a greeting to Colonel Adler, once the officer in charge of Hyam's band and recently appointed head of the earl's castle guard. But Hyam's attention remained fixed upon the wagon. He pushed his way through the crowd and leaned over the wagon's side.

"A veritable treasure trove!" Timmins tended to speak excitedly over anything to do with the written word. "The legends have become alive before our very eyes!"

The soldiers were mud-spattered and road-weary. They held mugs of cider and munched happily on bread and cheese, enjoying the scribe's antics. Timmins was a favorite among those who called the palace home.

Adler said to Hyam, "Meda tells me you slept straight through an attack."

"Of course he did!" Timmins bent down to lift a grandson clamoring at his feet. "That's all the man does! Most mornings Hyam walks into the scriptorium and asks for a quilt and pillow!"

"You talk utter rubbish," his daughter said. "Hyam works harder than all of your apprentices together."

"Well, that's hardly saying a thing, is it." Timmins peered myopically at Hyam. "How could you possibly have dozed through the blast that woke an entire city?"

Hyam paid him no mind. Timmins was as outrageous as he was poetic and rewarded his friends with fierce affection. Timmins was counted among the city's finest teachers and called everyone dunderheads, including the earl. He was never satisfied, no matter how great the effort. He was happiest when peering over a lost scroll or a book abandoned for centuries. He made the past come alive and put flesh to the long-dead bones of myths and legends. He had friends everywhere.

Hyam had no idea what he expected to find in the wagon bed. All he could say for certain was, the source of power lay there before him. The dusty tarp was thrown back to reveal several dozen scrolls scattered amid clay shards. Four intact clay vessels were propped on blankets and lashed to the wagon's sides. The vessels would have stood taller than Hyam if held upright. But such a position would have been impossible, for their bases were curved and pointed like crude clay spears.

"These dunderheads actually broke one of the precious amphorae," Timmins groused. "Didn't you know you carried the wealth of centuries?"

"The pot was already broken," Adler replied. "And these scrolls are so old their script has vanished with the years."

Hyam reached for the nearest scroll and instantly felt the power course through him. He shivered with palpable delight.

"Never mind that lot," Timmins cried, and pointed at the top of the nearside vessel. "Observe the crest on this amphora! The past is come to life!"

But Hyam would not draw his eyes away. The scroll was so ancient the act of unrolling caused tiny flecks to fall off like dry scales. Even so, the unfurled document stole away his breath. His fingers trembled so badly he feared he would rip the vellum further. So he propped himself on the wheel spoke, leaned over the side, and settled the scroll on the wagon bed. Gingerly he unfurled it one handbreadth at a time.

Adler set down his mug and leaned over to study the nearest clay vessel. Shona moved up beside the colonel. Shona was seventeen, and a beauty. The scribe doted on his only daughter, though he complained to all within reach that she remained the one scroll he could never read. Shona was blessed with her father's questing mind and her uncle's fair looks. She also held Hyam in something akin to awe. Her two older brothers were both married with children of their own. If Shona had any interest in men or matrimony, she hid it well.

A crest was stamped in gold leaf upon the vessel's mouth, and then inscribed twice in the clay itself. Adler read, "Property of the merchant of Alyss."

"Not *Alice*, you dunderhead. This holds no maiden's diary. Ah-*liss*. The most famous of cities."

"Never heard of it." Adler traced a hand about the sloping base. "Why is this jug shaped so oddly?"

Shona replied, "Amphorae were designed to fit snug along a ship's curved hull. Imagine hundreds of these clumped together like eggs in a crate of their own making. They were used to carry the most valuable of liquids, finest wines and rare oils and refined fragrances."

Timmins demanded, "How did these come to be in your possession?"

"Ten days ago I arrived in Emporis on regular patrol," Adler said. "As we approached the city, a troop of Elven warriors emerged from the glade across the dread vale. You know the one."

Hyam nodded. "I know."

"One of them spoke our tongue. He said a desert trader had arrived bearing a legacy from the lost times. Those were his exact words. Because of their nature, the Elves were forbidden from allowing them entry. But it was urgent that these artifacts be brought to you." Adler paused. When Hyam did not respond, he asked, "Does that make any sense?"

He continued to inspect the scroll. "It does. Yes."

"We had scarcely settled into the barracks when we were visited by a drover named Selim. He asked if rumors of the king's latest edict were indeed true. When I confirmed this, the drover said his master had instructed him to offer these amphorae to the earl. He said he would accept whatever the earl felt was proper payment."

Hyam glanced up. "What edict is this?"

"The height of idiocy," Timmins cried. "The king has forbidden the ownership and the trade in all documents not written in human script!"

Adler continued, "The drover claimed his master was bitter beyond measure after lugging those amphorae almost six hundred leagues."

Hyam touched one of the unbroken seals and shivered as the power coursed through his fingers. "Does the trader have more?"

"I asked that very question and received no response. Nor would the drover let me speak with his master." Adler drank more cider and wiped his mouth. "We were tracked the entire way back from Emporis by troops in forest green. They dogged our steps and searched the way ahead."

One of the apprentices asked, "So where is this Alyss, anyway?"

"You really are the worst dunderhead that has ever tried to eat me out of house and home," Timmins replied. "Come over here so I can thunk your thick skull."

Shona offered, "Alyss was the largest trading city of the lost realm. Before the Milantian invasion, Alyss was a city of unimaginable wealth. Poems describe how many of the palaces were roofed in pure gold."

Adler gestured to the amphorae. "So these scrolls . . ."

"Are over a thousand years old!" Timmins finished.

Shona traced one finger along a wax stopper. "The question is, why would they use amphorae to store scrolls? Even the most valuable were transported in chests."

"Perhaps a scroll in one of the intact vessels will be legible." Timmins almost danced in place. "Would that not be a wonder to carry us through the winter!"

Hyam reluctantly broke away from his study. "You can't read this?"

That turned them all around. Timmins demanded, "Read what?"

He lifted the scroll. "The script here is clear enough."

Timmins and his daughter crowded in on either side. Shona asked, "You see text? Truly?"

"And designs." Hyam resumed his inspection of the ancient vellum. "Do they not seem to move before your eyes?"

Timmins leaned over until his nose almost touched the scroll. "I see nothing save ancient vellum." He slipped back to earth and exchanged a long look with his daughter. For once, the scribe was both somber and still.

Shona said doubtfully, "Perhaps it is the sun's angle. Move aside, Hyam." She slipped into his place, squinted, declared, "Still nothing."

Hyam touched one of the scroll's designs. The image was

traced by the same fire that accelerated his heart rate. "Truly, none of you can see what's written here?"

"I have no idea what you're talking about," Shona said.

Timmins said softly, "Tell us what you see."

"The script is Milantian," Hyam replied. "It appears to be a teaching scroll."

"For what discipline?"

Hyam looked from one perplexed face to the next. "War."

3

As soon as Hyam described what he was reading, Adler insisted the amphorae be taken straight to the inner keep. The wagon rolled and jostled over the cobblestones and halted in the palace forecourt. When Trace was alerted, he ordered the scrolls be carried to the wizards' largest cavern. There Hyam broke the seals and began reading each document. He occasionally halted work when exhaustion overcame him, or when Joelle forced food into his hands. Someone brought in a pallet that became his only resting place. He neither left the palace cellars nor saw the sun.

Two and a half days later, Hyam finished sorting the contents of the five amphorae—the four whose seals had remained intact, and the one that had arrived broken. Three massive tables, long enough to seat forty students on a side, were piled with carefully unraveled scrolls. In all they held fifty-eight documents. A fourth table contained another two scrolls. This pair were much smaller, scarcely wider than Hyam's hand. They were also written upon what appeared to be flexible sheets of solid gold.

Hyam turned to the gathered assembly—Trace, Meda, Adler, Joelle, Timmins, Shona, the earl, various mages and court officials. Tired as he was, he felt a piercing regret. Whatever came next, he knew he would soon leave the cavern and the documents' potent force.

Hyam addressed the earl. "Sire, what you see here is one small part of a larger collection. Much larger. A veritable library would be my guess. Perhaps several."

Bayard strode to the nearest table and peered down at one scroll. "Describe for me what you see."

"The script is precise and constant. The shape of each letter is identical. As though one scribe taught a hundred acolytes. Or perhaps they adopted this process over time."

Timmins offered, "Professional scribes, trained to the discipline."

Bayard nodded slowly. "What is the purpose?"

"So no individual hand is revealed," Timmins replied.

The earl turned to Trace and demanded, "You see nothing?"

"For me and all the other mages, the vellum remains blank." Trace indicated four of the wizards clustered to his right. "These are the only wizards in Falmouth who show an ability with Milantian, which is an almost impossible tongue. They see nothing."

Bayard was a careful strategist, a leader who made a lifetime practice of doing battle only when he was certain he had already won. He took his time, moving to the next table, his steps measured. "Why do you call this an impossible language?"

Trace said to Hyam, "Speak the words for him."

Hyam knew they were safe here. A thousand years of spells secured them far more than the surrounding rock. But he had been beaten as a child and forbidden to utter the tongue he had first been forced to learn. The early conflicts rose with bile in his throat as he closed his eyes. Instantly the script he had spent two days and nights reading flamed into view. It was another of the traits that had always set him apart, this ability to commit any script to memory with one reading. He remembered everything.

He chose words from one of the more innocuous scrolls and intoned them carefully. He stumbled twice, as he had not uttered the tongue in years. But he doubted anyone noticed.

When he opened his eyes, the gathered throng all gaped at him. He looked from one awestruck face to the next. "What is it?"

"You breathed in and out at the same time," Timmins said.

"That's impossible," Hyam said.

"And yet it is true," Bayard insisted. "And you sang a constant note. Three voices, all together, in harmony, without break or hesitation."

"I merely spoke the words."

"What the earl describes is what I heard as well," Trace said.

"And I," Joelle said. "It was . . ."

"Beautiful," Shona said. "And terrifying."

"Enough." Bayard pointed at Hyam. "A library, you say."

"Only two of the scrolls are complete. Actually, the two together make up the only complete spell." Hyam silently amended, only two of those he could read. But he would leave that bit of news for later. "The rest refer to scrolls we do not have, and continue where the last left off. They are also numbered. The numbers do not match."

Bayard asked, "How high do the numbers go?"

"In the thousands." Hyam indicated the tables. "The division you see here is not arbitrary. These represent four different entities."

"Signifying what?"

"The first table here contains legacies of cities and ruling clans that no longer exist. The central table is spells of warcraft. Dread powers are described. Plagues. Ghouls. Mental enslavement. Tempests that create terror in the hearts and minds. Thankfully, sire, not one of these spell-scrolls is complete. Perhaps the intention is to carefully guard any reader from knowing everything required."

Trace said, "If other war scrolls should fall into the enemy's hands . . ."

"Burn them," Bayard snarled. "Burn them all."

Joelle spoke up from her place by the rear wall. "Sire, the Ashanta have already sent word to their Emporis banker, instructing him to pay whatever is required to hold this trader until Hyam can journey there."

Bayard asked, "Have they inspected these scrolls?"

"Twice. They also do not discern the script that Hyam

has described. But the air of this chamber is enveloped by a force they have never sensed before."

The earl indicated the third table, which held far fewer scrolls. "And this third lot?"

"Spells of healing and protection and binding. The only complete incantation among all these scrolls describes the making of a large shield. Big enough to go around a group, perhaps an entire camp." Hyam glanced over at the master mage. "No mention is made of an orb."

Trace cried, "What, none?"

"Not in any of these documents, not once."

Bayard demanded, "Tell me what this means."

Trace said, "One of two things. Either the orb's application is taken for granted. Or . . ."

"These were intended for use by spell casters without access to an orb," Hyam finished.

Bayard looked from one to the other. "I thought that was impossible."

Trace replied, "We instruct our young apprentices using simple spells where they draw upon their innate abilities. It forms part of the test for who is gifted. One such spell involves shielding the mage from their own force. But to protect an entire company, not to mention wield powers of warcraft, I would call that an impossibility."

Hyam thought back to his earliest introduction to magic, when he stood in an oval field at the forest boundary, caught up in what he did not understand. But he did not speak.

Bayard walked to the last table, which held just the two miniature scrolls. "And these?"

35

Hyam unfurled one of the slender golden cylinders. "I have no idea."

Bayard turned to his cousin. "You know this script?"

"Never seen it nor heard of its existence," Timmins replied.

"Nor, according to Joelle, have the Ashanta." Trace opened one and waved it gently. The surface writhed like ripples across a pond. Light weaved and danced. "Myths speak of this process, where gold is melted by magic and woven into a fabric as sheer as silk and flexible as water. And beyond the grip of time."

The two scrolls were filled with downward strokes, like they had been etched with a blunt trowel. Some of the dashes were short, others long, some narrow, others almost round. Nothing else. A series of perpendicular furrows.

Bayard returned to the tables holding the Milantian scrolls. "One thing seems clear enough. The only way we can determine whether the scrolls are valid is to try the shield spell."

"I've been thinking the same thing," Hyam agreed.

Trace warned, "May I remind you this is Milantian magery we are discussing."

"Only if the spell actually works," Hyam replied.

"Of course it works," Trace countered. "Else why would they hide it?"

The earl said, "We must know if these scrolls hold true power!"

Trace frowned, but remained silent. Hyam took that as the only agreement the old man would offer. He felt the thrill rise within him. He had yearned for this moment since first realizing the spell appeared to be complete. A faint spark shot from the first scroll to his fingertips. "Sire, perhaps you should step well back."

All the Falmouth wizards clustered about the cavern's entrance. None wanted to miss this application of Milantian magery. Such an event could well form legends and minstrel tales. If Hyam succeeded.

The spell was laborious, three scrolls in length, with weavings of the hands to start the process. As Hyam chanted the initial words, the droning cadence swept him up, filling the vast chamber. It seemed as though his voice rose in volume until it echoed and rang against the distant stone. Faint streams of light emanated from his fingers, forming a tapestry of pastel hues. Joelle stood just inside the portal, watching him with grave eyes. He wanted to shout, to sing the exultation of doing magic again. But he dared not interrupt the spell-weaving.

He completed the first portion, drew his knife, and scarred the flagstone with the opening inscription. Trace moved closer so as to watch Hyam's motions. Each syllable formed a drumbeat that echoed and resonated through Hyam. A trail of fire followed the blade.

When Hyam completed his walk around the dais, he drew the final talisman like a knot upon the first drawing. Instantly the flames that had followed his knife were doused. As he straightened, Hyam felt as though the cavern still resonated with his voice.

The earl called over, "Is that it? You're done?"

"I am, sire."

Bayard muttered, "What a waste."

Hyam saw the same dissatisfaction reflected on all the other faces. "You did not see the fire? What about the noise?"

Bayard shook his head. "All I heard was the scrape of your knife. As for fire . . ."

Trace called, "Wait, sire. Everyone, stay where you are." The old mage stepped forward.

Hyam warned, "Careful."

The earl's senior wizard crossed the scarred flagstone, hesitated, then reached out one hand. To Hyam the cavern's torchlight appeared to quiver slightly, like an unseen wave rippled the air separating them. Trace pushed harder. Then stepped back and said, "Remarkable."

Bayard demanded, "The shield exists?"

"It does indeed, sire."

The earl strode across the cavern, touched the solidified air, and said, "It feels cold."

"Like ice," Trace agreed.

"You know of no such spell?"

"Not even with the orb's application. And to have this done by spell alone, I have never heard of such a thing."

Hyam said, "The scroll's final words warn that no magery should touch the shield's exterior. Which suggests it may be more than simply defense."

Trace said, "Sire?"

Bayard nodded. "Test it, then."

"Clear the room, everyone." When the chamber was emptied, Trace shut one of the double doors and locked it into place. Then he called, "Ready?"

"The smallest spell you can manage," Hyam replied, and stepped behind the central podium.

Trace pulled the second door over to where it partly shielded him. Then he wove together a ball of light and cold fire, no larger than his hands. He sent it scurrying across the flagstones.

The instant the ball touched the shield, the entire chamber beyond the shield was engulfed in crimson flames.

4

As soon as Hyam left the wizard's cavern, exhaustion struck. Joelle and Shona half-carried him to the kitchen, where a cook served up gruel laced with meat, standard foot soldiers' fare, all she had that was hot and ready. Hyam ate with the savage need of a wild animal. He was not even aware Joelle had left the kitchen until the moment she returned with Adler. They guided him out the pantry exit and almost tossed him onto the saddle of a waiting horse. Warmed by the kitchen fire and dulled by the meal, Hyam dozed his way through the city, out the front gates, down the road, along the white-stone lane leading home. He managed unaided the walk from the stables to his bed. He was asleep before his head hit the pillow.

When he awoke it was well past dawn, of which day Hyam had no idea. Joelle lay there beside him, her eyes soft and welcoming in the early light. Later they fell asleep again, carried by birdsong through the open window. Hyam's last thought was how he would remember this melody for the rest of his life.

Soon after, Hyam found his awareness rising in bodiless form. This rare freedom carried a soft whisper of exultation, but not enough to awaken him. He was aware of Joelle rising from the bed. He sensed Bryna's arrival and observed as Joelle conversed with the Ashanta Seer. He knew they spoke of the scrolls and what he had read. He felt the affection between the two women and knew how good it was for Joelle to have this friend, this link to the race that had banished his wife for the crime of being half human. Very good indeed.

Joelle left after a time, and the isolation freed him to travel further. A few languid breaths, and Hyam was swept away.

He was transported to an unknown island rimmed by cliffs and froth. A small beach of slate-grey pebbles was hammered by relentless surf. Hyam had no idea how large the central mountains were, for he had no frame of reference. The island contained neither house nor castle nor animal nor ship nor men. Trees clenched the cliffs like living sculptures. The central peaks seemed very high, with tight vales so deep their bases were lost to shadows. The broader meadows were curiously formed, with great brownish lumps of some mottled stone dotting their expanses.

Then one of the brown knobs chose that moment to move.

The beast rose on wings large as an ocean-going vessel's main sails. It swept up, up, and came to hover directly alongside where Hyam hung in the air above the island's highest peak. The dragon's hide changed colors now that it was removed from the meadow's camouflage. The scales glinted a ruddy gold, with diamond patterns repeated along the edges of both wings and the long spear-like tail. The eye close to Hyam burned with yellow fire, fierce and intelligent. Hyam felt the beast's gaze strip away his dream-like ease, such that his heart hammered and his breath rasped. He was not afraid, simply as alert as he had ever been in his entire life.

The dragon spoke.

Hyam was certain it was speech. The timbre was low as a war drum and swift as a volcanic rumble. Tight staccato bursts. When he remained silent, the dragon emitted a final chattering burst, one that carried the force to rock Hyam's vision.

"I have no idea what you want, or why I am here," Hyam said.

The dragon erupted, its wings beating at him with the force of twin furies. Hyam spiraled away, a human leaf caught in a tempest of wind and roars.

The dragon chased after him, bellowing in rage. Hyam was falling and had no power to halt his descent. The dragon tucked its wings in tight and fell as well, catching up with Hyam. The beast blasted him with fire.

The inferno carried such power Hyam woke up screaming. He fell to the floor and slapped at the flames he had left back at the island. The agony was fierce nonetheless, almost as strong as the sense that he had failed at something vital.

When Hyam finally steadied, he found the house still empty. He devoured another meal. Afterward he bathed, and as he was dressing he heard a familiar voice call from the front garden.

"You're awake. Good." Meda stepped through the open front door. "You've been summoned."

He was already moving, grateful for a reason to run from his dream. "By whom?"

Meda followed him down the white-stone path. "Everyone."

The black walls of Falmouth Port predated the struggles of ten centuries past. Before the Milantians had invaded the realm, the city had served as a warrior's bastion and defended the realm against desert invaders. More recently, after the Oberons lost the crown to the realm's current king, Bayard had accepted defeat on the condition that he be granted this fief.

Bayard was known far and wide as an honorable man. When dark forces began swirling about Port Royal and the king's court, newcomers flocked here, eager to swear fealty to the earl of a forbidden realm. Ships arrived throughout the fair-weather season, carrying both refugees and seasoned troops who refused to serve the unnamed shadows. Newcomers brought tales of strange happenings and feral beasts that prowled the forests. Now even the best-traveled routes were threatened. They spoke of a ruler who was never seen and royal edicts that troubled everyone of good heart.

The road leading to Falmouth's main gates was lined with shops that had immigrated with their owners. The structures served cobblers and armorers and leather workers and smiths, bakers and butchers and fruiters, taverns and inns and bordellos and gambling dens, fortune-tellers and healers and midwives. The Earl of Oberon's strict oversight was more lax beyond the city walls. A new mayor oversaw what had come to be known as Lesser Falmouth. Two women shouted good-natured insults from upstairs windows but went silent as Hyam and Meda passed. He pretended not to notice.

As they approached the city's main gates, Meda said, "Something's changed about you. The shadows have lightened."

With most people he would have deflected the comment, for Hyam rarely spoke about himself. But Meda had been with him since the beginning. He replied, "The scrolls contained power. I feel it still."

Meda saluted the guards on gate duty. "Milantian power. That no one but you can read."

"The Mistress of the Long Hall near my home suggested my blood was tainted. Now I have read an invisible script written in a tongue most say cannot be learned."

Meda halted him with a finger to his ribs, rigid as a blade. "You may carry an unwanted legacy. It is true of many warriors. Someday if you're interested I'll share with you a few of my own shadows." The finger stabbed his chest a second time. "But those fragments of your past do not make you. They do not describe you. Tell me you understand."

"You are a good friend," Hyam replied.

"I try to be." She motioned them on. A few paces further, she said, "The earl is going to send a guard with you to Emporis. It's not my rotation. But I want to volunteer. If you'll have me."

Hyam intended to travel with the golden scrolls, in hopes a translation text might be found among the desert trader's wares. But as the scrolls held Milantian magery, he could not request passage through the Elven road. This meant traveling through the badland fiefdoms, a prospect Hyam relished. He had not left Falmouth since the Battle of Emporis.

Hyam replied, "I'd savor the chance to journey with you again."

Meda seemed to find enough closeness in the moment to say, "Joelle told me that losing your magic has been a trial."

They entered the inner keep, saluted the guards, and crossed the palace forecourt. "I did not know I lacked eyes until two years ago, when I discovered the realm of magic. I explored this new world with new senses for a few weeks only. Then I was blinded again."

"So touching these scrolls . . ."

"There is a glimmer of light. Just a glimmer. But enough to make my heart sing."

❖

Bayard paced the sunlit forecourt, ignoring the din of traders and troops readying for the journey ahead. Trace spoke with Joelle, who carried messages to the head wizard of the Emporis keep. The wolfhound Dama sprawled at her feet, panting in the heat.

Bayard motioned for Hyam to join him and said, "I need your help."

"Sire?"

"My son is eight and not well."

Hyam nodded. All the city knew the earl's only child was not responding to the healers.

"Perhaps my wife and I will have another child. Perhaps . . ." Bayard waved that aside. "I have put this off too long. I intend to name Shona as my heir apparent."

"It is an excellent choice, sire." Shona's brothers shared their father's passion and wanted nothing more from life than carrying on their father's work. "Your niece dreams of carving her own place in the world."

"You understand. Excellent. But Timmins and his wife have sheltered Shona. She has never been beyond Falmouth's borders. She does not know the world. She has no idea . . ."

Hyam supplied, "What a ruler must face."

"Which is why I want you to take her on this quest."

"Timmins has agreed?"

"Twice. And retracted twice. Last night I begged. Shona pleaded. But . . ." Bayard pointed at the gates. "Here they come now."

As soon as Hyam saw Timmins's angry scowl and his daughter's tears, he understood what Bayard had not asked. "Your cousin has become my friend during our time together, sire. Allow me to speak with him."

Bayard stepped away. "May you have more success than I."

Timmins had all his arguments ready and fastened his aim upon the earl. But Hyam stepped directly in front of him and declared, "Shona is leaving you."

"Her mother and I can't allow . . . What?"

"Not this year," Hyam said. "Perhaps not the next. But the scribe's life will not keep her. You and your wife both know this. Which is why you listened to Bayard at all."

Timmins drew his narrow shoulders back as far as they would go. "There is nothing wrong with my world."

"For you and your sons, it is ideal. For her?" Hyam glanced at the young woman. At seventeen, Shona was a rare beauty with a brilliant intellect, and the jewel of her father's household. Hyam admired her for the strength it took to remain silent. "She wants more. You know this."

Timmins sputtered, "I know nothing of the sort."

"You know," Hyam persisted. "Her mother knows as well. Shona will never be content with your profession. She will choose her own road. If you refuse her the chance to decide for herself, she will run away. Perhaps through a bad marriage, perhaps through rebellion. But it is coming. You sense this. And you fear this."

"She is *my* daughter. It is *my* decision. My cousin cannot *possibly* know whether she would make a capable ruler."

"Precisely. Which is why Bayard wants her to come with us. Even if she is not suited to lead, she can learn. And she will grow. And she will return enriched by the process."

Timmins struggled to hold his composure. "You will keep her safe?"

Joelle walked over and fit herself to Hyam's side. "We will do our best. That is all we can promise."

"She is her own person," Hyam said. "The road carries all the risks that worry you in the night. But you know us both. You know we will do all we can to protect your daughter and bring her home."

Timmins turned to his daughter and asked, "This is what you want?"

"More than anything, Father. More than my next breath."

He shuddered. "You understand what it means to accept the role of heir?"

"How can I? But I know that I want to learn. And be tested. And have this chance to see if I am worthy to lead. And to serve."

"Well said," Joelle murmured.

Timmins bowed his head, defeated. "Then go with my blessing."

Shona embraced him fiercely. "Thank you, Father. Oh, thank you!"

Hyam turned to where Bayard observed them and said, "We are ready."

5

Early on their third day, they entered the high reaches leading to Rothmore Vale, home to the badland tribe closest to Falmouth Port. The road curved and climbed, then climbed some more, up to a pass flecked by late snows. They descended slowly through severe cutbacks. Twice warriors as rough-hewn as the rocks emerged from caves and offered them a savage salute.

They shared the Emporis road with the earl's troops and a motley assortment of traders and wagons. Captain Meda was accompanied by a handsome young corporal named Alembord, who was clearly smitten with Shona. But if the scribe's daughter even noticed the soldier's existence, she gave no sign.

They traversed a high meadow rimmed by razor ridges the locals called fells, then rounded a silver lake fed by a myriad of streams. The wolfhound loped about chasing gophers until Hyam spotted an eagle and called Dama to heel.

The eagle's wingspan was broader than Hyam's reach. The snowy hunter clung to the blue-black sky and circled directly overhead.

Joelle said, "I wonder what it is like to fly."

"Like the Ashanta travel," he guessed. "Only better. Wings and wind and all the senses alive."

"Trace speaks of lost spells that permitted the orb carriers to soar."

Hyam nodded to the bird and the sky. He had heard the same.

She turned from the bird. "Husband, I sense something troubles you."

The call came for them to mount up. As they rejoined the trail, the eagle dropped from the sky like a feathered bomb. The wings snapped out at the last possible moment. The bird showed a dancer's poise as it snared a furry creature with its talons and winged away. Hyam waited until the eagle was a faint speck in the distance to say, "I will tell you tonight."

They rode the same shaggy-haired mountain ponies as all the other troops. Midway through the afternoon, clouds gathered and the sky boiled with sullen fury. They arrived at a cluster of corrals and simple stone huts just as the wind strengthened. Hurriedly they off-loaded the animals and took shelter.

Joelle loved such times and stood outside the doorway to watch the storm's arrival. The rain moved upon sibilant limbs, a hushed sound that flavored the air with a sweet fragrance. Hyam held his wife and reveled in her laughter every time the lightning illuminated their craggy world.

They shared their hut with Meda, Shona, Alembord, two

traders, and a red-bearded clan shepherd. The cottage roof was designed with such storms in mind, sloped away from the predominant northern wind, with a slanted hole that let out the fire's smoke yet kept their haven dry. Three sheep were secured in the corner, so pregnant they looked ready to explode at any moment.

As they shared a simple meal, Hyam noticed Bryna's appearance and Joelle's smile of welcome. His wife remained stiffly nervous around the Ashanta elders, but Bryna and Joelle had become fast friends. Hyam watched the Ashanta drift past the fire and settle onto the packed earth next to Joelle. The telepathic race knew no word for either greeting or farewell. But Joelle traced a hand along the space where the apprentice Seer's face should have been, as warm a hello as Hyam had ever witnessed.

He decided there would be no better time to confess, "I have been dreaming of dragons."

The entire hut turned toward him as he went on, "Actually, it has been one dragon, several dreams. Four, to be precise. They started the morning after I finished sorting the scrolls. The beast has returned before each dawn."

Meda asked, "But dragons don't exist. Do they? Have they ever?"

Shona replied, "They fly in numerous legends. But none that hold any truth."

"Bryna agrees with you," Joelle said.

Alembord asked, "Who?"

"Her Ashanta friend," Meda explained.

"She is here now?"

Joelle said, "She just arrived, yes."

It was hard to say who had the wider eyes, the shepherd or the traders or the corporal. The younger merchant said, "The legends come alive and dance in the firelight."

Meda asked Hyam, "What happens in your dreams?"

So Hyam told them. Precisely. Here there was no need to hurry. The fire warmed them, their bellies were full. The rain fell and the lightning punctuated his telling. Hyam described the moment of swift travel, the island, the mountains, the black shoreline. The meadow dotted with large green mounds. The dragon that unfurled and hovered in the air beside him. "The first three nights, the dream was the same. Deep bursts of speech, then rage, then I am blasted by the beast's fire. All morning I ache from the flames."

Meda asked, "A dream leaves you hurting?"

"I know it is absurd. But the soreness is real enough, I assure you."

Joelle interrupted at this point to say, "Bryna has never heard of such a place as this island."

Shona's expression was as awestruck as the traders'. "Nor have I ever read of such an island realm."

The fire crackled and hissed for a time, then Joelle asked, "You're certain this was speech?"

"Staccato beats. The same each time. As precise as a warrior's drum. At first I wasn't sure. But now, yes. The dragon seeks to speak with me."

Joelle asked, "Then the dream changed?"

"This very dawn. The dragon soared up to where I was trapped in the air. It examined me for what seemed like hours.

Over and over the beast spoke, low drumbeats timed so precisely I am certain it was an unknown tongue. Finally it grew angry, just like every time before. Only this time it did not blast me. Instead, it flew out, far over the sea, until it vanished in the distance. And then it returned."

"And all the while you remained imprisoned in midair."

"Yes. When the dragon returned, it held in one claw a golden scroll."

Meda and Shona and Joelle all breathed as one. His wife asked, "Like the ones you carry?"

"I wasn't certain at first. Then the beast flapped the scroll open. It drifted in the sunlight like a brilliant sail. It was the same. Only a hundred times larger. A thousand."

Alembord demanded, "Larger than what?"

Hyam reached into his pack, drew out one of the scrolls, opened it, and let the fire play over the golden surface. The shepherd muttered fearfully, and the traders were beyond speech. Hyam rolled up the scroll and returned it to his pack. "The beast spoke again. The impatience it has always shown me was even stronger now, but without the fury. I could feel the pressure of its words, like the storm we watched approach. A great, intense urgency. It shook the scroll and it spoke. It was still speaking when I drew away. It shouted, louder and louder, and the power made my departure even swifter. When I woke up, I was still vibrating from the force."

Hyam held out his hand, revealing the tremors that shook his entire arm. "Just speaking of it causes me to shake again."

Joelle asked for them all, "What does it mean?"

He shivered anew from the force of words he did not

understand, uttered by a beast who had never existed. "I have no idea."

By midmorning of the next day, all the travelers spoke of nothing save Hyam's dragon dreams.

The highland meadow narrowed to a ridge broken by a high pass, then broadened to where Meda and Shona and Alembord and Joelle all rode clustered around Hyam. Dama loped ahead, exploring in happy abandon. The storm had departed with the dawn. The sky was impossibly clear, the air crisp.

Meda mused as they rode, "A beast that large cannot fly."

"It doesn't need to," Hyam replied, enjoying the discussion enormously, for it eased the dream's grip. "Seeing as how it exists only in my head."

"Tell us again what happened during this morning's dream," Shona said.

So he did. For once, he did not mind being the center of attention. The shepherd who had shared their hut rode a stunted mountain pony, listening in silence as Hyam repeated his dream.

When he was done, Alembord spoke for the first time since they'd entered the new vale. "And then once again it held out the golden scroll."

"As long as the Falmouth gates are tall," Hyam replied.

Joelle said, "And marked with the same strokes as on the ones you carry."

"Identical."

The route narrowed as it crested a rise. They looked down

into Rothmore Vale, broad as a bowl and filled with a village of over a thousand dwellings. At its center rose a mound that was crowned by a larger hall of stone and wood. When they arrived at the valley floor, the shepherd rode on ahead, the pony making swift time.

Meda watched his departure, then returned to her earlier musings. "No matter how large the beast's wings might be, they couldn't lift that great a weight."

Joelle declared, "Perhaps the wings are not for flight at all."

"I've been thinking the same," Shona said. "They are for balance."

"And steering," Joelle said. "Exactly."

Meda studied the pair. "Then how can it fly?"

"Magic," Joelle replied.

"It stands to reason," Shona said.

"The beast does not exist," Hyam said.

"This we cannot say for certain," Meda countered.

Shona said, "Describe the speech."

"The pattern was intentional and repetitive. Of this I no longer have any doubt. Imagine a living kettle drum. Like that."

As they approached the village, a contingent of warriors emerged from the chieftain's hall and mounted steeds scarcely larger than the shepherd's horse. They cantered through the wooden palisade and started toward Hyam.

The lead man saluted Hyam with a lance. Upon the long slender blade was tied a highland banner that snapped in the breeze. "You are the hero who defeated the Emporis mage?"

At Joelle's insistence, Hyam no longer protested when others applied the word to him. *Hero.* "I am."

"The chief of Rothmore Vale salutes you and invites you and your company to be his guest this night."

At sunset they were feted in the clan's main hall—not, according to Meda, the normal greeting shown to the earl's troops. The warrior clans might hold the peace. But they were still a quarrelsome bunch who lived to make trouble. The earl kept the roads open by gold as much as by treaty. Normally the troops and merchants paid a hefty fee for their passage and fare.

This evening, however, everyone traveling with Hyam was invited to the feast, down to the lowliest trooper and smallest trader. Hyam and Joelle were hosted by the chief himself, seated with his wives and the clan leaders on a raised dais. Their chairs ran along just one side of the long table, so they could be viewed by all those gathered in the hall. The chamber was a full hundred and fifty paces across, beamed with branches from the largest tree Hyam had ever seen. At first he thought the mound supporting the chieftain's hall held a grove of many trees, but the chief assured him that this was the mark of every highland vale—one tree, iron roots, many limbs. Why only one such tree grew in each vale, no one knew. The legends differed from clan to clan. But such trees formed the heart of the tribe and fashioned the living pillars upon which every chieftain's hall was supported. A great flat plateau of rock and earth and root formed the center of every vale, so preserved by time and stubborn strength that not even the great central fire could scar its living timber.

It was also here that Hyam finally learned the reason why Shona held no interest in the dumbstruck Alembord or any other fawning young man.

Joelle had remained withdrawn since the banquet's start. Hyam knew something had upset her, and he feared it was his fault. Joelle was normally not given to silent brooding. When she was displeased, she wanted the world to know it. Her suppressed tension worried him mightily.

Over platters of roasted wild boar coated in honeyed wine, Hyam leaned in close and said, "What is it?"

Joelle showed him a blank gaze. "The girl is infatuated with you."

The words were so unexpected, for an instant he had no idea who she referred to. "You mean . . . Shona?"

Joelle's examination was so intense she might as well have peeled away his skin. "You did not know?"

"Joelle, I . . ."

She sighed away a fraction of her ire. "Shona has been captivated since the first day you entered her father's house."

"What?"

"More than that. She is in love."

Hyam could not help but glance down at the center table, where Alembord struggled as usual to make conversation with the beautiful young girl. In Hyam's home region, they could have called Shona's coloring midnight fair. Her hair was a dark russet that turned gold in moonlight. Bayard's strength was present in her features, but Shona gentled this with a womanly grace. She was striking now and would no doubt mature into a rare beauty. She would make a fine countess. Or queen.

Hyam asked, "How do you know?"

"She told me."

"The girl seated there, Timmins's own daughter. She told you, my wife, that she is in love with me."

"Shona asked if I would consider sharing you with a second wife," Joelle said. "I wish you could see your face."

"I cannot handle you," Hyam replied, "much less another woman."

Joelle showed him a cautious smile. But a smile nonetheless. "I would hardly call that a gallant response."

"What do I do?"

Joelle took aim at the young woman. Her voice was flat as beaten tin. "Be gentle. Be patient. But be firm when the time comes."

Hyam had the distinct impression his wife was speaking to herself far more than him. "I will try."

She turned back. "Truly, you had no idea of this?"

"Now that you tell me, yes, I suppose there were signals . . ." He sighed. "What a mess."

Joelle tilted her head, as though needing to inspect him from a different angle. "Are all men so blind?"

Hyam was saved from needing to respond by the chief rising to his feet. He was a massive red-bearded warrior who hammered the table with the haft of a two-bladed ax. The chief roared for silence, then declared, "The hero of Emporis will now tell of his dragon!"

The declaration was Hyam's first signal that he was to provide the night's entertainment. He might have objected had the task not been far easier than his conversation with

Joelle. So he rose to his feet and related the dreams yet again. One after the other.

The history of each badland tribe was an oft-repeated lore, seldom written down. These were people who loved nothing more than a new tale. They cheered each dream and quarreled over their meanings. As Hyam described the huge golden scroll, Joelle reached into his pack and drew out the smaller versions, which Hyam passed to the chief. The bearded leader marveled over them for a time, then motioned for aides to carry them about the chamber. Hyam needed over an hour to arrive at the point where he declared, "At dawn this morning, there was a new dream."

As he described the most recent encounter, the hall grew quieter than it had been all night. The only sound, other than Hyam's voice, was the faint echo from the hall's distant rims, where his words were passed down to those who could not hear.

In his latest dream, the dragon shaped a perch from one claw and carried Hyam over a distance so vast he might as well have been transported to a different world.

The dragon deposited him in a valley filled with ash. Hyam did not see the bones. But he knew they were there, hidden beneath the tragic blanket of ruin and defeat. Just as he knew who had been behind the destruction.

When he finished talking, the hall remained locked in eerie stillness. The clan chief rose to his feet once more and declared, "It is forbidden to speak of the dark days in this chamber."

"I apologize," Hyam said. "I did not know."

"Nor could you. Now it is done." He turned to the hall and raised his voice. "I say, tonight we break the oaths, and for the best of reasons. Who stands with me?" When the clan responded with a roar, the chief said, "Describe to us this vale."

Hyam responded with a question of his own. "How many clans were laid waste by the crimson mage?"

"Nineteen halls will no longer hear the songs of lore and clan saga. Describe and leave nothing out."

Hyam had no difficulty doing so. This was another remarkable component of the dreams, how they did not fade with time. "The valley was almost as wide as it was long. How great, I do not know, for there was nothing in the basin except ash."

"Dunnesend," the chief said. "Few are shaped as earthen basins. It has to be Dunnesend."

"A hill rose at its center, just like where we now gather."

"That helps us not a whit. It is one of the traits of all those vales where our villages are located."

The chief's wife leaned forward and said, "Someday you must return and hear the lore that binds us to our highland world."

"I would be honored."

The chief waved that aside. "Describe!"

"There was a broad waterfall to my right. It plunged a long distance and thundered where it fell. A lake was formed at its front, the surface black from the surrounding landscape."

The chief glanced worriedly at his wife, then called out, "Where is our lorekeeper? Come forward, Caleb."

An ancient sage rose from his place and swatted away the

hands that sought to help him. He leaned upon a tall staff polished by the years. The hall remained silent, watchful, tense. The only sound was the rapid tap-tapping of his stave.

"I live to serve, sire."

"Can you think of such a vale?"

"May I be permitted to inquire of the forbidden?"

"Ask!"

The sage's beard was long enough to be tucked inside the upper fold of his robe. But his eyes were clear and his voice strong. "Which way did you face, hero?"

"My name is Hyam. The sun touched the ridgeline to my right. But whether it rose or sank, I cannot say."

"You dreamed at dawn. Let us say north for now."

"A waterfall on the eastern ridge." The chief sounded more worried still.

"Go on," the sage said.

"Two towers rose from the highest peaks on either side of the waterfall. Or rather, their remnants. The stones were blasted with something so fierce they ran like wax. Turned to lava, they were. Only their stubs were left. One to the left and one to the right . . ." Hyam felt as much as heard the tempest that swirled through the hall, a whisper of something that might have been awe. Or dread. "What is it?"

The clan's lorekeeper pulled his long beard from his robe and stroked its surface, down to the tip by his waist. If the elder was touched by the emotion that rippled through the clan hall, he did not show it. "You saw the remnants of a wall?"

"In places," Hyam confirmed. "To either side of the towers."

Caleb nodded. Satisfied. He turned to the chief and declared, "It is as you suspect, sire."

"But . . . that vale holds no ash."

"Who knows what era the dragon revealed to the hero of Emporis. It can be no other valley, sire. The hero was taken to Ellismere."

The undercurrent had a voice now, a faint rustling and stirring. The chief looked at Hyam but directed his words to the sage. "What say you?"

"My grandson and I must journey with him, sire."

"It is forbidden," the chief said.

The old man's beard jutted out as he set his chin. "Who are we to tell the hero of Emporis what should be done? Hyam has been summoned!"

Hyam asked, "What is Ellismere?"

All eyes turned his way, but no one spoke until the chief himself said, "It is the name we no longer utter, though all know of it. It is the vale of woe. The place where the wasteland begins."

Caleb explained, "A thousand years ago, Ellismere served as the realm's first line of defense. Beyond that stretched the desert wasteland. When the first dire beasts attacked Ellismere, the clan chieftains journeyed three times to Port Royal, asking the king to honor his pledge and come to our rescue."

"The Milantian invasion," Hyam breathed. "It started there."

"No, hero. No. It began in the great forest that once rose north of Emporis. The glade known as Ethrin was the fabled home to the Elven king. First that vast forest homeland was defeated, and the green warriors were slain to the last man. Then the enemy attacked the highland clan guarding the only route connecting the trading empire of Emporis to Falmouth Port and the realm."

"And the king did not heed your warnings," Hyam said. "He did not honor his pledge, because he did not believe the invasion was real."

"The first King Oberon did not accept that the fabled crimson wizards were leading an army of beasts the likes of which none had ever seen before," the chief confirmed. "Not until the Earl of Emporis wrote to describe how his own troops had journeyed north and found that where Ethrin had once stood proud and secretive, now lay mile after mile of ash and death and woe. And by then Ellismere was destroyed, and the crimson foes led an army toward the realm's heart."

"Ellismere is our anguished legacy," the sage declared. "The bitter roots that hold fast our distrust of lowland rulers."

The chieftain's gaze had gone distant, as though reciting lessons from his youth. "The lowland's promises are forever stained by the ash that once was Ellismere."

Hyam found himself drawn by forces he could neither name nor understand. But as he started to voice his confusion, he glanced down. Joelle met his gaze with certainty and love. They did not speak. They did not need to. Hyam found what he required in her gaze. "I must go there," he said.

"You will not find it without us," Caleb replied. "For three ruined vales lay between there and here. Nine years back, the crimson mage announced his arrival by attacking those valleys that surround what once was Ellismere. The trails are empty, with no living clans to aid your trek."

Hyam nodded. And waited.

Caleb said to the chief, "Sire, again I ask your permission."

The chief studied his elder scribe before asking, "You are up to such a journey?"

"I have spent my entire life waiting for this. When I was the age of my grandson, my own grandfather took me there. We stood within the ring of stones, and he described to me all that I have related and more besides. He made Ellismere live once more, at least for a single sunrise. It is time I take my own heir and help him make homage to that which is now gone."

6

As the caravan prepared for a dawn departure, Hyam watched as Meda drew Alembord to one side. Hyam did not need to hear the heated exchange to know what was being said. The previous evening Meda had told Hyam that Alembord's interest in the earl's niece had reached an unacceptable level. Meda had taken Hyam's silence as agreement. Now the guards captain was ordering the corporal to leave their group and join the merchant caravan. Hyam watched as Alembord protested in the strongest possible terms. In response, Meda took aim at Shona and spoke words that blistered the trooper's face with shame. Hyam saw Alembord speak through a clenched jaw, and Meda reluctantly agree.

As Meda and the red-faced corporal joined Hyam on the rise, the chief emerged from the great hall, accompanied by the lorekeeper and his grandson. "The three valleys between here and Ellismere were once connected by a well-traveled road, as these were the vales closest to our own by blood and lore. Now the villages are silent and the road is cursed."

Caleb went on, "Young men and women go hunting treasure. It is forbidden, but the pickings are rich. Those who seek a wife, a new field, or just adventure, they go and none can stop them."

Meda asked, "Why does this trouble you?"

"Because recently some have not returned," the elder replied. "Twenty-two days back, three of our strongest young warriors went adventuring. You understand?"

"They were not likely to be caught unawares by bandits," Meda said.

"We suspected their disappearance was the work of another highland clan," the chief confirmed. "In earlier days we would have trekked from hall to hall, searching out the culprits and challenging them to single combat."

The sage continued, "But Caleb went looking for his friends and returned two days before your own arrival. Tell them what you found, lad."

His grandson took up the telling. "They told me they were headed to the furthest vale destroyed by the crimson one. When we could not find them there, we followed the ancient road to Ellismere. Where the road crested the final ridge, it looked as though the rocks had been chewed."

"Torn apart," a woman from the chief's guard said. "Deep gouges in the ridge, like claws as broad as I am tall."

"And now you hear of my dream," Hyam said, "and wonder if this dragon feasts upon the flesh of men."

"You yourself spoke of being blasted by flames from its nostrils," the chief said. "And of the beast's frenzy."

"Every dream has held a frantic urgency," Hyam agreed. "But I do not think the beast means me ill."

"We are speaking," Meda reminded them, "of an animal that none have ever seen."

"But it flies in legends and songs," the sage said. "Old as mankind."

"None have ever been proven to hold to truth," Shona said.

"But other legends have come to life around us!" The sage pointed north and east, to the ridge that separated them from the desolation. "A crimson mage appeared and destroyed the peace of ten centuries. A hero rose from the ranks of humans and joined the crimson mage in battle. The sky was blasted with flame and magic, such that we ourselves witnessed the event, fourteen days' hard march from Emporis!" Caleb's beard trembled with indignation and certainty. "I, Caleb the Elder, tell you that a dragon has arrived! If it is a threat, the hero of Emporis will bring it down! And I, keeper of the Highland Lore, will bear witness to all the generations yet to come!"

❖

Despite his advanced years, the lorekeeper held to an impatient pace. "One of those missing was my favorite nephew. A wastrel if ever there was one, but a fine warrior just the same." Caleb rode a stubby mountain pony, not much larger than a donkey. The beast proved sure-footed and swift as they climbed the steep northeastern ridge. Caleb swung his staff at his grandson riding ahead of him, a handsome youth with a winning smile. "The one you see there is hardly any better. The pair of them claimed to be in love with a different woman every other week."

"Terrible," Joelle said, smiling at the youth. "How dare he."

The youth carried his grandfather's name and was known simply as the Younger. He possessed a crop of black curls that would have done a maiden proud. He winked at Shona and said, "How can I deny the ladies when they ask to taste the wine?"

The old man watched Shona snort in derision and urge her horse to greater speed. Then he noticed Hyam's grin and snapped, "I suppose you think you are an expert on the subject as well."

Joelle said from behind them, "Hyam knew next to nothing about love when we met. But he is proving to be an adequate learner."

It was the old man's turn to cackle. "Is he indeed."

Meda asked, "How far to our destination?"

"Three days, if the weather holds," the Younger replied, and sniffed the wind. "Which it should."

"The highland fiefs encircle Emporis on three sides, like creases in a long ribbon," his grandfather explained. "Sixty-one clans still hold to the highland ways. Some are little more than brigands. Others have inherited talents from the ancients and commune with all manners of beasts."

"My latest lady is from such the northern reaches. We met when she was down trading with her father. She calls me her wolf cub." The Younger howled at the blue-black sky.

The ridge did not fall directly into the next vale, as Hyam expected. Instead, they passed through a meadow turned yellow by the winter that seemed reluctant to release these high reaches. The wind carried a severe bite, and they halted long enough to pull traveling cloaks from their bundles. The meadows were shared by goats and coal-black sheep and stubby cattle that fled from them like half-wild beasts. The shepherds who exchanged greetings with the two Calebs spoke in voices that creaked from disuse.

They trekked for hours through a thick forest. When they emerged, they knew without being told that they were reaching the next valley. The silence was a blanket that stifled any will to speak. No one objected when they made camp, using the forest as a shield against the rising wind. They tethered the mounts where they could crop the golden grass, gathered wood, and started a blazing fire. No one spoke as they set two pots on the cooking stones, one for tea and the other for stew. Then they followed the lorekeeper along a path only he could see, and halted where the world fell away.

They surveyed a wasteland. Not even the grandson's good cheer could defy the bleakness of that ash-covered vale.

Shona said softly, "The crimson storm assaulted first the Elven forests and then the highland world. In both places they left nothing but ash and bone. So read the scrolls from ten centuries ago. Three vales they demolished, one after the other, carving a swath of destruction along the border with the yellow sea. Then they vanished from the high vales, carried like smoke on the wind, straight into the heart of the human realm."

The elder Caleb studied the young woman. "You are apprenticed to a lorekeeper?"

"My father is Timmins, scribe to the Earl of Oberon."

"Your father is by all accounts a good man. You will carry a message to him?"

"I will."

"Tell him that Caleb the Elder salutes him and the earl both. It does an old heart good to know the leader of Falmouth and his sage keep tribal lore alive in the generations to come."

"You do me and my brothers great honor," Shona replied. "I will tell them."

Caleb turned back to the grey-black vale. "This was the second fiefdom attacked five years past by the crimson one. The first lay three days east and north of Emporis, a half-tamed clan that few will miss, if truth be known. When news came of that first attack, I discounted it as the work of brigands and those who scorn our legacy. This time I came to see for myself." He scowled over the silent reaches. "The lorekeeper of this vale and I were friends."

Caleb the Younger added, "Bayard came the instant he heard. He offered the clans his port city as a haven and gathering point. He lost hundreds of warriors keeping the roads open."

"Time and again the Earl of Oberon has earned the clans' trust." The lorekeeper studied the vale, his gaze wintry and narrow. "Come. We must eat and rest."

The wind died with the dusk. They ate without appetite and unfurled their bedrolls. Hyam awoke an hour or so later when Dama huffed softly. He opened his eyes to find Meda, Alembord, Shona, and Joelle standing by their blankets. He started to ask what it was, but Joelle motioned him to remain silent.

He pulled on his boots and followed them toward the ridge. They halted where the two Calebs came into view. The clan's lorekeeper and his grandson stood in the moonlight, their arms lifted over the empty vale. Their voices were joined in a duet that was both lyrical and spoken, rising and falling in unison. Caleb the Elder droned a long verse, answered by his grandson's warbling grief. The voices echoed out over the valley, far into the distance, into the night.

Hyam and the others stood and shared the lament for a time. Then they returned to the camp. The two lorekeepers were still chanting their highland dirge when Hyam fell asleep.

❖

The dragon dream returned in the pre-dawn hour. But this time, Hyam did not travel to the island. Instead, the dragon came to him. The beast swept over the meadow that bordered their camp and drew Hyam up so that he flew alongside.

In one sharp, twisting swoop of its wings, the dragon turned and looked down over the ash-draped vale. Though the night was still black and the moon already set, Hyam was convinced the dragon saw the valley for what it was, a record of wizardly crime, a place of recent death and woe. What was more, the beast was mightily confused by what it saw. And troubled. The dragon swept over the vale, back and forth a half-dozen times. It chattered to Hyam in that deep drum cadence.

Finally the beast returned Hyam to his sleeping form, then stretched its wings and flew off. As it departed it continued the drumbeat cadence, calling back to Hyam, urging him to forge on.

Hyam knew he would sleep no more, so he slipped from the bedroll and pulled on his boots. Joelle murmured and sent a hand drifting across the blanket, searching for him, then she quieted and went back to sleep.

Hyam stood there for a time, studying Joelle's silhouette in the vague pale light. Her dark honeyed hair was pulled back from her neck, revealing a tattoo she had inked herself in the darkest hours of her own hard nights. Hyam would never confess the thought that rose then, not even to the windless dawn. But in such moments as this, when he marveled over the fact that such an amazing woman had gifted him her heart, he knew a vague gratitude over her imprisonment. For Hyam knew that Joelle's love was an unspoken thanks for his rescue. He had freed her, and she had imprisoned herself again. She had chained herself with a love so fierce it scalded his very soul. Joelle was born to fly, to soar, to hunt upon the winds. He saw this too, when she opened herself to him and revealed the hawk's fierce intent emblazoned far deeper than the ink embedded in her skin. At such times he felt almost consumed by her love. He had no way of thanking Joelle for the gift, except to do what he did now. Stand amazed and filled to overflowing by the gift of her wings.

He knelt beside Joelle, stroked her face, and kissed the

delicate point where her neck met her hairline. She stirred and murmured, "Is it time?"

"Sleep, my love. Sleep."

"Oh good. I thought it was . . ." Then she drifted away.

He pressed his lips to her ear and breathed, soft as the first hint of breeze on the dawn, "I love you, Joelle. With my heart and my days. I cherish you for all you are and all you are helping me become."

She rose with a dancer's grace, gripping her blanket in one hand and his neck with the other. She kissed him, a long and languorous closure. Then she led him barefoot into the soft rustling grass that led to the forest border. When they were hidden away from the camp, she found a space where the moss grew so thick it might have waited centuries for their arrival. Hyam felt the strength of her arms bind them together.

In the days to come, after the world was tilted to an uncommon course, Hyam would often think back to that velvet dawn. And be grateful that he had spoken the words while he still had time.

7

They skirted the valley rim along a smuggler's route. The silent journey took them most of the day. The trail became increasingly vague the farther they traveled. On the vale's opposite side they entered another highland meadow covered with golden grass and trees burnished by the spring. They overnighted in a shallow bowl that was surrounded by a hedge. The barrier was important, for the sunset wind was fierce and carried a northern edge. They ate in silence and slept uneasily, surrounded by a legacy of ash and defeat.

In his dream that next dawn, the dragon landed atop a knob that overlooked their present camp. Hyam felt himself lifted and drawn to stand alongside the behemoth, which chattered at him in the low drumbeat. The dragon remained confused, concerned. Though Hyam understood nothing of the speech, he was certain the beast conveyed a desperate urgency.

That morning they continued along the border trail, which

turned treacherous from disuse and the steep ridgeline. They traversed the next valley in the early afternoon. When they arrived at the far side, they found no route leading onward.

Meda asked, "There is no ridge trail?"

"There is no reason to maintain one," the young Caleb replied. "Beyond this lies Ellismere, and then the desert wasteland."

The lorekeeper added, "For a thousand years, the neighboring fiefs have never entered Ellismere. Not even when the droughts struck and they were desperate for fodder."

"Why not?"

"Those who went spoke of strange mists that strode about Ellismere like armies. Our clansmen were certain they were doomed if they remained."

They arrived at the ridgeline bordering Ellismere just as the sun was setting. They passed rocks gouged by claws broader than a man was tall. Hyam answered their unspoken questions with, "I do not think the dragon would have consumed your men."

The vale was the largest Hyam had seen and contained a mound vastly larger than the one holding the Rothmore hall. They retreated to a defile rimmed by spear-shaped rocks, each three times the height of a man. The stones rose in jagged unison to stab at the moon and stars. The lorekeeper showed his years for the first time, gesturing for his grandson to come help him down from the saddle.

They ate a cold meal, listening to the wind rush between the granite staves. Directly across the valley, the rising moon illuminated the remnants of a once-mighty wall. At its center rose two knolls, and upon these pinnacles stood ruins of towers. The stones resembled a candle that had melted down and flowed to join the peak.

Meda watched Shona walk to the nearest stone and run a hand along its edge. Meda explained, "Such stone circles are called places of accord, bound by oaths so old they predate the Milantian invasion. All within these boundaries were safe. Anyone who disturbed the peace in such places was banished for life."

"You heard correctly." Caleb studied her intently. "Where did you see such places?"

"I served my first tour in the fiefs north of Emporis." Meda continued to watch Shona. "I was seventeen."

Teeth shone through the sage's beard. "So you survived your time among the wild clans."

"Barely. There were many nights when I kept breathing only because of such stone circles. I never again want to call any highland clan my foe."

Caleb asked, "Why did you become a warrior?"

"I was the youngest of seven, with six brothers who relished any chance to pound on me. I learned to fight and discovered I loved it." Meda stretched out on her bedroll. "I have seen much and lived well in the process."

They bedded down as usual, with Shona nestled up close to Joelle's other side. Hyam was drifting into sleep when he heard his wife whisper, "What will you do when you return to Falmouth?"

He heard Shona reply, "You mean, if I pass this test of the road?"

"You will pass. You are learning, you are one of us."

"Bayard has said he will name me his squire. I shall serve him at table, and in formal events stand behind him as cupbearer. I will act as his secretary, and I shall learn what I can."

"For how long?"

"A squire's normal duty lasts for seven years."

"A long time for a beautiful young lady to hold her tongue."

"I have often thought the same thing. But Bayard is as good a teacher as Father. And I shall be rewarded. That is . . ."

"If you hold fast to your duties, yes?" Joelle gave that a moment, then said, "It is good to hold a clear vision of your future goals, is it not? This adds a vital clarity to the tasks at hand."

"I suppose . . ."

"Your duties are tied to your present and your future. Both are vital. Lives depend upon your doing well." Joelle settled further into her bedroll. "Good night."

Hyam rolled over, slept, and did not dream. Until the dawn came.

❖

The hour before sunrise, the dragon swooped down and pulled him away. Once more Hyam sensed the anxious impatience that fueled the beast's repeated appearance.

They came to rest upon the knoll beyond one ruined tower. The empty vale was huge enough to swallow Falmouth, a vast swath void of all movement. The dragon chattered in its deep-throated manner. Only this time there was not the customary fierceness. The urgency carried a gentle note, pleading and apologetic. As though whatever awaited them was important enough for it to treat Hyam as a partner in its mysterious quest. Asking for help. Imploring.

The dragon curved its great neck so as to inspect Hyam first with one gold-green eye, then the other. It emitted another war drum of sound and pointed a talon toward the distant floor. As if to emphasize the point, the dragon extended those great wings and swooped down, down, until it came to rest upon the large mound at the valley's center. The wings extended to full span, and the neck stretched up to where the body became a spear pointed straight at Hyam. And the beast bellowed. A huge roar of need and fire and resolve.

Hyam woke to the first faint wash of morning. He rose and walked to where Meda stood on watch, gazing out over the Ellismere vale. She greeted him with, "The dragon?"

"Yes."

"You all right?"

"Yes." He started to explain that the dreams were not unsettling. But just then his attention was snagged by a strangeness. "Meda . . ."

"I see it."

Tendrils of night mist emerged from caves farther along the ridge. Only, this vapor defied the wind. Instead, it drifted toward where Hyam and Meda stood. The cloud grew in length but remained poised atop the ridgeline. Dama padded over and stood beside him. There was no growl, nor sense of worry from the beast.

Meda drew her sword, the blade snickering against the scabbard. Hyam started to point out that steel would have little effect on smoke. But he found himself gripping his own scabbard and simply asked, "Have you ever heard of such a thing?"

"Never."

The haze extended a thousand paces and more along the ridge. Then the fog divided in two and began encircling their camp.

Hyam yelled, "Hold fast!"

The cry was enough to waken the camp. Behind him he heard soft cries of sleepy alarm. But at least the haze had halted.

"I am Hyam, conqueror of the Emporis mage." He had no idea whether he should speak, or whom he addressed. But the mist hovered halfway around the stones. His wife was with him. And his friends. If a sword would not work, he had nothing save his voice to protect them. "If you want me, I am here."

Joelle protested, "Hyam, no, you—"

"Stand back!" For at that moment, a clump of the fog separated from the rest. It moved forward a half-dozen paces. Behind it, the vapor split, then split again, until they faced hundreds of spectral shapes. Then hundreds more.

The first blade of sunlight rose above the eastern ridge. Hyam half expected the specters to dissipate. Instead, they coalesced further, as though they needed density to withstand the force of daylight. The first figure of mist took one step between the stones and halted.

Hyam forced himself to walk to the lone shape and demand, "Why are you here?"

Behind him, the elder lorekeeper said, "My great-grandfather told me tales of these tower guardians."

Meda asked, "They were clan warriors?"

"Some were. Others were soldiers of the realm. Assigned duty as the first line of defense."

"I have read of them," Shona said. "In some of my father's oldest scrolls."

"The first king of your line, daughter of Oberon, charged them with a vital duty. Before the Elven kingdom north of Emporis was destroyed, desert merchants brought word to the realm of dangers rising from the yellow realm. The first Oberon king sent forces to join with the clans. Together they manned the wall you see upon the opposite ridge, a line of defense against whatever the desert spawned. But the realm's first guardians grew bored and sullen and many deserted. They despised these lonely reaches. The night the Milantian horde invaded Ellismere, the winter wind was so fierce it could freeze armor to the skin. The soldiers who remained on duty were all clustered in the tower, gathered about the fire. They failed the clans and the realm."

Joelle said what Hyam had been thinking. "If they faced an army of mages, there was little they could have done."

"They broke their oath," the elder Caleb insisted. "The legends claim that in death they fashioned a new vow. To return to their station whenever a threat arose."

Hyam turned back to the waiting mist. "Hear me! We are no threat! We have been called here—"

He stopped because the spectral haze directly in front of him condensed further, fashioning a warrior of white.

Moonlight glinted off helmet and breastplate and spear and shield.

All around them the mist reformed, until they faced a forest of phantom soldiers holding unsheathed blades.

The ghostly troop moved in unison, forming a two-sided phalanx. They rimmed the path leading from the circle of stones down, down, to the vale of Ellismere.

As one, they saluted the empty trail between their ranks.

The lone warrior beckoned to Hyam. *Come.*

Joelle demanded, "Why should we go anywhere with such as these?"

"I was thinking the very same thing," Meda said.

Hyam stepped closer, to where he could make out misshapen teeth in a mouth that had not existed for a thousand years. "I know you not. Nor do we see a reason to accompany you."

In response, the sentinel rose from the earth. He hovered just above Hyam's head, up where his wraithlike form became silhouetted by the sun. Gone was the warrior of old. In its place appeared a great conjured beast, whose outstretched wings bore diamond patterns along their leading edges. Talons raked the space between it and Hyam, and a sweeping tail lashed out, mist-like against the stones.

Then the sentinel returned to earth and resumed his warrior guise. He motioned once more. *Come.*

"I will go," Hyam declared.

Joelle responded, "Then we all journey with you."

8

The spectral troops stood ranked to either side of the narrow path. Those flanking the drop-off hovered in midair, while those on the opposite side melted slightly into the cliff face. They were certainly not pleasant to look at, with their sightless eyes and grim demeanors. And yet Hyam felt somehow comforted by their presence. There was a binding together of his dreams and the quest, a sense of arriving at answers to questions he had carried since long before the scrolls appeared. Such as, whether some objective might be great enough to carry him beyond the loss of magic. As he descended into this dread vale, flanked by an honor guard of ghosts, Hyam welcomed the mysteries.

Midway down the ridge, they paused on a broad plateau watered by an underground spring. The waterfall across the valley sounded much louder here, the noise resonating off the wall behind them. Hyam settled next to Joelle, the smooth rock cool against his back.

Meda hunkered down on Hyam's other side and passed over sacks of dried fruit, nuts, and a skin of tea. "A soldier's breakfast. Alembord, Shona, Calebs, join us." She studied the valley floor with the tight gaze of an officer gauging enemy terrain and asked Hyam, "That mound is our destination?"

Dama huffed down by Hyam's feet, snuffed the handful of fruit, and turned away. Hyam replied, "That is where the dragon directed me."

"Then I'd say you, Joelle, and I should reconnoiter the terrain. Alembord should stay on guard here with Shona and the highlanders."

"Agreed," Hyam replied.

Alembord said, "My lady, I should—"

"Follow orders," Meda replied.

The younger Caleb complained, "I did not come all this way to be left out of a battle!"

"No," his grandfather said. "You came to do as you are told!"

Neither young man liked it, but when it was clear they were not protesting further, Meda said, "Let's head out."

Joelle tightened the shoulder scabbard holding the Milantian blade. "Dama, come."

As they arrived at the valley base, the contingent of silent warriors split into fighting groups and spread out across the floor. Their silent alertness only added to the tension.

The route they followed was a wretched thing, a mere hint of what once had been a mighty road. The vale was a pale and dusty plain in the early light. Anywhere else, Hyam would have counted it the start of a fine day. The air was crisp but not uncomfortably cold. But down here it merely illuminated the absence of hope and life both. To either side of the road, the grass was stunted and colored a sickly orange. Not a tree interrupted the vast empty plain, not a shrub, not a gopher. Only the gigantic mound that was their destination, lumpish and scarred.

Much of the central hill had wasted away, leaving only rock and a tangled petrified forest. The uncovered limbs were massive, thick as tree trunks, and grey as old bones. The spectral forces formed a ring around the hill and did not approach.

Joelle asked, "What do we do now?"

Hyam recalled the dragon's vantage point and replied, "Climb up."

The top of the mound was flat as a plowed field and unevenly furrowed. Joelle and Hyam picked their way carefully, for the drops between some roots were wide enough to swallow them whole. Dama, however, loped with carefree ease.

Joelle stopped near the center, her eyes widening. Hyam asked, "What is it?"

"The power you showed me, deep in the earth. You remember?"

"By the Emporis tower. Of course. You feel it now?"

"I'm not . . . I think so. Yes. Faint. Like a taste on the wind." She smiled. "It's nice."

"I'm sure." He lingered there longer than he should have, held by the thought that hers could well have been the first smile in the Ellismere vale for centuries.

84

Which meant he was caught utterly off guard when the call sounded from the distant ledge.

The younger Caleb proved to have a remarkable set of lungs. Hyam, Meda, and Joelle turned together and saw the sunlight glint off the sword Alembord waved over his head. Then Dama howled, drawing them back around.

A shadow appeared where the waterfall began its long descent, one that reared and wrenched itself from the rocks. The behemoth glared into the vale, taking aim straight at where they stood. Then it lifted its head to the sunrise and bellowed. The blast filled the vale with the stench of death.

Joelle asked, "Is that your dragon?"

"No. Definitely not." Hyam was already moving. "Call Dama to you."

As the monster tumbled over the ledge, Hyam began casting the Milantian shield spell. The beast had a snake's ability to roll and writhe, and fell to the valley floor as fast as an eagle on the attack.

Hyam used his blade to scour a hasty circle, racing about the mound's perimeter. Twice he almost tumbled into the shadowy depths. Dama punctuated his footsteps with snarls. The monster landed on the valley floor with enough force to shake the entire mound.

Hyam fell flat, caught himself, and scrambled up, all the while puffing out the chant, hoping with adrenaline desperation that the shield spell had not been interrupted.

The behemoth extended six legs like fluid barrels and pummeled the earth as it raced toward them. Howling. Screeching. Raging with a ravenous fury.

The spectral warriors formed a broad phalanx of smoke and translucent swords. They clambered onto its mighty back and stabbed with their weapons. But the magic that had formed the beast offered protection from such an attack. It rolled upon the earth, cast them aside, screamed its bloodlust, and headed for the mound.

But the warriors' attack granted Hyam the time necessary to complete his unsteady course. His blade scoured the last roots and rocks. He leapt over the final gap, trailing over shadowy air. Their lives depended upon the shield.

He completed the final flourish just as the beast scaled the mount.

The monster slammed into the shield, then tumbled back to the base. The impact caused the entire root system to vibrate like a tuning of the harmonies of doom. Hyam was knocked flat again. He was separated from Joelle by less than five paces, but it might as well have been a thousand. He wrapped his arms and legs around a root and clung to the sunlight.

Somehow Meda managed to hold to her feet. Both Joelle and Dama, however, were flipped off their perches. Dama disappeared into the cavernous root system. Joelle clutched to a handhold and shrieked, "Hyam!"

He clawed his way across the distance as the monster thundered back up the terraced rise, bellowing with the lust for fresh blood. "Take my hand!"

She grabbed and clambered her way back up top just as the fiend hammered the shield once more. Meda stepped back and almost fell into another gap, but managed to right herself. The beast slammed into the invisible wall a third time, but this time they were ready.

From somewhere beneath Hyam's feet, the wolfhound howled. In the far distance, Alembord and Shona and the younger Caleb drew blades and raced down to offer what aid they could. Their approach only added to Hyam's need for haste, for he knew with utter certainty they sped toward their doom.

The monster resembled nothing Hyam had ever seen or heard of. The legs were barrel-like stumps that ended in fan-shaped claws. The hide was mottled and hairless, a crude pattern of orangish green. Its head was by far the most fearsome component. Six furious eyes rimmed a crown of thick bone. A trio of nostrils smoldered a putrid fume. The being had two mouths, one inside the other, that opened like alternating petals of a flesh-eating bloom. The six triangular lips were rimmed with teeth the length of Hyam's sword. The fiend roared and clawed the shield and roared again.

Joelle searched through an opening in the roots, then called, "Dama is too deep to reach!"

It was one thing to tell himself the shield protected them, and another thing entirely to turn his back on the behemoth. Yet that is what he did, carefully making his way across the web of petrified roots, following the wolfhound's snarls.

Meda cried, "The beast tracks you!"

Hyam realized it was so. The fiend rounded the crest so as to keep its head aimed at him. Hyam dropped to his belly and leaned into the crevice. Far below he could hear Dama snarling and scrambling. It sounded to Hyam as though the dog was actually moving away from them, but with the beast's bellows he could not be certain of anything other than the fact that the wolfhound would have to wait. Which was a shame, because Dama was a most ferocious ally.

When he rose to his feet, he turned and waved to Alembord, gesturing them to hold back. Meda came up beside him and did the same. Only when they stopped did Hyam return his attention to the beast.

Joelle called, "What do we do?"

He had only one idea. He leaned in close to the two women and yelled, "Find two gaps on opposite sides. You both need footholds so you can come up fast. I'll act as the lure."

"Hyam, no—"

"Listen! You have the Milantian blade. I'll break the shield, dive into a third hold, and stab up. If the beast comes after me, both of you go on the attack."

Fear turned Joelle's gaze liquid. "What if it can get to you?"

"The roots are like stone." Meda's sweat-streaked face was grim with anticipation. "It's a good plan."

Hyam said, "I'll use a crevasse too narrow for the claws to reach in."

Joelle gave the fiend another look, her terror clearly mounting. Hyam knew he had to move now, before she froze. He clenched her tight.

Joelle's face felt hot against his cheek, her breath molten as she shouted into his ear about love and safety.

He released her and yelled, "Stab once, stab deep, then duck back down!"

Joelle glanced at Meda and must have found what she needed to tighten into the warrior mage who had been forged in flames all her own. It gave him the confidence to yell, "We will do this and we will walk away!"

9

Joelle and Meda both found suitable openings and carefully lowered themselves inside. Joelle then drew her sword and gestured to him, followed by Meda. By then Hyam had found his own perch, a narrow ledge with space for him to crouch and thrust his blade.

Hyam signaled the ladies and approached the fiend.

To have Hyam stand safely a mere sword's distance away drove the beast to a new level of frenzy. It clawed and chewed at the shield, blind to all save the prey.

Hyam poised at the brink of his opening, waiting for the beast to rear back. Then he drew his blade across one point in the magical line and broke the spell.

He was only halfway into the shelter before the beast was upon him. But Dama struck with such force the beast stumbled.

The wolfhound had evidently burrowed through the roots and stones, all the way to the shield. The instant Hyam broke the spell, Dama burst from her burrow and flung herself at the fiend.

Dama struck between the two rear legs and clenched the monster's underbelly. The wolfhound weighed a fraction of the behemoth. But her fury granted her a force so potent the creature was knocked from its perch and sent tumbling off the mound.

"*Dama!*" Hyam and Joelle and Meda all shouted together, then scrambled down the terraced steps.

Hyam yelled, "I'm going for the head!"

Meda leapt down upon the beast's back, landing at the juncture of the two rear legs. She stabbed once, twice, then was tossed well clear.

Joelle remained focused upon rescuing Dama. The fiend was curved around the wolfhound, attacking with claws and the flower-mouth. Or it would have been, but Joelle scoured the opposite flank all the way from the middle leg to the beginning of its tail. The Milantian blade could cut through steel like a sickle through grass, and the fiend's side proved no stronger. The behemoth howled and swung its head around just as its guts spilled into the dust.

Hyam scaled the slimy back and plunged his sword up to the hilt in the nearside eye.

The monster shrieked a new pitch and convulsed down its entire length. Hyam was tossed free of the legs and rolled to safety.

Joelle leapt impossibly high as the tail scissored about.

She tumbled hard but came up running, and when the tail swung back she sliced off the tip.

Meda clambered back up and stabbed once more at the spine. She was now joined by Alembord and Caleb and Shona, who distracted the beast long enough for Hyam to reach the head once more.

Hyam gripped the slimy scalp with his knees and rammed his sword deep into another eye. The beast shook him off, but the frenzy was lessening.

Then Joelle slammed her milky blade into the chest, plunging the blade down all the way to the scabbard. Hyam climbed up a third time and stabbed where the massive skull met the spine.

Only when the beast ceased its struggles did Hyam realize he was shouting a war cry of his own.

One moment the monster shuddered in death throes. The next Hyam tumbled to the earth, with nothing beneath him save dust. The brownish cloud drifted momentarily in the wind, smudging the meadow. Through three heaving breaths, Hyam watched the cloud disperse.

The meadow was silent except for soft whimpers from the wounded dog.

Hyam raced back to his wife, stroked her face, asked, "You are hurt?"

"Bruised, shaken, but fine," she gasped. "The beast?"

"Gone."

Dama's yelping cry pierced them both. Together they limped over to where Meda stood. The wolfhound lay crumpled on her side, her back and rear limbs at angles that clenched Hyam's heart. "Dama, no."

The dog whimpered softly, panted, and keened a tight breath. Her side was laid open, her pelt matted with blood and the beast's ash. Hyam cradled the dog's head, stroked her, and repeated, "You beautiful, beautiful friend."

10

Joelle suggested they use Dama's tunnel as her resting place. Hyam nodded agreement, gripped the dog's pelt, and began pulling. Shona helped with the others, her thoughts split precisely in two. On the one hand, she was thrilled to be alive. The chilling rain felt exquisite against her skin. How easily it could have been her that they pulled and shoved toward her last resting place. The cold breeze whispered to her that every breath was a gift to be savored.

And yet at some fiercely private level, Shona complained bitterly. Was this what her uncle the earl had sent her out here for, to struggle and twist and tug in the dark, hauling a dog into a mound of petrified roots? What would her parents say to this, except come home? And home was certainly where she wanted to be just now. Away from fell beasts whose howls turned her every breath into a keen of fear. Away from ghost warriors whose vaporous tendrils clutched at her like spiderwebs when she raced through them. Old men who spoke of clans dead for centuries, bad food, and stony earth for beds. And for what? So she could be spurned by a man she loved?

Dama's fur had soaked up the water. Her pelt was so slick it was hard to find a decent handhold. As the tunnel narrowed, only two people at a time could handle the carcass. Shona and Meda and Joelle took turns up front, while Alembord and Hyam and the younger Caleb shoved from the other side.

When Dama became stuck in the narrow passage, Meda puffed, "Perhaps some other location might work better."

The elder Caleb replied from just beyond the opening, "Though the valley has been empty of all save ghosts for a thousand years, the heart of Ellismere remains hallowed ground." The old man pointed back to where the ghostly troops stood at attention, their ranks shimmering in the rain. "They seem well content with our actions."

With the sweat streaming down her face and burning her eyes, Shona saw her mental tirade from a distance. She crouched in the cave-like dark while Meda took her turn, and realized the unspoken protests reflected a childhood that was no more. The road and the quest were working on her. The rather spoiled young woman who had argued with her mother over dresses and jewels and dances was gradually fading away. This was why she had come, Shona knew. Or rather, why the earl had wanted her to go. Not to see tragedy, though no doubt he knew she would experience her share of hardship. But rather to grow up.

When the tunnel opened, Joelle moved about setting mage-lights in place. They discovered a vast chamber framed by cathedral roots. Chests of gold and jewels littered the floor, while spears and shields decorated the wall. They gathered there, awed by the remnants of a once-proud warrior clan that breathed no more.

Together they lifted Dama and settled her into an alcove formed by the massive roots. Joelle spoke first, offering tribute to their fallen friend. Then Meda. Finally Hyam offered what few words he could manage.

It was then Shona noticed the ghostly general had joined them. "Hyam."

When he lifted his tear-streaked face, Shona pointed to the translucent soldier. "We have company."

The troop leader stood at the entry to another alcove. He waved a hand, beckoning Hyam forward. When Hyam stepped toward him, Joelle illuminated the recess with a mage-light, then gasped at what she had revealed.

Inside was a giant scroll. The spool rose twice the height of a man. Hyam reached out an unsteady hand, traced two fingers over the centuries of dust, and revealed the sparkling gold beneath.

Together they maneuvered the scroll back into the main chamber. With the others' help, they unfurled the golden sheet enough to know it contained the same jagged writing as Hyam's miniature scrolls. Only here there was something more, for between each line of jagged furrows lay a script Shona had never seen before. "What is this writing?"

Hyam's voice carried both raw grief and awe. "Elven."

Joelle now stood beside Shona. "So this is . . ."

"A teaching scroll." Hyam turned to Caleb and asked, "May we take this?"

The elder stroked his long beard before replying thoughtfully, "A dragon that has never existed leads you here in a dream. We are greeted by spectral warriors who have guarded an empty vale for a thousand years. You defeat a beast that heralded our first war with the crimson riders. You lay your friend to rest at the clan's heart. A ghostly general points you to this hidden treasure." He glanced at the translucent leader as though seeking approval. "I would say the fief that once stood here would be proud to call you clansman. In that case, the scroll is yours by right."

11

Meda had bruised her ribs and Alembord had a nasty gash down one shin, which he didn't even notice until Joelle pointed it out. They spent the next nine days recuperating and searching for the creature's lair. Their hunts proved futile, for there was neither game nor any sign of another beast. They were forced to halt their search when supplies grew low.

The trail leading north was little used, for the next three vales had been attacked by the crimson one. Every time they crested another ridge, the view was as desolate as it was stupendous. To their left ran another empty vale, to their right an even emptier desert. The yellow reaches were flat as a seabed, the above a superheated blue. Each midday the sun drew dancing ribbons from the vacant plains.

When they reached the inhabited valleys, Caleb insisted upon a gathering. The lorekeeper spun new tales of dreams and dragons and monsters and battles. Thus the highland clans learned of this latest threat.

The trip from Ellismere to Emporis required twenty-seven days. Hyam did not complain overmuch. He marched and he mourned and gradually he healed from the worst of the sorrow. And the giant scroll kept him busy.

When fully unfurled, the scroll stretched eleven paces, the gold so thin it rippled in the slightest breeze. Hyam studied the translated words and committed them to memory. He also used the scroll as a teaching tool, introducing Joelle and Shona to the Elven tongue. Together the three of them copied the entire scroll onto sheaves of parchment, often working late into the night. By the third week of study, they spent time each day conversing in the language of forests and myth.

Every day of their journey, Hyam spied a desert eagle spiraling high overhead, apparently tracking them. For what purpose, he had no idea. Nor could he say why the dragon no longer appeared in his dreams. Perhaps it was the loss of Dama or the work on this scroll. Whatever the reason, his dawns were no longer punctuated by the beast's arrival. Nor did he have an opportunity to discover whether the scroll indeed taught the tongue of legends.

This last morning before arriving in Emporis, Hyam slowed his pace so that he and his wife could travel well behind the others, enjoying a rare private moment upon the road. They walked hand in hand, leading their sturdy highland ponies and speaking about things that mattered little. The rough trek, the heat, the pleasure of a bath, and the company of other wizards.

They caught up with the others at the top of the final ridge. Sweat stung his eyes as Hyam joined them in studying the yellow vale. He did not need to ask why they had stopped. The sense of dread resonated through his entire body.

Meda said, "The enemy's shadow lingers. I can smell it."

"Taste it, more like," Alembord agreed.

There was an eerie silence to the valley separating them from the Emporis gates, a quiet that went beyond an absence of sound. The valley ran north to south, with the city of Emporis far up to their left. The ruined tower where Hyam had vanquished the crimson foe rose above the city's ancient walls. The valley stretched before them like an overheated crypt.

The elder Caleb said, "The clans have renamed this place Specter's Vale. It is here that the crimson mage demolished a clan's army, then stored his ghost battalions in the rocky earth. Travelers speak of screams rising from the valley floor on moonless nights, and drifting fogs that choke the strength from the bravest warrior."

Then Joelle announced, "We are not alone."

Hyam turned and saw that his own spectral army had re-formed behind them, a horde of mist and fierce translucent forms. They had been last seen upon their departure from Ellismere Vale.

"Their leader says he will see us through to the far end," Joelle declared. "At least, I think. His speech is oddly formed."

Hyam asked, "You hear them like you do the Ashanta?"

"Not exactly. It's like . . ." Her features creased with the effort of trying to describe. "His voice is a whisper upon the winds of time."

Hyam decided that mystery could wait for another hour. He turned to the spectral warrior and asked, "Is there danger here?"

Joelle replied, "Not for you or your company."

The ghostly Ellismere warriors split into four companies and marched fore, aft, and to either side of their small band. Hyam watched the troop pretend to march, their legs moving across the dry earth without raising a dust mote. The desert eagle circled high overhead, tracking their progress across the empty vale. Nothing else stirred.

Midway down the gorge, Hyam stopped and peered at the ridge opposite the city's gates.

Meda asked, "Something wrong?"

Hyam pointed to the glade of dusty pines. "There is a portal leading to the last Elven kingdom. Or rather, there was."

Joelle explained to the others, "The armies who defeated the crimson mage gathered along that ridgeline."

"The scroll we carry is written in Elven," Hyam went on. "It is as much theirs as anyone's. And it will be safe in their keeping."

Joelle gentled the pony as Hyam and Meda unlashed the scroll. Hyam and Alembord shouldered the burden. When they arrived at the ledge, Hyam pulled the silver chain from beneath his shirt, fitted the crystal pipe between dry and cracked lips, and blew.

They waited in the silence and the heat. Hyam turned and glanced back across the vale in time to watch the eagle rise from the Emporis castle's central keep. It shrieked once, a piercing call.

Then a voice spoke to him in Elven. "We have long hoped to hear from the emissary."

Hyam faced a trio of green warriors. "I have a report to make."

The Elf inspected the ghostly warriors arrayed along the ledge and down the ridge. "You are in need of such allies as these?"

"They are part of my report." Hyam recognized the Elven spokesman. "You accompanied me into the citadel's garden."

"Aye, Emissary. I did. That was a rare battle indeed." He offered a warrior's grin. "Make your report."

"It is long. Do you need to write it down?"

"I will deliver your news word for word."

Another of the Elves added, "We are here to correct any mistakes he might make."

The soldier bridled. "I do not err."

Hyam paused long enough to translate for the others. Then he related it all, starting with the arrival of the scrolls. Twice he stopped to drink from the waterskin Joelle offered him. Even so, his throat closed up at the end and he could not finish.

Shona spoke the Elven words for him. "Hyam lost his wolfhound to the beast."

The soldiers blanched. "Dama is no more?"

Hyam managed, "Her sacrifice is why we stand here today."

"We salute the sacrifice of our fallen friend." The Elves unsheathed their swords and came to attention, blades to their foreheads. When Hyam translated, Meda and Alembord and Joelle and Shona did the same. Caleb and his grandson lifted staves.

Joelle said quietly, "Look behind you."

Hyam turned to discover the spectral soldiers were saluting as well. The sight of that translucent formation, arrayed in ranks that carpeted the ridge with soldiers of smoke all saluting his fallen friend, struck Hyam hard.

The Elves sheathed their weapons and the spokesman asked, "The Ellismere fiend was not accompanied by a crimson one?"

"Thankfully not."

"And when you struck the blow that felled it, the monster vanished into dust?"

"Not a speck remained, not a drop of blood, no sign it had been there at all except for the claw marks and our fallen friend."

"This sounds like mage-work from the era we thought forever buried."

When Hyam translated the words, Joelle responded in Elven, "And there was the attack on the glade about our home."

"The trees sang to us of crimson force," the Elf agreed, then sighed. "This is calamitous news. Darwain must be informed."

"There is one thing more." Swiftly Hyam recounted his dreams and finding the scroll.

This time even the Elves could not hide their shock. "A dragon? Truly?"

"Many of them. Resting like living hills upon an emerald isle. But only one tried to speak with me."

"We have no record of any such . . ." The soldier stopped talking as they untied the burlap covering and revealed the scroll's leading edge. "Wonder upon wonder."

"The words here are Elven," Hyam pointed out.

The soldier struggled to maintain his composure. "Once all the Elven kingdoms paid fealty to a realm north of Emporis."

"Ethrin, the forest destroyed in the first Milantian attack," Hyam said.

"There are tales of such scrolls, fashioned by forces long forgotten, left with the Ethrin rulers by the last of the Ancients. This is the first trace of Ethrin's lore we have seen in a thousand years."

"Take it," Hyam said. "It is yours once more."

The Elf stepped forward and ran one hand along the shimmering surface. "Emissary, your coming was truly a gift."

12

Hyam led his company back down the ridge and through an avenue lined by his wispy warriors. As they recrossed the valley floor, he again felt the dread force, as if the crimson warrior's army was only temporarily contained. As they approached Emporis, the plateau fronting the city's main gates became deserted. Hyam heard the patter of footsteps and caught fleeting glimpses of heads peeping over the parapets. There was not a whisper of sound.

Hyam turned to face his silent troop and said, "I thank you for your company and your protection."

Joelle's voice sounded overloud in the quiet. "Their leader says, stand in open terrain, away from any glade or forest. Blow the Elven pipe if you have need of us. We will come."

Hyam asked, "What is your name and rank?"

"He says that names are for the realm of the living," Joelle replied. "And titles for those who still have the power to choose their fate."

"How can I free you?"

"We are not yours to release. We failed in our duty. We pay the price."

"But if I want to help you, as you helped me . . ."

"We are the lost. There is no help," Joelle softly replied for them.

"There must be," Hyam insisted. "Tell me what I must do!"

Their leader stepped closer still, until Hyam could see the close-cropped beard, the cavernous cheeks, the gaze from beyond the reach of time. They stood like that until the leader turned and signaled to his troop. The spectral force became mere wisps of fog, blown apart by a wind Hyam could not feel.

As Hyam and his company approached the city's portal, a voice called from inside, "Are they gone?"

Hyam saw Joelle smile in response, then Shona rolled her eyes. He replied, "They are."

A dandy in a wizard's robe stepped from the shadows. "And here I thought I was a brave man."

Joelle said, "Greetings, Connell."

"My lady Joelle." He peered over the ledge, down into the empty vale. "Might one ask who accompanied you?"

"Allies from an unexpected quarter," Hyam replied. He had seen the young man in the company of Falmouth wizards but did not remember ever speaking to him before.

Connell was about Hyam's age and wore tailored robes with magical symbols sewn into the fabric. He bowed low, arms extended like a courtier's. "My lord Hyam, this is indeed an honor. Forgive my quaking knees. I have always been frightened by specters. Not that I have ever met one."

Joelle said, "Connell has been appointed head of the Emporis wizards."

"Only because I was the sole mage who asked for the job."

"The Mistress Edlyn claims Connell was the most adept student she ever trained," Joelle went on.

Connell stuffed the handkerchief back up his sleeve. "The Mistress grew a bit addled there before she departed."

Shona bridled. "She most certainly did not."

"And my heartfelt greetings to you, Miss Shona. You are dazzling as always."

The younger woman sniffed and looked away.

"As pleasant and winsome as ever, I see." He turned back to Hyam. "I asked Miss Shona to marry me. I was eleven. She was six. She refused my entreaty. I've never fully recovered."

"You were a pest through my entire childhood," Shona replied. "I see nothing has changed."

Hyam said, "We are in need of baths and hot food."

"Your servant, my lord." Connell bowed a second time. "Welcome to the oldest of cities. But most certainly not the fairest."

Everything about Emporis spoke of years beyond man's ability to count. Age and danger seeped from the stones and infected the air. Soon as Hyam passed through the main gates and started down the central thoroughfare, he saw tight gazes on men and women alike. Most strode the yellow lanes with hands firmly grasping sword hilts or metal-tipped staves. Hyam had never seen so many weapons. When he commented on it, Meda responded, "A city once vanquished heals slowly. And the crimson mage was hardly the first despot to conquer Emporis."

As Connell led them toward the ruined citadel, Hyam gawked at the desert garb of dusty robes and curved blades, beasts he could not name, stallholders hawking every manner of oddity. He breathed the pungent mix of spices and men and epochs and danger. His face stretched into the first smile he had known since leaving Rothmore Vale.

"A number of mages resented how fast Connell rose," Joelle said. She pitched her words so all the company could hear, including Connell. It was clear the pair genuinely liked one another. "They claim he is favored because of his family, which leads the richest merchant clan in Falmouth."

"Merchant and shipping both," Connell said. "In truth, my family was enraged over my choice of profession. I'm the eldest son of the eldest son, and the first wizard my clan has produced in living memory. My father still calls me the black sheep."

"Connell has proved himself the ablest of instructors," Joelle went on. "The young people love him."

"They don't know any better," Shona declared.

"Quite right," Connell agreed. "Poor little lambs."

Meda asked, "Why didn't a more senior wizard want to come . . ." She answered her own question. "The orb."

"Precisely," Connell said. The conversation did nothing to dim his boyish enthusiasm. "They saw this posting as banishment from their source of power. But I was being restricted access. Had it not been for Trace, they would have made my life impossible."

"Trace wanted a trusted ally in this position," Joelle told Hyam.

The chief wizard of Emporis was tall and handsome, with the clear blue eyes of a midsummer dawn. He wore his blond hair standing straight up, like a yellow brush. His blond goatee ended in a woven strand as long as his thumb. He did his best to provoke—outrage, humor, attraction—any response would do, Hyam suspected, so long as it was robust. Connell was everything Hyam was not and never would be. Hyam already liked the young man immensely.

When they passed through the citadel's gates, the plaza fronting the palace was silent and empty of all save the morning shadows. Their footsteps rang over the stones like echoes in a man-made cavern.

Shona asked, "Where is everyone?"

"My students had best be at their studies. As for everyone else, no citizen of Emporis will set foot inside the palace keep," Connell replied. "Our victuals are left in wicker baskets on the doorstep. Those who survived the red-robed Milantian want no contact with his former residence."

Caleb spoke for the first time since entering the city. "Some of our tribesmen who visit Emporis claim the palace stones can be heard to scream on moonless nights."

Hyam saw how the old man and his scribe had to force themselves forward, and offered, "We will gladly put you up at one of the city's inns."

Clearly the old man was tempted, but he asked, "And who then will make an account of the hero's journey? You?"

Shona said, "I will serve as keeper of records."

Caleb halted midway across the stone plaza. "You will travel with the emissary to the end of his journey?"

"That is my aim."

"You promise to maintain a careful account of all that happens?"

"So do I vow."

Caleb used his stave to salute the company. "In that case, I and my grandson wish you success with your quest and bid you farewell."

When they turned away, Hyam asked, "Don't you want a meal? A bed for the night?"

But the pair were already moving away. "I have no desire to take another breath within the shadow of the crimson mage's abode. We will reside with clansmen who have made their homes in Emporis."

Hyam called, "What of provisions for your return journey?"

"With the tales we carry, the clans will compete to host us." The elder's stave tapped loudly across the stones. "Farewell, Emissary."

The company of twenty-six acolytes and seven mages hovered behind the chairs holding Hyam's company and Connell. They were all present at Hyam's invitation. Connell's study was not crowded, however. The chamber was a full forty paces long and two dozen wide. The framed metal speaking portal on Connell's office wall sparked, swam, and fashioned itself into a window that revealed Bayard and Trace and several members of the earl's inner council. Hyam had never seen a communications mirror at work before, and the brilliant connection that spanned their weeks on the road was startling.

The earl spoke with the formality of a leader in council. "Greetings, Hyam. You are well?"

"I and most of my company, sire, thank you."

Bayard was seated at the head of the council table. He smiled at his niece. "How has the road treated you, Shona?"

"I am learning, Uncle."

"Your father is eager to speak with you when we finish."

"And I with him."

The Earl of Falmouth turned to Hyam and said, "Give us your report."

Hyam's account took well over an hour. Golden light lanced through the open window and turned the stone molten. Hyam heard crows greeting the coming dusk from the empty courtyard below. When he was done, and Bayard frowned in silent concentration, Trace asked, "What is your assessment of the dragon tongue?"

"It is incomplete."

"How so?"

"Many words within our own language are meant to convey hidden depths or parallel meanings. The dragon's speech takes this to a completely different level."

Bayard said, "One word for many meanings. All languages have them."

"Not like dragon speech, sire. At the end of the Ellismere scroll are the Elven words, 'This speech predates the Ancients.' I believe the language was seldom used. As in, the connection between Elves and the races who used this tongue was tenuous."

Bayard demanded, "What of the two small scrolls—can you now translate them?"

"That I can. One is a treaty between dragons and men, Elves, and Ashanta. We are called to aid the dragons whenever they request, for whatever reason, however it may cost us, wherever we might be required to go. There is nothing written about dragons aiding us. In fact, they are commanded not to enter the three realms of men, Ashanta, and Elves."

"Curious, that," Trace mused. "Have you ever heard of such a thing, Highness?"

"Never," Bayard replied. "And the other scroll?"

"Another treaty, worded exactly the same as the first. But who binds this one to the dragons, I have no idea, for the name for these people is not in the lexicon."

Trace reflected a moment, then asked, "You have had no more dragon dreams?"

"Not since the night before we faced the beast in Ellismere Vale," Hyam replied.

Bayard said, "The Ellismere beast was the result of Milantian magery?"

"The highland elders claim these very same monsters fought alongside the first Milantian hordes," Hyam confirmed.

Joelle added, "Don't forget the attack on our home."

Trace said, "Our spies send us troublesome reports of

darkness spreading through Port Royal and the king's household."

"I think we should assume they are all linked," Hyam said.

Bayard asked, "Are the dragon dreams part of this threat?"

"It is possible, sire. But my gut says no."

"And yet the dreams lured you to the valley where you fought the Milantian beast. And since you survived, the dreams have not returned." Bayard mulled this over, then changed directions once more. "When do you meet with the scroll merchant?"

Connell replied, "Tomorrow morning, sire. The Ashanta banker is bringing him here."

"Then we will expect your report at noon." Bayard rose from his chair. "Shona, your father would have a word."

Hyam rose very early the next morning. Their chamber had a small window, little more than an arrow slit. He padded across the stone and glanced up at a starlit sky. The moon was a hook of purest silver. Of the dawn there was no sign. Hyam dressed anyway. He would sleep no more that night.

Joelle sat up in bed. "What are you doing?"

"I thought I'd go watch the dawn from the citadel." He had gone up the previous dusk with Connell and found the view fascinating.

"Wait and I'll come."

"You should rest."

But Joelle tossed the covers aside and reached for her clothes. "Did you dream?"

"Not of the dragon. I dreamed of home." Which was very strange. He could not recall the last time that had happened. "Not our cottage. My field."

"The oval one in the forest," Joelle said, dressing swiftly.

"It was as vivid as the dragon dreams. It was night. I saw the same moon as here. Like I had been taken there."

Joelle sat on the bed and slipped on her boots. "Perhaps you were."

"The field was fallow. No one has touched it since I . . . since the day I left." He had a sudden image of newly discovered magical abilities being put to use, saving himself by opening a great fissure in the earth and sending warriors and their steeds plunging to their deaths. Hyam pushed that memory aside and refocused upon the dream. "I felt the power surge through me."

Joelle stopped in the act of reaching for the door handle. "Then you must go."

"Perhaps it was just the recollection of bygone days."

"You would let this stop you from seeing if the dream holds a message for your future?" She gave him a chance to object, then opened the door and said, "We will go as soon as this quest is accomplished."

As they stepped into the corridor, Meda pushed herself off the side wall. "Mind a bit of company?"

"Don't tell me dreams woke you as well," Joelle said.

"It was the kids, up for an early meal and noisy as a flock of angry geese. Connell wants to get them into the day's lessons before he departs with us." Meda followed them down the long corridor and up the citadel's winding stairs. When they arrived at the top, she added, "I like Connell. He puts on airs of a dandy, but I sense a deep affection for his charges."

"And the students adore him, both here and back in Falmouth." Joelle sidled up beside the officer, where they could peer out over a low point in the wall, and breathed the city's air. "Hyam had a dream of home."

"I do that sometimes. Always seems nicer than what I remember upon awakening. How was your region called?"

"Three Valleys." Hyam faced directly east, where a first faint hint of greyish rose traced its way across the sky. "The planting festival will be over now and they'll be entering into high summer. Early crops will be coming in soon, berries and corn and possibly wheat if the season's been kind. If I was there I'd be working dawn to dusk and beyond. Weather is everything. Every time I meet a neighbor, we study the sky."

Joelle was watching him now. "Do you miss it?"

"In truth, I haven't thought of it in months. Longer."

"Do you wish you had stayed?"

"Not even once since meeting you," he replied.

She smiled at him, then turned back to the dawn.

The citadel had been largely destroyed when Hyam blasted the crimson mage into oblivion. Despite the tower's stunted shape, the view was stupendous. Emporis crowned a high conical hill that stood well apart from its neighbors. The desert reaches opened like a vast pewter sea in the early light, silent and empty and beckoning. Hyam could see the faint indentation of the road used by the wilderness travelers. It called to him in a strange way.

The boundaries of Emporis had been set down in some

lost epoch, marked by walls built from stones broader than a man was tall. The streets were narrow and winding, the crowds dense, the air thick. The city woke early and worked hard. Hyam heard the rhythmic sounds of hammers striking metal and breathed the pungent odor of lamb roasting over cedar chips.

He confessed, "I like it here."

Meda humphed her disagreement. "My first commanding officer said to treat this city like a viper, the only snake that kills for pleasure and always without warning."

Hyam nodded, for he sensed the latent threat from all sides. "Even so."

"You like the mystery," Joelle offered. "The chance of new beginnings."

"There are more endings here than fresh starts," Meda said. "More menace than mystery."

They stood in silence until the sun crested the horizon. Gradually the city revealed its true form, the callous edges and harsh sounds. Surrounded by razor cliffs and yellow wasteland. Hyam drank it all in.

A gong sounded from somewhere below them, Hyam assumed calling them to breakfast. He had turned away when Joelle cried, "Look there!"

A great desert eagle landed on the juncture where the citadel's stones met the flat roof. The tower's ruins were as tall as the level where they stood, such that the bird looked directly at them. The eagle was a soft russet, more brown than red, with streaks of gold upon its head and down the tips of both wings. Hyam thought the bird was beautiful as the dawn.

"A desert hunter," Meda said. "Though I've never heard of one so large."

The bird chattered softly. It was the sound a parent might make to a nesting chick, an almost melodious rattle.

It caused the breath to catch in Hyam's throat.

Meda stepped over beside him. "My first liege captured such birds from their nests and trained them to hunt—"

"Quiet," Hyam murmured.

The eagle ruffled its feathers. And then made the sound again.

The drumming was far swifter than when uttered by the beast in Hyam's dreams. But he was fairly certain the sound represented the same speech.

The eagle repeated the sounds a third time. Precisely.

In dragon speech, the bird said, *Come. Dusk. Alone.*

Hyam had yet to try the noises. But he did his best, forming a mild cough deep in his throat. His efforts were slow and halting. To be certain, he repeated the one word.

Understood.

The eagle extended its wings, growing mightier still. From tip to tip the span was broader than Hyam was tall. The sun rimmed the bird's wings with fire as it rose into the air.

13

Shona rose well before dawn. Though she was bone-weary from the trek, the hours of lost sleep would not be missed. Not after what had woken her.

She dressed and left her sleeping chamber. Like all the citadel's rooms, hers was a vast stone cube. She had not once felt lonely on the journey until the previous evening.

As Shona walked the long corridor, gradually the slap of her sandals became overlaid by a faint din. She halted by the dining room's entryway and listened to the happy chatter. She stayed there, her hand resting upon the aged wood, and thought of her father. She recalled other students taught by a teacher they both loved and wanted desperately to please. She pushed open the door, wondering how it was possible to be both delighted with the journey and aching with remorse for having ever left her home.

She was eighteen years old that day.

Connell's chair scraped overloud in the sudden silence as

he pushed from the table and rose to his feet. "Miss Shona, did we wake you?"

"No, I . . ." Shona had no idea what to say. The entire group was watching her. She could feel the gazes, especially those of the older boys and the male wizards. She had been followed by men's eyes for years now. Why it should bother her so this pre-dawn, she had no idea.

Connell rounded on his students and roared, "You lot could wake the dead! The ghoulish army would find you a nuisance! Eat up! Class in ten minutes!"

They laughed at his pretended ire and resumed their breakfast. Which was clearly what Connell had intended. He stepped in close enough to be heard over the noise and asked, "Are you hungry?"

"No, well . . . Can I speak with you in private?"

For one brief instant Shona glimpsed the man behind the mocking jollity. Connell's gaze became sparked by a deep and compassionate wisdom. He asked, "Bad night?"

"Not bad. But the dawn was . . ."

"Unsettling."

"Very."

"No amount of cleansing spells can erase all the shadows this palace has known," he replied. "We can speak in my chambers if you like, but I do not meet privately with anyone. You understand?"

She took a moment to study Connell. He wore the traditional robe, tailored to suit his broad shoulders and narrow waist, yet otherwise unadorned. The severity suited him. Shona said, "I have misjudged you. For years."

The impish gleam flashed in his eyes once more. "Nice to know I have the capacity to surprise."

She tried for a smile of her own. "Astonish, more like."

"Come. Why don't we sit here." He led her across the hall to an empty table. "Their noise will create walls. Would you like breakfast?"

"Perhaps a tea."

"Tea it is." He turned, and instantly a young man rose from his place and hurried over. "Bring our guest a mug of tea, will you, Fareed?"

When they were alone once more, Shona told him, "I was woken by a dream. I stood before a tall candle. I reached out, and I picked up the flame with my bare fingers. Not the candle. Just the fire. And it didn't burn me."

Connell was so intent he did not notice the student's return. "Did the dream end then?"

"No. I held the flame for a time, then I set it down. Not on the first candle. On another. I watched the flame burn on this second candle, and I felt . . ."

Fareed watched her with the same intensity as Connell. The mug smoked unnoticed in his hands.

Connell said, "Tell me."

"I felt so excited." She knew her face burned with embarrassment. The whole thing seemed ridiculous now. "Like I had finally discovered something I had been searching for my entire life, and didn't even know it until that very moment."

Connell fished in his pocket and came up with a ring of keys. He handed them to the student and said, "You know where to find them?"

"In the corner of your study, Master Connell. Where they always are."

"Don't call me that."

"Yes, Master Mage." Fareed shared a conspiratorial grin with Shona as he handed her the tea. Then he hurried away.

Connell asked, "You are seventeen, are you not?"

"Eighteen today. Please don't tell the others."

"Why ever not?"

She could not bring herself to say more than, "I don't want any fuss."

He started to protest, then shrugged. "Eighteen is very late for such an event. But it does happen. Occasionally."

"What do you mean by event?"

"For your abilities to wake up." He drummed his fingers on the table. "Twelve is the most common age. I've one student, the girl you see over there with the white hair, she became aware at nine. Three of my charges started at fourteen."

"You mean, I have . . . I might be . . ."

"We'll soon see." Once again he showed her the somber intensity. "You need to eat something."

"I'm not the least bit hungry."

"That doesn't matter." He rose, walked to the central refectory table, and filled a plate with bread and fruit and cheese. He returned and set it down before her. "It's important that you eat all you possibly can."

She selected a grape and almost gagged when she swallowed. "I can't."

"You must. Here. Take some of this cheese."

She broke off a sliver and took it like medicine. "It tastes vile."

"You only think it does. Now some bread." He pared an apple and held out a slice. "Eat it, Shona. It will ground you in the material realm."

She forced herself to do as he ordered. "What is happening?"

"The older the individual upon awakening, the more intense the transition. There is every risk of someone your age losing touch with the substance of this earth."

She swallowed another morsel and felt the meal settle in her stomach like a brick. "What happens if I lose touch?"

"We'll discuss that later. Right now . . ." He glanced over as his student entered the dining hall. "Here we are."

The candles were thick as her wrist and were planted in iron stands almost as tall as Fareed. At their appearance, the din cut off for the second time that morning. Connell did not seem to notice. "Set them down there by the far wall. Come with me, Shona."

Gone was the mocking tone, the boyish flirtation, any hint of the wealthy, insolent young man who had once teased her constantly. Connell was gentle and severe at the same time. "Shona, this is Fareed. Trace actually bought him from a desert merchant, but that is a story for another time. He serves as the class monitor when he is not causing me endless grief. It is customary for another student to join in this process. Fareed?"

The young man was a year or so younger than Shona and delighted at taking part. "Think back to your dream. Before you touched the flame, how did you protect your fingers from the fire?"

Shona asked, "The dream is common?"

"All your questions must wait," Connell replied. "Answer Fareed."

Shona did her best to ignore all the mages and acolytes who watched them. She recalled, "I concentrated on my hand. It tingled."

Fareed cast a look at his teacher. Shona saw their shared excitement and felt a tremor course through her. As though she was entering into a secret shared by only a select few. The wizards of this realm.

"Do you feel the energy now?" Fareed asked.

"I . . . yes." Her hand felt on fire, and yet it was a pleasant sensation. As though her limb vibrated to the excitement shared by everyone in the hall.

"Draw it around your entire body. From your head all the way to your feet. Feel it encircle you with an aura of protection. Tell me when you are fully shielded."

By the time he finished speaking, it was already done. The energy flowed up and around and around, until it rang in her voice. "I feel it!"

"This is your safeguard. Each time you draw upon it, you also strengthen it. You must practice this daily. Do you understand?"

Her heart was racing now. She wanted to sing, to shout, to fly away and never return. She understood. Not just the shield, but the need for the food she had eaten. It anchored her. "Yes!"

Connell turned and called to the acolytes and mages who watched from the far table, "Shield yourselves and this room!"

One of his fellow teachers called back, "It is done!"

Connell said to his student, "Light the first candle and step back."

Fareed grinned at Shona, his eyes dancing with whatever was about to come. He touched the candlewick with his finger. A flame ignited.

Connell said, "When you are ready, lift the fire and claim it as your own."

With those words, Shona's entire world was rearranged. She still felt the energy course through her, deeper even than her bones. A sense of knowing filled her. The fire was an opportunity. She could both focus on it and draw upon it. In an instant of otherworldly awareness, she had realized that the fire was not something outside her. She did not merely hold the flame. She *joined* with it.

With the realization had come a new ability. One to draw upon the same force she now used to shield her fingers from being burned. It coursed through her like a surging torrent, demanding release. Which she did, by doing as the master mage of Emporis instructed.

Lifting the flame from the candle was the most exciting event of her entire life.

"Stretch out your arm," Connell said. "Extend the flame beyond its normal boundaries."

Shona did not ask what Connell meant because she did not need to. She took a deep breath and extended her force, bonding and releasing at the same time.

The fire exploded outward, blinding her momentarily as it surged through the dining hall. Shona was horrified by what she had unleashed and fearful she harmed the others. She retreated by taking an indrawn breath, and she sensed that Connell assisted her in damping down the force.

But when the fire was diminished and her vision was restored, she could see the entire company of mages and acolytes were grinning. At *her.*

Connell then said, "Fareed?"

"There is a formal closure to this event," the young man told her. "You must show that you have the ability to reduce your power to safe levels. Being a wizard is not only about releasing the mage-force. Even more important is *controlling* the power. You must now take the flame and light the other candle."

The act was both simple and telling, for the temptation to release the force a second time was very strong. The power still surged and roiled, beckoning her to create more havoc. Resisting the temptation caused her fingers to tremble as Shona transferred the flame from one candle to the other.

Fareed nodded. "Whenever you are tempted to act without full control of your abilities, do you give your word that you will always remember this act and what it represents?"

She breathed, "I will."

He beamed. "Then I welcome you to the company of acolytes."

14

Hyam, Joelle, and Meda were walking down the citadel's main corridor when a light shone around the door frame leading to the dining hall, brilliant enough to stop them in their tracks. It faded swiftly, and a cheer erupted. Hyam could hear Connell say something but could not make out the words. There was a second cheer, this one punctuated by laughter. Then the doors opened and the acolytes came tumbling out, a delighted, chattering mob. And Shona was at their center. She halted in front of Hyam and smiled shyly. Proud and embarrassed at the same time.

Connell came up alongside her and announced, "This one came close to burning us out of house and home."

"You told me to claim the fire," Shona replied.

"And so you did!" Connell beamed like a proud parent. "With a whirlwind's force!"

Joelle asked, "You have magical abilities?"

"Since two hours ago! She has the makings of a master

126

mage, this one." Connell went on to Shona, "Mind, you need to practice that shielding every day."

"I will," Shona said. "Every hour."

Joelle said, "I want to hear everything. But first we have news of our own."

"All that must wait," Connell replied. "The banker and our desert trader should be outside. That Ashanta representative is never late."

But neither banker nor merchant awaited them. Instead, a man Connell identified as Lord Suthon's clerk paced nervously beyond the citadel gates. The clerk was middle-aged and balding and carried all his excess weight about his middle. Even before Connell completed his introductions, the clerk was already urging them westward along the city's main avenue.

"Lord Suthon was in a rare state, I tell you. Rare indeed. Sent me off to fetch you with a shout, wouldn't even let me finish my morning coffee." The clerk's ink-stained robe bore dark patches of nervous sweat. "That's unlike Suthon, I tell you. He's a man who insists on order and decorum."

As Joelle moved to his side, Hyam sensed a new presence among them. She murmured, "Bryna is here. She says something terrible has occurred. What exactly, they are not sure."

Hyam had no chance to ask anything further, because on his other side Connell was asking the clerk, "What did Suthon say was the matter?"

"Don't have the slightest idea. When I asked what I should

tell you, he shouted at me a second time. Make haste, was all he said. Which is precisely what I did."

Hyam asked, "Why doesn't Suthon live in the palace?"

"He wanted to," the clerk replied. When Connell snorted softly, the clerk insisted, "It's true, I tell you. His lordship had every intention of moving in. But a bevy of Emporis merchants met him on the road and begged him to reconsider. None of them would set foot in the palace, nor enter the main keep, nor cross before the palace gates on a moonless night."

"All that's true enough," Connell said.

"The merchants urged Lord Suthon to lay claim to a manor vacated by an ally to the crimson mage," the clerk went on. "It stands two doors down from the Ashanta banker."

"The absent merchant supplied victuals to both the palace and the mage's army," Connell explained. "The day of your victory, a group of rather irate citizens went looking for him. But he'd vanished, him and all his clan. Bayard has offered a sizeable reward. He hasn't been seen since."

Three hundred paces from the palace, they left the markets behind. The avenue broadened and became partially shaded by trees planted in raised stone tubs. A great crowd of people moved with them, though they were careful to keep a distance from Hyam's group. The homes grew larger the closer they came to the city's western wall. Finally the avenue ended at a stone plaza fronting grand residences. Here the crowd was at its thickest. The murmuring wash of voices stilled at their approach.

"Make way!" the clerk cried, but it was hardly necessary,

for already the throng pressed back, forming a path through which they passed.

Their destination was a manor on the plaza's opposite side. Two guard towers rose from the wall's corners. The Ashanta symbol for treaty was stamped into the filigreed metal archway above the main gate. Or rather, what was left of the gate, for it had been mostly destroyed. As had the right-hand guard tower. And the manor's front door.

Connell indicated the foppish gentleman rushing down the front walk. "Suthon, the earl's representative."

Suthon greeted them nervously, "Thank heavens you've come."

A voice called from among the mob rimming the plaza, "Has the fiend returned?"

Suthon jerked as though the citizen had read his own thoughts. Connell, however, was made of sterner stuff. He turned and addressed the crowd. "The crimson mage was destroyed. His power has been vanquished. Many of you were witnesses to the battle and the triumph."

Another from the crowd called, "What happened here?"

"I do not know. Yet."

"We want answers!"

Hyam could sense the crowd's fear. Tension seethed across the open plaza, dense as fog. He stepped up beside Connell. "Should I speak to them?"

"It might actually save the day," Connell muttered.

Hyam raised his voice. "You know who I am. The crimson mage and Prince Ravi ruled this city with terror and dark forces. But no more! I am here, along with the Lady Joelle, the wizard Connell, and both the earl's representative and the earl's niece. We aim to keep you and the city safe."

A woman's voice shrilled, "What *happened* in there?"

"I have no idea. But if you will be patient, we will make a thorough investigation. Then I will come back out and together we will tell you everything we have found."

"Everything?"

"You have my word."

He stood and felt the tension dissolve into a muttering worry. He had no trouble with that. He was worried himself. Hyam turned to the others and said, "Let's go."

There was no front door to the Ashanta banker's residence. In fact, there was nothing upon which a door might have been placed. The frame was gone. The surrounding stones were seared a greyish black, their surface turned molten-smooth. Beyond the absent portal, a layer of ash covered what remained of the floor. This cone-shaped destruction extended back from where they stood.

Hyam climbed the front stairs with Meda at his side. Joelle and Connell followed. The others remained out front, where the mob could see them and hopefully hold to patience.

From his position at the entryway, Hyam looked straight through what had been the manor's rear wall. He said to his wife, "Ask Bryna if she detects the presence of a mage inside."

A moment's pause, then Joelle replied, "She senses nothing save the energy of what has already passed."

"All right. Let's go."

Joelle unsheathed the Milantian blade as they moved forward. Their footsteps were muffled by the ash that covered every surface. The conical hole at the rear of the house was the same precise shape as in front, only ten times larger. A moon-shaped segment of the flooring was gone. Remnants of two windows dangled overhead. There was no movement. No life.

Hyam skirted the missing segment of the kitchen floor and crossed the rear garden, back to the city's western wall. A clutch of guards stared down from the wall's parapet. Hyam traced one hand over the ancient stones, which remained untouched by whatever had demolished the banker's residence. He called up, "Did any of you see what happened here?"

A trooper leaned over the parapet and pointed to the nearest tower, five or six hundred paces to his right. "We were up top there, your lordship. The first sign any of us had was smoke rising from the ruins."

"What of anyone leaving afterward?"

The guard slipped back out of sight as Connell stepped up beside him. Hyam asked, "What do you know of this wall?"

"Legends claim the Ancients sealed these stones with a force powerful enough to defy time," Connell replied.

The guard returned and called down, "No one saw anything, your lordship."

Hyam waved his thanks and turned back to the ruined manor. He asked Connell, "Was there family?"

"A wife and two young daughters." Connell fell into step beside Hyam. "Lovely girls. I thought one showed the makings of a mage."

A shout rose from inside the manor. They hurried along the track their footsteps had made in the ash and clambered up inside the house to discover Shona and Alembord standing beside Joelle.

Shona declared, "Someone is here."

❖

Even as Shona had stood by the demolished manor's front gate, she continued to tremble slightly. Despite the moment's exquisite nature, Shona could sense the crowd's tension. They massed across the plaza from where she stood, an unmoving wall of flesh and fear. But just then her mind resonated with Fareed's words welcoming her to the ranks of acolytes. *She was a mage.*

She walked a half-step from Alembord and faced the ruined villa. It was easiest to locate the shield in the fingers of her right hand. Soon as she closed her eyes, she felt the power. She drew it up and around her, creating the same shield as before. She opened her eyes and pretended to study the gaping ruin where the front door had previously stood. Her shield remained in place for a time, then drifted silently away. She drew the shield back into place. Again. Over and over, reveling in the coursing power. Amazing herself in the process.

Gradually the initial thrill died down to where she could study the internal effects. She felt the subtle power course across her, delicate as a breath of wind. With each new creation of the shield, her senses grew sharper. The impact did not last long, a few seconds only. But for those brief instances, she felt as though she could see around corners and through walls.

She was tempted to turn her attention to the people on the other side of the plaza. But their anxiety was already an unpleasant stain upon this amazing day, far more potent than the manor's destruction. Whatever had caused this ruination was long gone. How she could possibly be so certain of this, she had no idea. But she stared at the manor's stone façade as she drew the force around herself once more. In the tiny fraction of time that it was available to her, little longer than a single breath, she tried to push her awareness outward. Extend her senses in a definite direction.

She tasted the ash, and overlaid upon this was an acrid stench she had never known before, yet instantly knew it represented death.

Immediately she retreated back into herself and felt the shield gradually dissipate. She took a long breath and drew the power back up and around herself. And then redirected her senses, out in a different direction.

Shona drew back, so terrified she did not realize she had screamed until Alembord rushed over. "What's the matter!"

But Shona was already racing for the manor's front steps.

❖

The manor's lower level was mostly intact, save for one sliver of missing ceiling at the back, through which the sun now shone. The stairs emptied into a long antechamber with a vaulted ceiling that ran the entire length of the house. A number of doors opened off, most of them locked and barred.

Hyam asked, "Where did the sound come from?"

"It wasn't a sound, exactly." Shona pointed at a door with a high peaked top. "There."

Connell tested the door and found it locked. He settled his forehead on a band of iron that fortified the stout oak, placed his hands upon the lock plate, took a deep breath, and pushed. The lock rattled and complained, but the door opened. He leaned on the stone frame and breathed hard. "I detest dealing with iron."

Joelle stepped inside the dark chamber and with a gesture lit the chamber's many candles. The illumination revealed the banker's wealth. Silk carpets and brightly colored tapestries masked the windowless stone. Ledgers bound in leather and stamped in gold ran down two walls, held in glass-fronted shelves with gilded columns. The desk was oiled mahogany, held aloft by carved pillars covered in gold leaf. The chairs were covered in soft hide, the inkstand gold.

"There is no one here," Connell said.

Shona pointed at the tapestry rising between two of the ledger cabinets. "Behind that."

The tapestry showed an island rising from a sunlit sea, the waters a stunning mixture of russet and gold and blue. It hung on rings, suspended upon a long brass rod. Connell swept it aside, revealing only stone. Frowning, he ran his hand over the wall.

Joelle stepped up beside him. "Bryna senses very old magic at work, spells from the Ashanta's earliest contact with mankind . . ."

Meda asked, "Can she detect anyone?"

Joelle held up her hand, silencing them all. She continued to draw her fingers slowly over the stones, as though her motions were guided by an unseen hand. Then Hyam heard her speak the Ashanta word "Open."

The wall became framed in fire and slid soundlessly back.

A man's voice called fearfully from within the hidden chamber, "Are you friends?"

15

An hour later, Hyam walked back across the square. Joelle and Meda accompanied him, while Connell remained behind to question the banker. The crowd held to such a still attentiveness he found it unnecessary to shout. "Who among you saw the attack?"

A woman cried back, "Is that what it was? The mage—"

"I will answer your questions. First answer mine. You heard there was an assault on the banker's home. Did anyone actually see it?"

A man stepped forward, dressed in dusty clothes and a builder's leather apron. "I heard it, your lordship. And saw a bit. I was putting a new roof on a house one street over. You can't see it from where we're standing, but I was high up."

"Tell me what you saw."

"There was a great crack, like the sky itself was split open. The earth shook enough to topple over my ladder, carrying my boy with it."

"Is he safe?"

"Aye, your lordship." He tugged on the sleeve of a young man taller than himself. "This is the great lout here. Shaken, but that's it."

"So you heard a blast. What did you see?"

"I was mostly watching after my boy. But I saw . . . Tell the truth, I can't say for certain what I saw. The air seemed to shiver above the wall, like. And there was this great tumbling roar from the house. Then nothing."

Hyam thanked him, then asked the group, "Did anyone else see what took place?"

A woman called, "I saw it."

An older woman standing beside her protested, "Don't speak up."

"He asked and I'm saying." The woman was young, slender, and dressed in the grey cotton frock of a maidservant. She pointed to a cluster of houses at the plaza's north end. "I was ironing in the upstairs front room of the home back there, your lordship. It was just as the builder says. I heard a great blast, then the earth shook hard enough to crack the window where I was standing. Dust rose in a great billowing cloud, out the front door and the back both. Then it all went quiet as the tomb."

"Aye, she's right," the builder said. "I forgot about the dust."

Hyam asked, "Did you see anyone leave the manor?"

"Nary a soul, your lordship, and I was watching close."

Hyam thanked her and raised his voice a notch. "Everything these good people have reported confirms what we have found inside. Some dread force has attacked the Ashanta banker and destroyed his home."

The crowd gave off a single rustling breath, then a woman demanded, "It's as I feared, the mage is back?"

"No. That I can say for certain. The crimson one who ruled this city has been destroyed. Whoever attacked here does not carry the same threat. This is a lesser force, but dangerous just the same."

Another voice called, "What of the banker?"

"He is safe. As are all his family and servants. No one perished in the attack."

A man called, "And our money?"

"That too was untouched by the attack." Hyam gave the crowd time to chatter, then continued, "Here is what we know. A new force lurks in this city's shadows. And we need your help to identify who or what it is. The enemy is not so strong as to operate in the open. Keep a careful eye for the unnatural, the stranger, the one whose presence is threatening. Do not provoke it! Come to us. We will do what is necessary, and defeat it."

The querulous woman demanded, "You'll keep us safe?"

"Come to us," Hyam repeated. "We have been sent by Bayard, your rightful earl, to identify this threat, destroy it, and ensure your safety. Remember, Emporis is your city! Help us keep this threat at bay!"

⬧

The communications mirror served as a window most clearly at its center. Around the borders its surface became tinted by the pewter backing, and the images wavered somewhat. Bayard had brought his entire council this time. They all shared the same grim countenance as Hyam made his report.

When he was finished, Bayard pondered for a time, then said, "Tell me of this desert trader."

"His name is Jaffar, and thus far no one has seen him, including the banker." Hyam gestured to Connell, who was seated to his right, with Joelle to his left. "Your master mage questioned the banker while I dealt with the crowd. I would ask that he relate this portion himself."

Bayard demanded, "Crowd?"

"Drawn by the blast," Hyam explained.

Connell said, "Several times the banker sent for Jaffar, but the merchant was always represented by his chief drover, Selim. A roughish man by all accounts. Selim claimed that Jaffar is secretive by nature, and this was what has kept him alive so long. He also claimed that his bird had instructed Jaffar to not set foot within the city walls. For if he did, he would perish."

"A desert trader claims to receive instructions from a bird?"

"A great eagle with desert plumage," Hyam said. "A magnificent bird with wings broader than my arm span. Let Connell finish and I will explain."

Trace asked, "What else did the bird say?"

Bayard examined his chief wizard. "You believe the trader speaks with a bird?"

"The banker and his entire family survived," Trace replied. "I have no choice but to accept the man's report as true."

Connell went on, "The night before the attack, Selim slipped past the Ashanta banker's guards and entered their dining hall. He claimed to have done so to demonstrate how the real enemy would be arriving. Perhaps within the hour, certainly within a day. If the banker wanted to survive, they would hide where none could find them, for already the enemy was watching the house's only exit. He gave the banker a sack, one his master had been instructed to deliver to the hero of Emporis."

"More instructions from this bird, I suppose?"

"Precisely, sire. Then the banker said Selim left through the kitchen door, crossed the rear garden, and scaled the city wall like a spider." The mirror's illumination tinted Connell's features with a severe metallic gleam. "The banker and all his household spent a frightened night crammed inside the secret treasure chamber. Sometime around dawn, the earth shook so violently they were all bounced around like pebbles in a stone box. One strap holding gold bars to a shelf broke and knocked a guard out cold. The chamber was filled with the most horrid odor of ash and cinders, and they assumed the entire house had been set alight. But there was neither heat nor smoke."

Bayard pondered this, then asked Hyam, "What did the sack contain?"

"A scroll, a note from Jaffar to me, and the merchant's own private seal," Hyam replied. "The note stated that Jaffar was ready to take me wherever I needed to go, whenever I was ready to depart. The seal was offered as a guarantee. The scroll contains another Milantian spell."

"Which none save Hyam can read," Connell added. "To my eye it is utterly blank."

"The spell is there, and it is complete," Hyam assured them. "Jaffar wrote that the bird claims this scroll is vital to our enemy. Jaffar apparently did not even know he carried the scroll until the bird told him. He broke open one of the amphorae to find it. The bird told Jaffar to keep the scroll safe until we arrived. It is a binding spell, that much I can tell you, and centers upon transforming some kind of gemstone. To what purpose, I have no idea. The scroll merely says, 'Use a shard of heartstone, and draw together all that remains.'"

Bayard frowned at Trace. "Does that make any sense to you?"

"I am still grappling with the idea that a merchant has offered his services to a man he has never met," Trace replied. "On instruction from a bird."

Bayard turned back to Hyam. "What do you propose to do?"

"What we must," Hyam said. "Try to determine what secrets the new scroll holds that grants it such importance to the enemy. Then draw our foe away from the realm of men, out into the yellow desert."

"Risky," Trace muttered. "Perilous in the extreme."

"And yet the correct move," Bayard agreed.

Hyam asked, "Do either of you know what might be meant by the term *heartstone*?"

"None whatsoever," Trace replied.

"Perhaps Timmins can help," Bayard said, rising from the table. "But first he wishes to have a word with his daughter."

16

That afternoon Shona crossed the castle's silent court-yard beside Joelle, who had suggested they visit the central market together. Meda had volunteered to serve as guard and companion and remained two steps behind them as Shona asked, "Why are we doing this now?"

Joelle replied, "I want to buy you a birthday present."

"Connell told you?"

"As he should have," Joelle replied. "What sort of gift would you like?"

"I have no idea."

"It needs to be something that marks your entry into adult-hood. A gown, perhaps."

"Please, no. My mother is always after me to dress like a lady."

"Then let's pretend I did not even suggest it."

They passed through ancient stone arches and entered the crush of the city's main bazaar. Every manner of beast and race was on display, both for sale and crowding the cobblestone lanes. The first line of shops held birds in cages and on leashes. They screamed and shrilled and sang a welcome that buffeted Shona. The three women walked slowly, taking it all in, winding their way deeper and deeper into the market's heart. The lanes were roofed in long streamers of translucent gauze, violet and pink and ivory. Sunlight bathed the covering, and they walked through a shaded rainbow.

They stopped for lunch at an elegant teahouse whose interior was formed from polished blond wood. Without being asked, Meda settled into the table next to theirs. The waiter was an old man with merry eyes who pretended to swoon with delight over serving two lovely ladies, then urged them to try the house specialty of roast lamb with mint and desert sorrel.

When he departed, Joelle leaned across the table and said, "Hyam has had a second conversation with Bayard and your father. They all agree that our best hope for drawing the enemy from Emporis is to set off across the yellow realm. You are not to go with us."

"What?"

"They feel it is too dangerous."

The same trapped feeling she had known for years surged up, accompanied by fresh bitterness. "I suppose you're pleased."

"Hyam objected strenuously. I also thought you should come. Already your abilities have proven of vital importance. But your father insisted. Bayard refused to intervene." Joelle paused as the waiter returned bearing two cups and a ceramic pot. When he had poured their teas and departed, she went on, "Tell me what it is that most excites you about Hyam."

Shona studied the woman seated across from her. Joelle's eyes were flecked with traces of violet, evidence of her Ashanta heritage. Shona could find no hint of mockery, either in her voice or in her gaze. "His strength and his weakness. His joy and his sorrow. His . . ."

Joelle nodded and finished for her, "His mystery."

Shona felt a tear course down one cheek. The words tumbled out of her, a plea that could not be held back. "I have a thousand little moments. They are with me always. He loves books more than any man except perhaps my papa." She had not called her father that in years, and yet now it was the only word that fit. "He is part of my family. They love him as a brother and a son. We have our secret place, Hyam and I. At the top of the house is a garret that faces north. Hyam found it looking down from the castle walls. The door had been painted over . . . He goes there after a long day. He told me he loves the solitude and the way the sunset touches the mountains. We talk. I tell him how hard it is to be . . ."

Again Joelle finished the thought for her. "Ensnared by a family and a heritage and a love that has nurtured you since birth. Kept in a world that is too small to hold you and your dreams."

She swiped impatiently at her cheeks. "How do you know this?"

"Because I know you and care for you," Joelle replied. "And because I have endured my own share of unanswered yearnings. And because I want to turn you from a course that will only lead to heartache and—"

"Twice my family has invited suitors in to meet me. Twice I brought home young men I fancied. Four times Hyam has said they are not good enough for me. Four times."

"He knows your potential," Joelle said. "He wants you to soar with your dreams for wings."

"No. He never said it, but I'm certain he told me to send them away because . . ."

Slowly Joelle shook her head, back and forth, each motion erasing Shona's ability to object. "Hyam does not love you."

Shona felt the words clench her heart.

"He cares for you deeply. He is protective of you. He *believes* in you. But he does not love you." Joelle moved closer, her quiet words laden with a woman's force. "He is my husband. And mine alone."

Though tears veiled her vision, still Shona saw the woman across from her with a new clarity. Joelle was a woman complete in herself, a warrior vixen and a mage and a telepath with the ability to pierce the unseen. She was an orphan who had created a new family with this man. Hyam. Whom Shona loved.

The meal passed in a silent haze. Shona supposed she ate, but she did not taste a thing. Joelle did not speak again except to thank the waiter. When they finally rose from the table, Joelle took hold of Shona's hand and offered her the silent gift of strength. As a friend would. They left the restaurant hand in hand, trailed by the guards captain, and continued to walk down one market lane after another.

Joelle remained silent, granting Shona the chance to reknit her world.

❖

Hyam left the castle in the company of Alembord and Connell's assistant, Fareed. The acolyte was tall and skinny in the manner of a youth who had risen to man-height almost overnight. Fareed possessed a shy smile and the dark gaze of a gazelle, his features carved by sun and desert winds.

They headed south by west, away from both the bazaar and the wealthy residential areas. When the western wall came into view, they passed through barriers guarded by desert warriors holding pikes whose blades were as long as Hyam's forearm. Fareed passed the guards and led Hyam into the Emporis caravansary.

The central square was segmented into corrals, all fed by a spring rising into a circular trough of yellow stone. The corral to Hyam's left held a jet-black stallion that danced nervously against his lead, throwing up clouds of yellow dust. An auctioneer took bids from the jolly throng. Here on display was the clash of cultures that defined Emporis. Wild clansmen rubbed shoulders with city merchants and berobed travelers from beyond the yellow sea. Past the square rose the city's outer wall, where guards lounged in the shadows of the western gate.

They passed a stall anchored by the stables, and the smell of roasting lamb reminded Hyam that he had not eaten since dawn. They feasted on flatbreads split lengthwise and filled with lamb and spring onions. They drank cup after cup of cool mint tea. Between bites, Fareed explained how the area beyond the western gate held the main portion of the convoys. This section inside the walls held only the most valuable animals, the auctioneers, the middlemen, the baths, the strong rooms.

Hyam asked, "Do you know the desert merchant, Jaffar?"

"I have never met him. Few have. He prefers the shadows, that one. Many say he has never set foot inside the Emporis walls, sahib."

"My name is Hyam."

"Yes, sahib. Here in the caravansaries, Jaffar's reputation is very good indeed. Those who travel with him say he is the most honorable of men."

"What of the trader you worked for?"

"He was not a good man, sahib." Fareed dropped the remainder of his meal into the dust at his feet. "Wait here, please. I will search out Jaffar's chief drover."

Hyam and Alembord wandered across the plaza to the western gates. They stood in the shadows and gaped at the vast expanse of people and beasts and piles of goods that spilled down the hill. The slope was carved into seven ledges shaped like crescent moons, each over a quarter-mile wide. The caravans and animals and makeshift shelters stretched out to where they became lost in the dust and weaving sunlight. There were hundreds of travelers, perhaps thousands, and ten times that number of beasts. Cook fires created ribbons of smoke that lined the still air. The din was as ferocious as the heat.

Fareed slipped up beside him and said, "The chief drover's name is Selim, sahib. He awaits you in the stables."

They recrossed the plaza and entered a stable's cool shadows. Man-sized blocks of hay were stacked like interior walls, segmenting the space and flavoring the air. Fareed led them to where a man knelt and wiped down a newborn calf with fistfuls of fresh hay. The mother was very tall, with gentle eyes and the most curious hooves Hyam had ever seen, great pads broader than a frying pan.

"What manner of beast is this?"

"The one who will save your life many times, if indeed you plan to journey upon the yellow sea." The drover's voice was barrel-deep and oddly accented.

"I must," Hyam replied.

"And it's true, you lost your magical abilities in the fight with the red lord?"

"That is correct."

Selim lifted the newborn and helped it move upon unsteady legs to the mother. She nuzzled her offspring, sniffed it from tail to head, then began licking it with great strokes of her broad tongue. He said to Hyam, "If you are indeed weaponless against the desert mages, all those who travel with us should first consign their souls to the infinite. I shall tell them that as well."

"What can you tell me of the wizards in the yellow realm?"

"Not a thing, sahib, not even if they exist. But you have seen the damage wreaked upon the banker's home. And those traveling from the realm's interior speak of dark troubles. Nothing overt. But perilous just the same."

Hyam found himself liking the burly drover. He discounted the man's hostile gaze as merely part of the challenge ahead.

"Jaffar is indeed fortunate to be served by such an astute chief drover."

Something flickered in the drover's gaze, but he merely sniffed and demanded, "Who are these two?"

"Alembord is a trusted soldier from the earl's own garrison. Fareed is an acolyte serving in the Emporis citadel."

"This one I have heard mentioned before." Selim examined the young mage. "You served the trader Kasim?"

"Aye, sir. I did."

"Is it true he sold you to the Falmouth mages?"

"Soon as I showed the first bit of talent," Fareed confirmed. "Kasim dragged me into the earl's palace at the end of a rope."

"He is the worst of a bad lot. How old were you?"

"Eleven. The Mistress Edlyn paid him ten gold florins. It was the finest day of my life."

"Careless with the lives of his charges, is Kasim. And a liar." The drover shifted the newborn back to where it could suckle. He then rose to his feet and nodded to the servant holding the mother's leash. "I'm surprised one of his own lot hasn't done him in by now."

Fareed kicked at the straw and did not reply.

The drover grunted and turned his attention back to Hyam. "I have served this noble house all my life. Many times I have lived with astonishments. But none like this." He scowled at Hyam. "I am ordered to place my master's caravan at your disposal! Have you ever trekked through desert?"

"I crossed the Galwyn Hills. Once."

The drover spat. "They are nothing! Ripples across a gentle

lake, nothing! Out there, the yellow sea waits to devour your bones! You think the fiends will hesitate because you once could call upon magic? The yellow realm holds mysteries beyond measure, dangers beyond count!"

"Do you share the merchant's ability to speak with eagles?"

Again there was the flicker of something deep within that slanted gaze, but Selim merely replied, "I have more important duties. Like trying to keep my charges alive. The question you should be asking, effendi, is whether you are ready."

"We'll soon see," Hyam replied. "I want to leave at dawn."

"Dawn is not possible." The drover gestured at the still-shivering newborn. "Three days, perhaps four."

"We leave tomorrow."

"Hurry breeds death, effendi." He waited, clearly expecting more argument. But when Hyam remained silent, he grudgingly allowed, "Perhaps the caravan could be readied by noon."

17

Shona walked through the market at Joelle's side. With each step, her response to Joelle's words sharpened. She grew ever more certain that Hyam would, in time, come to care for her. But just now that had to be put aside. Another issue had to be resolved first. Immediately.

Shona was determined to travel across the yellow sea. She would see the quest to its end. Her father did not know, he could not have any idea, what fury she was about to unleash.

All her life she had lived under the exquisite joy and heavy burden of being an only daughter. And yet ever since childhood she had chafed under the restrictions set upon her life. As she walked toward the market's heart, Shona knew what she most wanted was the chance to prove herself.

The words that Joelle had spoken about Hyam not loving her had hurt badly. But for now she had to push everything aside, the pain and the yearning and the sorrow and the love.

That was for later. There would be time for all that and more. Once they left Emporis behind.

The lane they followed took a sharp turn to the left, and they entered the spice market. The heat was gentled somewhat by the gauze draped overhead. But this also trapped the fragrances, which were pleasant yet overpowering. Great baskets of brilliantly colored powders rose to either side. The vendors called to them, their singsong cadence as old as the city. The merchants claimed their wares had the capacity to bring new joys to the table, ignite hearts, inflame passions.

Shona passed beneath a ceremonial arch. Faint carvings of vines wound up the pillars and around the stone overhead. Then something else caught her gaze, an image that flickered across the gaps in the translucent coverings. Shona realized it was an eagle, high above the city, hovering directly overhead.

She was about to comment on the bird when Joelle exclaimed, "I don't believe this! Do my senses deceive me?"

The vendor was a woman, tall and heavy and draped in veils of red and umber and orange and russet. "The lady must be a child of the forest."

"I am, yes. Or was." Joelle stepped between the outlying baskets, drawn to an ornately carved wooden trough, an arm's length long and filled with white blossoms. "Oh, how I have missed this fragrance."

The woman proved to be very strong, for she lifted the trough effortlessly and held it up to Joelle's face. "Wild white rose, the only bloom that defies the forest's deepest shadows. Breathe deep, my lady. These flowers have traveled far, so that you might find pleasure in this moment."

Joelle buried her face in the petals. "It takes me home again."

The woman turned slightly, offering Shona the trough. "Here, my lovely. Indulge yourself and taste what few have ever known, the sweetest fragrance in all the world."

Shona started to lean forward, but a fitful wind found its way down the narrow market lane, causing the colorful gauze overhead to toss like desert sails. She caught another glimpse of the eagle. Directly above them. Hovering with claws and beak extended. As though readying for a dive and a kill. "There's something odd—"

"Well, never you mind. The forest perfume is not for everyone. Won't you ladies come inside? Let me brew us a tea. I have forest honey, fresh as the petals here."

"I would love a taste of honey, wouldn't you?" Joelle's gaze shone with rare ardor. She clapped her hands. "I know what to buy you for your birthday. Perfume!"

"This lovely maiden is celebrating her special day, is she? Then you've come to the right stall. For I hold the rarest of spices and oils inside." The woman used an elbow to draw back the shop's curtain, revealing an interior of silk carpets and cushions and wall hangings. "Together we'll create a special scent, lovely as the dawn, beautiful as you are, my dear. Come!"

❖

Hyam left the caravansary and headed toward the city's wealthiest shopping areas. He sought a jeweler who might know of the heartstone mentioned in Jaffar's scroll. Together with Alembord and Fareed, he entered the maze of cobblestone streets fronting the main bazaar, passing display windows showing off the finest goods that Emporis had to offer. Affluent patrons strolled the quiet lanes in flamboyant styles, bright as chattering birds. Young maidens wore silver bells fastened to wrist or ankle or neck, or all three, so that they jangled as they passed, signaling they were both rich and available. Their personal guards were as stern as the maidens were flirtatious.

Gemstone Lane was a stubby court that opened off the Street of Gold. The houses here were uniformly severe, with barred windows and guards patrolling in pairs. The shops had narrow façades, all just one door and one barred window wide. A fountain sang at the far end, fronted by two elegant teahouses. But as they approached the first jeweler's doorway, Hyam caught a faint whisper, clear and precise as the maidens' bells. "Wait. There's something . . ."

"Danger?"

"No, I don't . . ." Hyam turned from the shop and hunted farther down the lane, moving slowly, doing his best to ignore the gazes that tracked him from the teahouses. The farther he moved, the more intense grew the sensation. "There's something here."

Alembord touched the hilt of his sword. "What is it?"

"Sheath your blade. We're not threatened." Of that Hyam was certain, but little else. He knew he was making both men nervous, so he kept talking. "I sense the same thing I did when we found the Milantian scrolls. Some kind of force draws me . . . In here."

Where the next house should have stood opened an alley,

so narrow they could only pass one at a time. Whatever lay beyond the opening was sheathed in gloom.

Fareed protested, "Sahib, this place is forbidden."

"What lies down there?"

"The students call it Enchantment Alley. All manners of legends bind this place, many of them laced with dark forces."

"And yet I am drawn here." Hyam slipped into the alleyway and felt a burning hunger fill him, strong as rage. Fareed hesitated, then signaled Alembord, and together they followed Hyam.

The alley broadened into a tight stone cove, where six narrow shops formed a semicircle. Hyam aimed promptly for the third door. When it refused to open, he resisted the urge to beat it down. He knocked. Again. The longing was so strong now he could scarcely breathe.

Abruptly the portal swung open. Hyam stepped inside and found himself facing a wide-eyed old man who offered a courtier's bow. "The hero of Emporis is always welcome."

Hyam's voice rasped hard. "You have something of mine."

The old man was bent slightly to one side, burdened by the uneven weight of many years. His eyes widened, but he did not seem surprised. "Perhaps, my liege. Yes, perhaps."

"Something from . . ."

"From the battle. But of course, my lord. This way." He moved swiftly for an old man. Hyam followed the merchant inside the shop, his entire being focused upon what lay beyond the swinging doors, somewhere inside this litter-strewn second room.

The old man opened a glass-fronted cabinet, pulled out a wooden tray, then swept a bundle of parchments and scrolls off the central table. "In the chaos that followed your triumph, sire, I walked the castle gardens and keep. Searching for some small element that might someday prove useful. For what, I had no idea."

The tray was filled with charred fragments of Elven arrow tips and other metal items. Hyam's fingers trembled so hard he needed three tries to lift the tiny shard of glass. His chest was pierced by a song of triumph, a lament of all he had once possessed.

"I felt something," the old man said. "I must have, since I found this tiny element and brought it back."

"You were right to do so." Hyam panted through three tight breaths. "I am in your debt."

"Nonsense, your lordship. It is my honor to serve the one who vanquished the red lord." The old man bent in so close his breath touched Hyam's fingers. "Truly, this is from your orb?"

"Yes." Hyam let the old man peer for a moment longer, then slipped the shard into his chest pocket. Close to his pounding heart. "Alembord."

"Sire?"

"The money Bayard gave us. Let me have it, please."

Alembord untied the leather pouch from his sword belt and passed it over. Hyam opened the mouth and poured gold into the old man's hand.

The merchant protested, "It is too much."

"You have earned it all," Hyam assured him. He turned away and said to the others, "We go."

"Sire . . . a moment, please." When Hyam turned back, the merchant said, "I've spent my life serving the lesser desires of mortal men. But I've never done willing harm to another, unlike others I could name along this shadowed alley. Never sold what might be used to twist the fate of some helpless maiden or hapless spinster. Never dealt in poison or fiendish potions. And for a few bitter seasons I've almost starved as a result. Cast out during the red lord's reign, I was, left to fend for myself among the badland tribes and then working as a healer's apprentice in Falmouth. An apprentice, me at my age!" He dragged a sleeve about his face, then waved it all aside. "When I was younger I wanted nothing more than to study with the Falmouth mages. But I never showed an ability, more's the pity. Still, I held to the creed, my lord. I held to the creed!"

"I believe you," Hyam said.

The fire dimmed in those ancient eyes, and he withdrew a strand of silver wire that was slung about his neck. On it was a small key, which he fitted into a slit in the stone wall. "There's said to be a company of witches that call the yellow wasteland home. Years back, I met a drover who said he had discovered a treasure that once belonged to them. I wasn't sure I believed him, for he carried the look of madness in his gaze. But I bought what he offered just in case."

Hyam watched as the old man withdrew a wooden box and carried it back over. "In case what?"

"In case the instrument inside can do what the drover claimed." The old man's voice was hoarse now. With fear or eagerness or simple fervor, Hyam could not tell. "I couldn't risk allowing such powers to fall into the wrong hands, not and hold to the creed!"

Hyam started to open the box, but the old man waved him to a halt. "Not here, good sir. Not here! There are foul winds that still blow through Emporis on moonless nights. I detect the enemy's stench in the dark hours. Take this somewhere safe, do with it what you will. Only not here!"

The wood was scarred and featureless and very light. "What did the drover tell you?"

"Inside this box is an eye. If you peer deep and ask the right question, you can glimpse around time's boundary. But only backwards. Not into the future." The hoarse voice shook now, and Hyam realized the man was desperate to rid himself of this possible threat. "But seek a wrongness, the drover said, or seek for the wrong reason, and the forces locked inside will swallow you whole."

18

When Meda stepped inside the spice merchant's tent, she held the curtained doorway slightly open with the hand not resting on her sword hilt. Shona inspected the fancy shop, the benches with silk cushions, the ornately carved central table with its inlaid surface of silver and pearl, the gilded lamp hanging from the oiled ceiling timbers. Joelle seemed blind to everything except the white flowers.

The tradeswoman settled Joelle onto a padded bench and asked Shona, "Won't you sit down, my lovely?"

"I'd like to stand if that's all right."

"Whatever pleases you is excellent by me."

The tradeswoman turned to Meda, but before she could speak, Meda replied, "I'll remain here by the door."

"Of course you will, and how fortunate these two ladies are to have such a capable officer guarding their backs." She beamed down at Joelle. "When did madame leave the wood-lands?"

"I was born and raised in the great forest. I was fifteen when I left." Joelle's voice sounded far off, as though spoken from inside a dream. "I have not been back since."

"Far as the great forest I have not traveled. But I know of what you speak." The tradeswoman spoke in a sultry melody, almost crooning the words. She bustled about, setting out various vials and implements, lighting a gilded brazier that stood upon a polished steel tripod. "Far to the west, with the Galwyn Hills as its boundary, yes? It must have been a beautiful abode."

"The most beautiful place in all the world." Joelle's voice grew increasingly vague.

Shona asked, "Is everything all right?'"

Joelle opened her mouth to respond, but no sound emerged. Far overhead, the eagle screamed, and for a reason Shona could not understand, the sound caused her to tremble. She watched as the woman drew out a small silver chest, as ornately carved as everything else in the room. The woman took a rose-colored block, long as her finger, and set it upon the fire's heart. "Here, let's enjoy a bit of perfumed wood. That should spice things up nicely, don't you think?"

The smoke gradually filled the tented room, and as it rose the woman weaved her hands in an intricate fashion. She chanted softly, releasing a faint pink trail from her mouth. As the two smokes thickened, Shona realized she was imprisoned. She could not move. She could hardly breathe.

"There. That should hold you well enough. Don't you ladies agree?" Each word thickened the smoke, which strengthened until it formed snakelike tendrils that bound all three women.

Then the old woman moved to the entrance, took the curtain from Meda's frozen hand, and shut out the world. The sorceress inspected Meda, then smiled and declared, "You'll roast up nicely, you will."

◈

Hyam followed Connell down the winding steps into the citadel's lowest cellar. Fareed guarded the cellar's entry, there to keep any curious acolyte from following. Each stair was twice as wide as he was tall and wound about a central pillar that ten men could not have encircled with their arms. Everything about this ancient castle was oversized.

Down and down they went, past one high-ceilinged level, then another. At the stairs' base Connell said, "This is where Trace and Mistress Edlyn spent the most time with their cleansing spells. I dread to think what foul mischief the red lord concentrated on down here."

Hyam felt the sizzling energy course through him, strong as when he had first touched the scrolls. "Somewhere below us, four great rivers of power join together."

"So Trace informed me." Connell held the mage-light aloft and studied Hyam. "You feel it?"

"I sense something. You?"

"Nothing save the same faint dread I've always known in these lower reaches." He drew the light closer. "Perhaps a bit of your powers are returning."

Hyam had been wondering the same thing. But he merely said, "Let's get started. I have an appointment with a bird."

The castle's lowest level held just one vast chamber, larger than the Earl of Falmouth's main banqueting hall. Connell strengthened the light to where both men squinted against the brilliance, and still the hall's far end was lost to darkness.

Hyam sensed the weight of untold years. The stones seemed as implacable to time's passage as the city's walls. He thought he smelled a faint trace of more recent evil, but it lay upon the cavern like dust on a disused table. The force here was implacable. Ages of men, wars, and strife—all this meant little.

Connell dimmed the mage-light to where it did not hurt the eyes. They were instantly encircled by shadows. "What happens now?"

"I am going to invoke the spell. After that, I have no idea."

"The spell that no one else can read."

"It's there. Otherwise the enemy would not have tracked the desert trader across the yellow realm. Perhaps you should leave the light here with me and go back—"

"I am going nowhere," Connell declared.

Hyam did not argue. In truth, he was grateful for the company. He drew out the fragment of his former orb. The shard was no larger than his thumbnail and hardly as thick, a mere shaving of cracked and splintered crystal. And yet it called to him with an intensity that caused his blood to sing. He set it down in the center of the circle formed by Connell's light and began the incantation.

He knew that he was invoking a binding spell—that much

was clear from the scroll's structure. What would happen, the scroll did not say. But ever since he'd first touched this fractured remnant, Hyam's heart had flamed with the hope that the spell might rebuild his orb. Even when he knew too much of the material had been lost in the battle against the crimson one. Such logic held little sway down here in the ancient chamber, surrounded by forces older than the race of man.

When Hyam completed the incantation's first portion, he inspected the man standing beside him. "Do you sense anything?"

Connell shifted nervously. "Perhaps. Are you finished?"

"No. This is the midway point." Hyam saw how Connell peered into the shadowed reaches. "Tell me."

"Your voice was the faintest whisper, and yet . . ."

"You felt its resonance."

Connell nodded slowly. "And something else. Every now and then, the walls flickered. Like, well, I'm not sure what it was like."

"Energy coursing about us. I felt it as well."

Connell glanced down. "Look at the glass."

"I see it." The shard of his orb pulsed softly. A faint throbbing beat that his own heart echoed. "I'm starting on the second part now."

Hyam kept his eyes open. He wanted to witness. He wanted to *engage*. Which meant he was able to watch as the power surged about the chamber. Every pulse of the shard at his feet was repeated with great silent streams that flickered lightning-fast over the walls and floor and distant ceiling.

Hyam did not lift his hands so much as permit the force to fill him. Fire crackled from his fingertips. It raced out, loud and explosive now, as though the energy could no longer remain silent. The incantation grew to a booming thunder, then in a sudden flash exploded outward. Hyam felt the shift as much as saw it, a circle of shimmering fire that grew and spread until it vanished, all but a flickering echo.

Hyam hesitated a long moment, then invoked the next word. Instantly the force returned, a silent circular wave of power that rushed back inside the chamber.

Only now the force carried with it a cloud of colored dust.

Larger fragments sparkled with the same power that surged about the ancient stone. The incantation carried such energy Hyam saw tendrils of fire take shape with the words, binding the dust together. Initially the dust carried two distinct colors. Some held a putrid pinkish tone. More was violet laced with silver fire. But as the words and the power united the flecks, the color changed, transforming into a silvery lavender. A new shade for a new fabrication.

On and on Hyam recited the Milantian words, marveling at how the shards followed commands he scarcely understood, binding into . . .

Not an orb.

A *multitude* of miniature globes.

Each was perfectly fashioned, a diminutive orb. They all gleamed with the same force that resonated about the vast hall. All of them were a perfect circle. Except one.

Hyam finished and let his hands drop to his side. The silence resonated strong as the thunder. Connell's breath rasped in and out, as though the mage sought air for them both.

A glowing field of orbs lay scattered about them. The living fire bathed them with pulsating energy. And at its heart was a tear-shaped gem that burned brightest of all.

19

The market beyond the draped entryway was lost to Shona now. Even so, she heard a frantic echo as the eagle cried once more.

Fear swarmed like a mad blind thing inside her. Shona was unable to move. Her eyes could track, and she managed tight gasping breaths. Nothing more.

The woman paused in front of Shona, inspecting her carefully. The crooning voice sang the words, "I don't suppose you'll be needing that perfume after all, will you, my lovely."

Shona had been around warriors all her life. For years she had lived in the shadow of the crimson mage. Talk of war and the threat of defeat had been real and constant. But looking into those eyes revealed something she had never known before. Shona saw a malevolent force that took pleasure from another's misery. The promise of doom, the sucking penetrating force that devoured hope. All was revealed.

The woman traced one fingernail down Shona's cheek. It

scraped her skin like a talon. "The master's only interest is in the half-breed wed to the enemy. He said nothing about you. Which means you can be my toy, at least for a little while. I'll have to work up something special, my lovely. Yes, indeed."

The woman stepped over and inspected Joelle. "I wonder what all the fuss was about. You're not half the threat they described." She hefted the trough, took a huge breath, then blew the petals all over Joelle. "There you are, my dear. Your forest shroud."

Joelle appeared in even worse shape than Shona. Her eyes were blank, vacant as death. A petal landed upon her lower lip, another upon her left eyelid. Joelle did not respond. Shona was not even certain that she breathed.

The woman set the trough down upon the brazier and began chanting softly. Hidden beneath the petals was a lumpish red mass that the woman picked up, inserted into her mouth, and swallowed. Then she drew in a great breath and inhaled all the smoke, expanding to where she almost filled the chamber. Shona felt the acidic fumes sucked from her lungs, across the room, into the ever-expanding woman.

Then it was done, and the sorceress resumed normal size. "There. That's better." She turned and smiled at her frozen guests. "I disliked placing so much of myself out there, don't you know. Exposed and weak, it left me. But never mind. Orders are orders."

She drew from the brazier a knife whose blade was turned crimson by the heat. Her few steps back to Joelle became a sinuous dance. "Which brings us to the next order of business. You and your young man have been such pests." The sorceress crooned like she would to a lover. "Your Hyam murdered my sisters in the Galwyn Hills and stole their orb. Then he had you carry that Milantian blade about like it belonged to you. Then you two show up in Emporis with that great army of yours, surprising the red lord. And now you've destroyed my master's favorite pet. Shame on you both. Such actions as these must be punished."

Shona might as well have been chained at the bottom of the ocean. She struggled with a ferocity that threatened to wrench her joints. But to no avail. Despite her utter stillness, the sorceress noticed her frantic attempts and said, "Hold to patience, my beauty. It will be your turn soon enough."

The sorceress set the blade down beside the trough and drew a small crystal vial from the folds of her dress. She uncorked it with a smile and crooned to Joelle, "You have something my master wants."

The sorceress placed the vial beneath Joelle's nostrils. Then she placed her free hand firmly on Joelle's chest. The witch mashed her hand down hard, forcing Joelle's breath out of her frozen throat. "That's it, my troublesome young lady. I'll take everything but that last thread of life and deliver it to my master. Along with your hide, which I'll soon be skinning away. That will send a message to your man, one he'll never forget. One that will draw him . . ."

The idea came to Shona in a single terrified rush. Soon as it formed in her mind, she acted.

She sought the power. For a single heart-stopping moment, she could not find it and feared it was not permitted in this befouled chamber.

The mage stowed away the vial and reached for the knife. "I do so hope there's enough of you left to appreciate my skill with the blade."

Shona found the power where it had first been located, there in the fingertips of her right hand. She clenched the force and drew it up and about herself. Then she flung it at Joelle.

The sorceress leapt up, dropping the knife in her alarm. "How can this be?" She swung about, hunting, her eyes blazing bright as the superheated blade. She fastened upon Shona. "You!"

Shona sent the shielding force surging out in the opposite direction, flowing around Meda.

The sorceress dropped to all fours. She scrambled about until her talons gripped the knife's haft. As she rose she snarled at Shona. The crimson blade was now aimed at Shona's heart.

Shona frantically reached to the fire flaming in the brazier. And claimed it.

The chamber was blasted from within. Shona saw nothing but fire. It coursed about her. Shona's panic granted a ferocity to the flames.

She heard a long piercing shriek. When that faded, there was no sound but the crackling flames.

The shop was reduced to ash and cinders. The market's din swept about them now, cries and protests and alarm sounding from all quarters. Shona wanted to cough. The smoke caused her to gag, almost strangling her. But she still could not move.

Then she saw a tear course down Meda's cheek, and Shona knew it was safe to give in to the darkness of exhaustion.

20

Hyam locked the miniature orbs in Connell's study, while the master mage sent a message through the mirror that another conversation with Trace and Bayard was urgently required. Hyam asked a passing acolyte about his wife, and knew an instant's keening concern when he learned that the women had not yet returned from the market.

Despite the earl's wishes that Shona continue on with them, Timmins had insisted that she remain in the Emporis castle until the next squadron could escort her back to Falmouth. Hyam had repeatedly pointed out the value she had shown, the awakening abilities, the bravery. But he had gone silent when Timmins grew red-faced and demanded the right to decide the fate of his only daughter. Now they were out shopping, and the sun was descending, and the enemy was loose, and Hyam wanted to go find them. But first he had to speak with a bird.

He and Connell climbed the circular stairs leading up to

the ruined citadel, and Hyam tried to tell himself that the ladies were fine. The bird had told Hyam to come alone, but when Alembord asked to join them Hyam saw no reason to object. Connell took that as his cue and invited Fareed and the four senior mages along as well.

The stairwell was attached to the tower's outer wall, such that it curved around a central open space. As they climbed, Connell explained this was an ancient battle tactic, as attackers fought with one arm hampered by the angled stone wall, and there was no central pillar to protect the oncoming men from mages positioned in the tower. But the tower was gone now, and above them the jagged stone frame was open to the sky.

The sun had just met the western hills when they arrived up top. They stood shoulder to shoulder about the rim, and Hyam tried hard not to fidget. He would give the eagle half an hour to appear, then he was off to find Joelle. Unless of course the ladies returned, and then he would willingly give the bird all night.

The city was at its most appealing now, the desert harshness and the age both softened. Smoke from a thousand fires rose like mystical pillars. Everything was golden, and all the mysteries were on glorious display.

Connell breathed in the countless sunset fragrances and confessed, "At times like this I could almost love the city."

The wizard on Connell's other side was an attractive woman with two silver streaks in her brown hair, like the one that had run down Dama's back. "The instant you lower your guard, this place will strike."

"No doubt, no doubt." Connell grinned at her. "And then you would be promoted to chief wizard of Emporis and everybody would celebrate."

"Mistress of acolytes armed with training spells and no orb," she said. "Hardly something to look forward to."

Hyam broke into Connell's response by pointing at the sky. "Here comes the bird."

The eagle was sorely displeased by all the people watching its arrival. The bird landed and fluttered about, its wingspan broader than Hyam's arms. Reluctantly it approached and chattered, "I said come alone."

"You did. Yes."

"The master forbids this."

Hyam had no idea what the words signified, so he merely gestured to the others and said, "These are friends. They need to bear witness."

The bird squawked angrily and scrambled about the roof-line, its talons scraping the tiles, cross as an old crow. Finally the bird said, "You are to come. The master awaits you beyond the yellow realm."

Hyam translated for the others, who were both silent and agog. "What is our destination?"

"That is for later."

"What of the dragon?"

"The master will decide what to reveal, and when."

The nature of the speech, coupled with its newness, proved immensely frustrating. "I don't understand."

"Remember the treaty. Now you must hurry."

"I . . . The caravan is not ready. We leave tomorrow."

"The crisis is now." The bird squawked for emphasis. "The master says he can heal your mate."

Comprehension arrived in a panic such that Hyam did not even realize he spoke in the human tongue. "What has happened to Joelle?"

"The master says give your mate to the Elves for safe-keeping." Then the bird took flight.

21

Connell met up with them at the city's main gates, where Hyam had come directly from the bazaar. The master mage had brought his entire company of wizards and acolytes, leaving the castle guarded by the Ashanta banker's men.

Connell was puffing hard when he rushed through the gates. "I spoke with Trace through the communication portal. He will be ready."

This was the news Hyam had awaited. "And Shona?"

"The earl prevailed upon his cousin. Trace added his own weight to the discussion. As did I. This is no longer about the father's wishes. We spoke of battles that never end and enemies that have risen once more. Finally Timmins agreed. The lass is free to travel with your company."

"Thank you." Hyam returned his attention to Joelle. Her still form lay on the pallet they had used to cart her from the market. Shona and Meda lay on stretchers of their own, but they were recovering swiftly from their ordeal. Not so his wife. Joelle remained bound to this earth by the most fragile of threads. Her skin was cold and her features utterly still. The thought of leaving her in the care of others wrenched him painfully. But if he stayed, his wife would die. Of that Hyam was absolutely certain. Her only hope lay beyond the yellow realm.

Hyam stepped away from the city gates, faced the empty desert valley, lifted the crystal pipe to his lips, and blew once. The night was brilliantly lit by an almost full moon, the city ramparts utterly empty of life. Emporis was a city that survived by knowing when to hide. Not a soul was about this night, not a warrior nor a merchant. Everyone had heard of the attack in the bazaar, and all feared Hyam's wrath.

But Hyam had no interest in revenge, and it was not the city that had wronged him. He would give in to anger and grief when time allowed. Just now he had a vital mission to perform.

A mist gathered by the southern ridge and spread swiftly across the valley, though there was not a breath of wind. The acolytes stirred and muttered, but Connell silenced them with a single word. Because of Joelle's vulnerable state, Hyam needed their protection. Tonight he could not afford to take chances.

Hyam stood with the others and watched as the ghost troop formed itself into a double line that stretched to the glade at the vale's opposite side. He recognized the officer who had met him earlier, the one Joelle had addressed, the one with whom he could no longer communicate. The commander unsheathed his translucent sword and pointed Hyam forward. The way was secure.

Hyam's request to Trace was that he enter the forest glade beyond the Falmouth perimeter and create a magical storm. He had hoped the release of this energy would alert them to Hyam's need. Somehow Trace had accomplished the impossible, for arrayed on the opposite ridge was a myriad of green-tinted flames.

The acolytes all held lights of their own, save those who supported the three stretchers. The valley floor was visible through the ranks of silent warriors. The ghostly soldiers faced outward, weapons unsheathed, as though expecting an attack at any minute. But the desert valley remained silent, empty, and free of all threat save the one they carried.

Midway across the rocky vale, Meda protested weakly, "I can walk."

"As can I," Shona said.

Hyam ordered, "Stay as you are."

Elven warriors came down the slope. Hyam recognized their leader as the warrior he had addressed in their last meeting. Trace and one of Falmouth's mage healers rushed forward and knelt beside Joelle's stretcher. They were joined by a tall Elf, the first Hyam had ever seen who bore the stain of years.

The elder probed and muttered some incantation, but Joelle gave no sign she noticed anything. She had not moved since Hyam's arrival at the destroyed shop. Shona and Meda both propped themselves upright now and observed the proceedings with alert gazes. Hyam tried hard to convince himself this boded well for his beloved.

Trace asked Shona, "Describe for me exactly what happened." When she was done with the telling, Trace asked the Elf, "Have you ever heard of a mage being able to extract their own essential energy and fashion it into a spell?"

"Never," the Elf replied. "And to do so without an orb bodes ill."

"Such fell deeds signify a malignant being," Trace said.

"Poisonous to the core," the Elf agreed.

Trace lifted his gaze to Hyam's company and asked, "Did you locate the vial holding Joelle's life-breath?"

"Not yet," Connell replied. "The mages are still sifting through the ashes."

"Then we must assume the witch survived," Trace said. "She has escaped, and she took the vial with her."

"I agree," Hyam said, though it cost him three bitter breaths to form the words. "Can you cure her without it?"

The three rose slowly. The Elf replied, "We can make her rest easy. We can shield her from further harm. And we can wait."

"And hope," Trace added. "Whatever else can be done, will be."

Hyam resisted the urge to fling himself once more upon the immobile body of his wife. "The eagle returned at dusk. It said the dragon could heal her."

"Then you must go," Trace said. "And swiftly."

"How long do I have?"

The Elf moved in close enough for Hyam to read his grave concern. "We will do all we can. You must focus upon the quest, else all will be lost." At a motion from the Elven healer, two guards lifted Joelle's stretcher and started up the slope.

"Wait!" Hyam knelt by his wife's side. His entire being was wracked by all he had not said, all the love he had not shown, all the incompleteness of his days. All the hours they could no longer share. All the love now stolen. He touched her face, cold as porcelain, and moved in closer still so that his ear rested upon her lip. He heard her faint breath and felt it rustle upon his skin. He rose, knowing that was all the hope this night would offer. That she still breathed.

They formed a silent procession up the ridge and discovered the Elven king and his queen standing by the glade's entrance. Darwain greeted Hyam with, "Were it only a happier purpose that finally brings us together again."

Hyam watched his wife vanish into the green realm and felt his life threaten to shatter.

The Elven queen stepped forward, gripped his face with both hands, and said, "We will do all we can for her, you have my word."

The queen's hands and gaze carried a burning current, strong enough to reknit the night and his world. Hyam breathed easy for the first time since coming upon his wife and the others. "I have something for you."

He motioned to Connell, who stepped forward and bowed. Upon his shoulder was slung the leather sack he had brought from his study. Hyam accepted the pouch and untied the drawstring. As he counted out the ones he intended to keep, he described the merchant's scroll and the spell and the event. By the time he finished with the telling, Trace had returned to stand alongside the Elven king.

Hyam fed some of the miniature orbs into Connell's waiting hands, then offered Darwain the sack. "I'm keeping one for me, Shona, Fareed, and Connell. Another eleven to be held and used by the Emporis mages. That leaves fifteen for the Falmouth mages, and the same number for your kingdom."

Despite the night's somber events, Trace was so eager he almost danced in place. "May I, Your Highness?" When Darwain passed over the satchel, he drew out one miniature globe and held it up close to the nearest light. "Most remarkable. That explains many things."

Darwain asked, "These are the same as our orbs?"

"These are said to hold a smaller charge and cannot handle the more potent spells designed for an orb," Trace replied. "But they are nonetheless a source of power themselves. Any number of ancient scrolls speak of these, but most of my fellow mages treat them as myths, for none of the scrolls mentioned how they might be formed. Nor have I ever seen one before."

"Which explains why our foe chased the merchant across the yellow sea," Connell said.

Shona lifted herself to a seated position. This time, when Hyam ordered her to remain as she was, she ignored him. She pushed herself to her feet, then needed Connell's assistance to remain upright. She said, "The witch said she worked for another. A master, she called him. She said the beast of Ellismere was his pet."

Darwain said, "Describe the witch and tell us everything she said."

When Shona was finished, the king and his wife exchanged

a long look. Darwain said, "Our records of the first Milantian wars confirm much of what you say."

"A few master mages," the queen said, "accompanied by a crimson horde, and every soldier able to cast dark spells."

Hyam slipped the tear-shaped stone from his pocket. "This one speaks to me."

"And so it should. May I?" Darwain shared the gem with his wife. "This is the orb's heartstone. Two of our own have survived the eons."

His wife lifted up a hand to the moon and whispered a soft breath of music. The moonlight coalesced into a sliver that spun into a thread, and the thread became a band thin as a needle, yet intricately woven. She continued singing as she settled the heartstone into the band.

Darwain's smile was both sad and joyful. "The last time I heard that song was at our marriage feast. New crowns are spun from moonlight by each new generation of rulers."

Still his queen sang. The threads shimmered as they weaved about the stone, forming a nest of silver light. She sang as she reached out and fitted the band to Hyam's head, such that the stone nestled at the center of his forehead. "That is how one carries the heartstone."

Hyam protested, "I do not care to wear any crown."

"None will see this unless you choose, and you will never notice its presence. Only its power, and only when you draw upon it." Darwain tilted his head just a fraction and touched his forehead with one finger. The moonlight coalesced, revealing a thin band of woven silver and a tear-shaped gem nestled upon his forehead.

Hyam started to object a second time, though he could no longer feel the crown's presence. But the Elven queen halted him with, "Who can say what trials await you in the treeless realm?"

Darwain reached out a hand. "Give me those orbs you intend to keep for yourselves."

When Connell passed over the smaller sack, Darwain handed it to a pair of elders. They swiftly stepped into the glade, then returned holding sticks the length of a man's forearm. They spoke in a cadence that formed the Elven plainsong, and gradually the wood became engraved with elaborate script. The tips grew wooden fingers that reached out and gripped each orb in turn.

When Darwain gave them back, he spoke with the formality of an incantation. "Wear them as your swords, wield them with care, take the battle to the enemy, fight the good fight, and survive."

22

The first five days of their desert trek proved such a brutal trial Hyam could not even name which part of his body hurt the most. The heat was fierce, but worse still was the animal's uneven gait. The desert beast was lumpish and ill-tempered. Whenever Hyam tended it, she would snap at him. She groaned and she spat and she stank. Hyam's thighs became so chafed they blistered and bled. By the end of each day, his bones ached. Meda and Alembord and Shona were similarly afflicted. Each evening, the caravan's drovers found great mirth in watching them dismount and stretch and groan.

His first two nights on the road, Hyam limped away from camp and opened the box given to him by the merchant who had yearned to follow the wizards' path. The countless years had worn the exterior wood smooth. The box contained a simple ceramic bauble. Upon its creamy surface was painted a myriad of symbols that might have been Milantian script, but they flowed together in a pattern that left Hyam uncertain of their origin or meaning. At the center of this circular script was an eye. It seemed to glow in the moonlight, as though lit from within. The gleam strengthened as he studied it, until Hyam found himself able to leave behind the trek and the worries and the heartache. He plunged into its depths. And he remembered.

The bauble would not allow him to move forward, just as the merchant had said. But memories took on an astonishing clarity. He remembered with vivid detail whatever he called to mind. The love and the loving, the laughter, the feel of Joelle's arms, the scent of her breath. It was all his once more.

But when he drew away, the world and Joelle's absence attacked him.

Hyam knew the bauble held an addictive force. The memories were too perfect. Nothing unpleasant was contained in these recollections, not even the distress he had known over losing his magical abilities. Within the eye there was only the good, only the pleasurable, only the allure that drew him further and further into its depths.

On the third night, Hyam resisted the urge as long as he could. Then he limped over to where Meda slept, gave her the box, and told her to keep it from him and never open it herself.

Theirs was the only caravan departing Emporis for the yellow reaches. On their ninth morning outbound from Emporis, Selim took his tea and cold flatbread with Hyam's group, offering fragments of desert wisdom to this heartsore stranger and his small company. "Winter is the time for such treks. Only because of these strange orders do we venture now, in the approach to high summer. Soon the yellow realm will be struck by winds so fierce the sand will etch flesh from bones, and then turn the bones themselves to more dust. And the heat will grow worse still. Either we reach our destination soon, or we and the animals perish."

They slept the brief period permitted them, then rose while the moon was still a tight sliver to Hyam's left. Dawn was another three hours away. They traveled until the heat made each breath a struggle. At midday they sheltered and rested, then ate a cold meal and trekked through the sunset and into the night. Hyam welcomed the uneven rhythm, the fog of fatigue, the pain. It gave him something concrete to struggle against. It would do until their true foe was revealed.

After another brief night, Selim again joined them for the pre-dawn meal. As they stood around the cook fire, Selim demanded, "Tell me, stranger. Why do you suppose the enemy attacked your mate and not you?"

Hyam saw the rage spark in Meda's gaze and knew she was ready to bark at the drover, both for his question and his tone. Hyam held up his hand, silencing her. He merely gave voice to the thoughts he carried through each day. "The enemy attacked my weakest point."

Behind them, drovers prepared the caravan while the beasts protested with their brassy moans. Selim studied him intently, clearly not expecting a direct answer.

Hyam went on, "They had sent a beast against us in the valley called Ellismere."

"Even I have heard of this place. The vale of dire beginnings, with its legacy of war and destruction." Selim paused. "A beast, you say."

"A magical fiend that turned to smoke and ash when we defeated it. The creature killed my . . . closest friend. But the rest of us survived."

"And then in Emporis they went after your woman and your guard and the young scribe."

"Weakening me further in the process." Hyam pressed his hands into the small of his back, wishing he could ready himself better for another day on the road. "And drawing my small company out here."

"To the yellow realm. Where you are exposed and vulnerable. Where your demise can be blamed upon the waterless world." Selim smiled without humor. "I do not give our survival good odds."

"There is the matter," Hyam reminded him, "of the bird who spoke to your master and to me."

Selim said, "Perhaps the enemy has methods to make the bird speak their lies for them."

"The bird, perhaps," Hyam replied. "But not the dragon."

Selim was already in the process of calling up his caravan when he realized what he had just heard. He seemed reluctant to turn back, as though curiosity was a weakness. But Selim could not resist the temptation. "The what?"

❖

Selim rode alongside Hyam as the caravan traveled east into another desert dawn. The glow turned the world into molten wonder. The air was deceptively comfortable, a miracle that would vanish an instant after the sun rose full over the horizon. The stars faded into a wash of palest blue, the moon set, and all that lay ahead was endless wasteland.

Hyam's description of his dreams took them into the full heat of day. When he was done, Selim rode for a time through the fierce light before he finally asked, "Why do you tell me these things?"

Hyam did not respond.

"You speak to me as a friend." The thought turned Selim angry. "We are strangers. You think because we share the road I have been named your comrade? You think my master's folly makes us allies?"

Hyam still did not reply.

"Such thinking can kill a journeyer of the yellow realm." Selim flicked his quirt, accelerating his beast. He tossed over his shoulder, "I regret meeting you, stranger. I dislike digging graves, even for people I do not know."

Shona and Meda nudged their animals in close to his. Meda said, "Much as I detest the drover's attitude, I too wonder why you spoke so openly."

Hyam nodded. "It was a risk. I decided to take it."

"But why?"

"Because," Hyam replied. "Something tells me Selim is far more than he wants us to think."

That day was like the ten that had come before. The camels groaned and rocked and made slow progress. The flat yellow earth became an anvil, the sun a relentless hammer. At midday they halted. Hyam and his small team followed the drovers' example and fashioned open-sided tents using their camel's broad humps as a tether. He dozed off, only to be stabbed by dreams. A face smiled at him in joy and in love. Hyam rose to a sitting position. The blinding light was preferable to being assaulted by his terrors.

Too soon Selim called them up. They stood slowly and the beasts groaned for them. A few hours later, a series of jagged hills formed to their left. They formed an oddly shaped ridge along the otherwise featureless plain. By late afternoon, the hills were perhaps an hour's trek away.

Early evening was the hardest hour for Hyam. The day was still baking hot but already held the promise of dusk. These hours of waning light and rising chill were as close as the desert came to true beauty. The sun set behind them, the moon rose ahead, the shadows faded gradually, the land glowed flaxen, and then the stars emerged. Hyam hated these soft hours. Joelle's face came to him, her features bathed by the Elven torches as he handed her over to others. So that he could depart on this futile quest.

Hyam was jerked back to the present by Shona calling, "The bird is with us."

All his company followed her direction. The eagle soared high and to the west, back where the departing sun might reflect upon its wings.

Meda maneuvered her beast up alongside him. "Is that truly the one who spoke with you?"

"Definitely."

"How can you be certain?"

"The bird showed us its silhouette." Hyam pulled on his reins. "Tell Selim we stop here."

"He will not like that."

"I was not asking." Hyam started out into the plain, separating himself from the others. He turned and called to Fareed, "Join me. Bring Selim and Alembord and Shona."

23

Fareed was the only one of Hyam's company who rode easy. Neither the heat nor the trek appeared to bother him at all. His animal also seemed more comfortable with its burden, and Hyam suspected it had nothing to do with the youth's lighter weight. Hyam waited until there was a good distance between them and the caravan to say, "I suppose I'm doing a dozen things wrong with this animal."

"A hundred, sahib," Fareed replied cheerfully. "A thousand. More."

"So why haven't you taught me?"

"It is not the servant's place to correct the master."

"You are not the servant, and I am no—"

"You remain wrapped in a trouble we all share, sahib. I am here to serve. I and the others have waited for you to speak."

"From now on, I am the student and you the teacher."

Fareed sketched a salute with his quirt. "It shall be as you say."

From behind came the tread of a racing camel. When Selim came within shouting range, he demanded, "You dare order my caravan to halt?"

"So it's your caravan now."

Selim lashed the space between them with his whip. "We hold to our pace for a reason. That reason is *life*. If we halt upon your whims, we *die*."

Meda said softly, "Ho, the bird."

Hyam watched the eagle settle to the earth between them and the ancient hills. "Dismount. Tether the beasts. We proceed on foot. You too, Selim."

The bird ducked and weaved as they walked, clearly disliking the approach of so many humans. Selim's constant muttering did not help things. Hyam stopped a good dozen paces away from the bird and said, "Shona, Fareed, make lights. Not too bright, mind."

The bird weaved a bit faster. Standing on the ground it looked oddly vulnerable, despite the vicious beak and its size. The eagle's russet coloring was turned the shade of simmering lava by the dusk and the magic torches. It stuttered, "Danger."

Hyam pointed to Selim and replied, "This one says there is danger on all sides."

"Then he knows the realm through which you travel."

Hyam asked the question that had drawn him this far. "How is this helping my mate?"

"That is not the question."

"That is *precisely* the question!" Hyam roared with all the rage and pain that had carried him this far. "That is the *only* question!"

The bird eek-eeked and unfolded its vast wings. "Insolent! Rude! Uncivil!"

"You told me you could help me save my woman!"

"Not I! Not I! The one I serve!"

"Then where is your master?"

The bird ack-acked and flapped its wings, but remained bound to the earth. "Go to the hills. There is a company who awaits you."

But Hyam was not letting go so easily. "Tell your master this! Either I receive my answers this very night, or I and my brethren return to Emporis!"

"You disobey! You defy! You violate!"

"Eleven days and nights I've waited for word on how to save Joelle. Hear this. I go to the hills. I ask my questions. Either I receive answers, or I return to Emporis and hunt the enemy. Not one step more. Make sure your master—"

Hyam stopped speaking because the bird took flight, acking and eeking in fury as it swooped up into the moonlight and away.

❖

They ate a cold meal brought to them by Fareed. Selim muttered angrily as they mounted up and started toward the hills. The strengthening moon did not make their destination any more appealing. The hills were shaped like a prehistoric beast, as empty and lifeless as the desert. Or so they thought.

When they approached the base, a fiery globe appeared on the summit. Then another. And more. Gradually a string of magical lights slipped down the slope toward them. They moved with an oddly weaving grace.

Then Selim muttered, "What manner of legend is this?"

Before Hyam turned around, he knew. Before he looked into the drover's eyes, he was certain. The validation he had sought for eleven impossibly long days had been revealed.

Selim had spoken in Elven.

Hyam gestured to the others. "Dismount. We continue on foot."

The company who descended the hillside did not dance, as Hyam had first supposed. The beings limped and staggered and stumbled down the steep slope. Their mage-lights remained poised directly above each head. As they lurched over the uneven terrain, the lights shifted and jerked and weaved.

The first of their company halted where the hillside met the desert floor. A querulous voice called out, "Which of you wears the healed diadem?"

Hyam's hackles rose. Not from the question, which he did not understand. Rather, from the woman's speech.

She addressed them in Milantian.

If the crone told Hyam she was five hundred years old, he would have accepted it as fact. An uglier woman, if indeed she could be called that, Hyam had never seen. Her skull was canted, such that her left eye was half a handbreadth higher than her right. Her hair sprouted in patches from a skull that appeared only partially covered by skin. Each clump of hair was a different shade, woven into a rope thick as Hyam's wrist and worn about her neck like a noose. As he approached, Hyam realized the clasp at the base of her scrawny neck was fashioned from a skeletal hand.

The others who accompanied the woman gathered to either side, none taking the final step off the hillside. The woman's voice was a scattering of sounds, a rush of wind over dry reeds and a bark from beyond the grave. She declared, "Before you stands the queen of what you cannot fathom. My realm was old before your forebears claimed the title, human. Do not *dare* to keep me waiting!"

Hyam said, "I am not certain that I understand your question. But I speak your language."

"And do so with an appalling accent. Who taught you to butcher the most regal of tongues?"

"Mages. Human wizards. They spoke it worse than I do."

She cackled, all rattles and dry coughs. "Who are these that accompany you?"

"Friends," Hyam replied. "They share the yellow road."

"There is no road where you go, strange one. There is no compass heading, nor safety. You and your friends will most likely perish."

"I have tried to tell them as much. They have insisted upon coming just the same."

She chewed on that for a time, her jaw muscles bunching beneath the parchment covering. "Well, I suppose it is not altogether bad to die in good company. I ask again. Do you wear the healed diadem?"

"I don't . . . If you mean a jewel fashioned from an orb, yes."

"Show me."

"I can't. I lost my powers in the battle against one of your own."

"Well, perhaps the era of humans has come to an end after all." There was no room in that desiccated face for sympathy. She observed him for a moment, then shrugged as though it was none of her concern. "Who fashioned the diadem you claim to wear?"

"Elves."

"Speak the word for *reveal* in their tongue, strange one. Then touch your middle finger to the orb's healed remnant. I must see that you truly carry the sign."

Hyam did as he was told. Instantly the center of his fore-head burned with an intensity that was both pleasant and almost blinding.

Even the crone was taken aback. "Touch it again!" When Hyam had done so, she peered at him more closely still. "Truly, you have lost your powers?"

"I have."

"Then this is another mystery added to this impossible night." She waved it aside. "Will you come?"

"Where do we go?"

"What are words, strange one? You cannot fathom what awaits you. Either you come or you do not. I was commanded to invite. I was commanded to keep you safe. Nothing more."

"Who commands the hidden queen?"

She liked that enough to cackle a second time. "Who in-deed. Come and you will see. Though the seeing may cost you everything."

"May I take a moment to speak with my allies?"

"The invitation is for you and whoever you select as your company." She waved a scrawny hand. "Speak."

Swiftly Hyam related what the woman had said. He finished with, "I cannot ask you to accompany me."

Selim demanded, "What is the tongue you speak?"

"Milantian. The language of the crimson mage."

"And yet I do not detect any danger," Shona said. "I do not understand."

"Nor I," Hyam agreed. "Even so, this woman may take me to my doom."

Meda replied, "If she takes you, she takes us all."

"Meda, I am grateful—"

"Enough. We will not ever have this discussion again." Meda's gaze was fiercer than her voice. "We are your company. Finished."

Hyam searched for a way to tell her what that meant but could come up with nothing adequate, so he remained silent. He glanced at each face in turn and found the same grim resolve. Even Selim.

He said to the crone, "We will come."

24

As they climbed, Hyam remained held by the language spoken by the witches surrounding them. Milantian was the speech of death and war and darkest mage-force. He knew his company were frightened. He knew he should try to reassure them. But he would not color this trek with fable.

He asked the crone, "Are you our foes?"

"Foes, you say? Do foes light your way to the realm of mystery? Do foes reveal themselves, breaking vows older than the race of man?"

When Hyam translated, Selim hissed in response, "The old woman's race has been our sworn foe for just as long."

The crone glanced back from where she led her company. "What strange scent do I detect lingering about this one?"

Hyam had no intent of answering, so he deflected with, "Is there no better route to the top?"

The crone and her company shrieked with glee. "What use is a path when few come and none depart? Except for you and your company, by command of the covert one. A path is as worthless as a name for empty hills in the midst of the empty reaches. And so all the world has thought. Including our own kind. And thus have we survived."

Hyam caught the hint of a lie but only said, "We will keep your secret."

"So the covert one has vowed." The crone shot him a look that was sour and bitter both. "Even so, we shall mark your departure with dread and foreboding."

The going was very steep in places. They climbed long enough for Hyam to lose every vestige of the night's chill. The shifting mage-lights cast the slope in shadows that flickered and twisted and hid crevices that almost tripped him twice.

When they finally crested the rise, there was nothing to see. The others gathered around him, panting hard. The desert stretched out behind, a sea of dusky moonlight, lifeless and silent save for the tiny bundle of campfires where their caravan waited.

Before them opened a central valley carved down the length of all four hills. The gorge was dark as a giant's open grave. There was no sound. No life. No reason to have come here at all.

The crone noted their confusion. "And so all have seen since the dawn of man's era, save those who have chosen to come and never leave. Not even our own kind who returned here have seen anything else."

Again Hyam sensed veiled untruths. "The crimson mage came here?"

She waved his question aside. "Here stands Lystra, strange one. This grand city once marked the boundary of the Milantian realm. Before the time of man, before the lure of shadow forces captured our finest, we were." She reached toward the heavens with both scrawny arms. "Observe, newcomer. Behold the lost empire. Behold the majesty of former epochs."

The crone's hands and fingers began an intricate dance, joined by all the others of her company. Together they weaved a complex script of moonlight and mage-force. Their elaborate motions transformed the night into a loom.

They weaved a city.

The hills became a bastion, from which sprung towers of lyrical splendor. These grew ramparts and palaces and grand chambers. The long cavern sprang to magnificent life, filled with silver fire and the music of a hundred fountains. A road of polished pewter opened before them, illuminated by living lanterns with diaphanous wings.

But the greatest change of all was in the crone and her company. Gone were the ghastly figures with their wretched faces. In their place stood women whose beauty dimmed even the city's allure.

The queen of Lystra shone with a regal power beyond the reach of time or human comprehension. The women who surrounded her gleamed with a magnetic splendor. They seemed to dance even when they remained still. They smiled with their entire beings. They sang a welcome even when silent.

Hyam and his company could only gape in wondrous astonishment.

The queen of Lystra was clearly satisfied with the effect of their creation. She laughed, the sound as lovely as crystal bells, as deadly as a silver dagger. "Come."

25

The valley was now a palace's central keep, several thousand paces long and framed by pillars tall as great forest trees. The floor was mosaic artistry, portraying scenes Hyam could not comprehend, all set in blocks of semiprecious stones.

As they descended the pewter road, Shona asked, "Are there no men?"

Lystra's queen showed satisfaction at the question. "Our males are kept in strictest purdah. But none against their will."

When Hyam translated, Fareed said, "There are desert legends of drovers who sleepwalk away from campfires, lured by beauties who lock them in silver cages, beyond even time's reach."

Hyam disliked the conversation's course, but translated nonetheless. The queen replied, "True enough, young sir, save for the cages. All our men are free to go. Which makes

our shared pleasure sweeter still when they choose to stay."
She frowned at a pair of young beauties who flirted with
Fareed. "But we harbor no human mages within our keep.
They are forbidden."

The last word was a lash, softly spoken yet enough to twirl
the ladies away. They spun back and around, pouting until
their attention focused upon Alembord.

The queen clearly approved of their new prey, for she said,
"This tall one with the flame of adventure in his eyes, he
would be made welcome. As would the drover. I prefer my
men to carry the spice of secrets. Their flavor is exquisite
when finally revealed. Shall my ladies sing for these?"

"Later, perhaps. First I have questions."

She seemed to expect it, for she took this as an invitation
to command, "Dance then, ladies. Dance!"

There was nothing Hyam could do except leave, and he
could not depart, not until he knew whether there was truly a
hope for Joelle in this realm of Milantian witches. He asked,
"What is your bond to the eagle?"

"Not the bird. He merely serves as courier for the covert
one."

Hyam hoped desperately that Alembord would prove able
to fight the lure. He did not want another lost soul on his con-
science. But the ladies were unabashed in their play as tempt-
resses. They were beauties of every age, dressed in diaphanous
silks that revealed far more than they hid. Silently they swept
about Alembord and Selim in a sinuous chain. Inviting them
to depart the human realm and know only pleasure.

Hyam turned so he did not have to observe the ladies and

asked, "What can a dragon offer the queen of this ancient realm?"

"What indeed." She clearly took pleasure in watching her ladies weave their spell. "We are bound by a treaty older than your race's memory. Old as Lystra. Older!"

"What is your bond to the crimson mage?"

She disliked the question intensely. But Alembord and Selim appeared captivated by the dance. Worriedly so. She seemed to find enough satisfaction in this to answer, "You humans think all Milantians are evil by nature. Phah. Your history is blind, strange one. Blind! Mage power is but a doorway. You enter and choose which way to proceed. We selected one direction. Mages like the one you destroyed chose another. So it has been since Lystra's earliest days. We have nothing to do with his ilk. Nothing!"

A third time Hyam sensed she was lying, at least partly. But the next question was the one he could not ask. About his own heritage. So instead he said, "What can you tell me about the dragon?"

"Nothing! I can tell you not one iota. How you even know of his existence is a mystery!" She gestured angrily at her minions. "Enough of your questions, strange one. Now it is time for my ladies to sing!"

"One moment," Hyam said. "I wish to ask—"

She clapped her hands, silencing his tactic. "Sing!"

Hyam had space for one thought, or rather, a single glimpse beyond the lure. He realized that Shona and Meda and Fareed were gone. Then his thoughts swam into a delirium of yearning so powerful his entire body ached.

The women sang of a different realm, one where neither sorrow nor worries could enter. Their lurid dance was no longer a ring of beauties, for they had joined somehow, the sound of their voices linking them into one unified whole. Magnetic. Pleading. Inviting.

Hyam felt the hint of a name sweep through his mind. He felt a keening sense of disconnect and realized he had a choice. Either he could join in the joy of unknowing, of pleasure beyond the ability of his senses to deny. Or he could recall the name and all it had meant to him.

He managed to utter one word. "Don't."

The dancers hesitated. Hyam had not meant it as a command so much as a plea. Yet his word shattered the spell, at least for one moment. And it released the queen's ire. She turned to him in regal fury. "You dare command a ruler in her own fief?"

Hyam drew his thoughts into some form of sensible order. "I am your guest. These are my company."

She sniffed. "Do not such as these have the right to choose for themselves?" The queen snapped her fingers at her ladies. "Sing!"

As he struggled to shape another protest, a witch slipped up to the queen's side and whispered a few words. Instantly the palace went silent.

Alembord cried in genuine anguish. The loss of the song was a vacuum Hyam felt deep in his bones.

"The covert one has signaled his arrival." The queen lashed the air with a vexed hand. "Ladies, join me."

The company of witches followed their queen, casting

mournful glances back at Alembord and the others. They gathered at the nexus of the central keep, formed a circle, and began weaving another spell.

Hyam forced his leaden limbs to carry him over to where Alembord stood. The soldier's features were taut with the hunger of a lonely young man. Hyam gripped his arm and said, "They are witches."

Alembord's only response was another rasping breath.

"They will feed upon you for as long as you survive." Hyam tightened his grip. "But it is not just about you. They seek a captive. One of our own. It would bind us to the vow of secrecy. If we were to speak of this place once we departed, you would die."

Alembord blinked once. Again. And struggled to see who it was who spoke to him.

"These are not human beauties," Hyam said, shaking Alembord's arm. "Remember how the witches looked before we climbed the hill."

Alembord shuddered. Coughed. Wiped his face. And was back. "I almost . . ."

"I know." Hyam breathed a trace easier. But the danger still remained. And Shona and Meda and Fareed were nowhere to be seen. He spoke to Selim in Elven. "You are all right?"

Selim looked shaken but intact. "The race who destroyed my homeland cannot hide behind spells. I see them for who they are."

Alembord asked, "What tongue do you speak?"

Hyam shook his head. That would have to wait. Now

the queen beckoned to him. Hyam said to Selim, "Will you join me?"

Selim clearly had no interest in approaching the witches again. "What can possibly be worth attending them?"

"Answers," Hyam replied. "Mysteries revealed. I hope."

26

The circle of witches weaved and worked their midnight loom. They forged a silver bonfire whose brilliant flames rose five times a man's height. Pewter sparks shot into the star-flecked sky.

Gradually the flames refashioned themselves, and the dragon grew within the silver fire's heart. His eyes sparked like the stars as it searched and craned. When his gaze fastened upon Hyam, the beast rose to his feet, and in that one motion he dwarfed both the bonfire and the central keep.

The dragon stretched out wings broad as a ship's mainsail and chattered the drumbeat Hyam had come to understand. The beast's greeting consisted of just one word, "Treaty."

It was the same word carved into every boundary stone lining the Ashanta settlements. Hyam suspected it served the same purpose here. He stepped forward and stretched out his arms, a human's equivalent of the behemoth before him. Unarmed and exposed. He responded in kind. "Treaty."

The dragon's silver-flamed head swiveled from side to side, inspecting Hyam closely. "You understand the word's true meaning?"

"I understand these are bonds untouched by time or race," Hyam replied. "I understand that in the past we united in moments of dire need. I accept that another such time has come."

The dragon remained an ethereal form, fashioned by moonlight and cold fire. He tucked his wings back and turned to the queen of Lystra. "Leave us."

She bridled. "This is my keep! My realm! My subjects!"

Hyam said, "She has hidden away three of my company. Two women and a young mage."

"Release them," the beast commanded.

"We need assurance that our secrets remain ours alone!" The queen stamped her foot. "We broke the oath of eons to admit them!"

"I will seal their lips," the beast chattered. "None will speak because none will be able. Now free this one's company and go."

Hyam waited until the witches retreated to ask, "Why am I here?"

"My people face a crisis that could end us forever."

"My question remains the same," Hyam replied. "I accept the treaty. But why me?"

"When all hope was lost, the west wind spoke to me. It carried your name. It revealed your face."

Hyam was swamped by the futile pain of fear without answers. "I lost my mage-force in the Emporis battle. Then some new foe attacked my beloved. I am alone. I have nothing to offer."

Selim spoke for the first time since entering the fire circle. "Not alone, Emissary."

The dragon shifted his ponderous form and spoke to the drover. "I salute you, child of Ethrin. Once your kind were our closest allies among the small folk. Will you grant me the boon of serving as guide to this one?"

"I have confirmed this to your messenger." Selim revealed a solemn dignity in his bow. "If it is within my ability, I will do as you have asked."

"Hyam must be brought to the port where your ancestors established their lineage."

Selim shuddered. The fire crackled. The sparks rose. Hyam waited with the beast, not understanding. Finally Selim said, "Sire, Alyss is no more."

"Nonetheless, that is his destination."

"Sire . . . in living memory, none who have taken this route have ever returned."

"I am aware of the risks, child of Ethrin. The bird will accompany you and serve as scout. Perhaps you will survive. Perhaps."

Hyam asked, "If the road is so perilous, why can't you fly over and bring me back?"

"It is forbidden for my kind to enter the human realm. A treaty more ancient than the ones binding our races forbids this. Even speaking through your dreams threatens the treaty's fabric. Even revealing myself in the witches' flames. But the alternative is my kind's destruction. Either way is filled with dread portents. So I have come this far. But no farther."

"What of my beloved?" The words scalded Hyam's throat. "What of Joelle?"

He ruffled his wings. "We have much in common, you and I. Forces beyond my ken threaten my own mate's next breath. I suspect the Milantian foes who robbed you of your most precious element had a hand in my mate's calamity. But I cannot detect either the method or the purpose."

Hyam's hands might as well have been stained by Joelle's blood. "What can I do, a mage who is mage no more?"

"There is no purpose to this discussion, human. Not until you complete the journey. Travel to Alyss. You will save us. How, I cannot say. Nor do I need to. For the west wind spoke to me and said this would come to pass. The west wind does not lie."

Hyam replied as he must, for there was but one possible course. "I will come."

The dragon unfurled his great wings. "Dawn arrives. I cannot allow the sun to notice my presence. Farewell, human. Survive the quest. Go to the port of Alyss. Stand at the harbor's mouth, face the sea, and await me there. By your coming you shall save us all and earn a dragon king's gratitude."

The dragon lifted up and drew the flames with him. The entire bonfire fashioned itself into wings big as the keep. The dragon flapped once, twice, and leapt into the sky. Instantly the form was gone, and the fire with him. A billion pewter sparks rose and joined with the first faint light of dawn.

27

Shona moved through the next two days in a heat-drenched stupor. She waited for Meda or Fareed to speak of what had happened during their captivity. But neither did. In fact, it seemed as though neither was aware of being imprisoned at all. But Shona knew. She remembered everything.

She had been frozen as tightly as when the Emporis witch had chained her with smoke. A bevy of witches had dragged her to one of the giant pillars lining the central keep. The stone column had grown a portal, or rather, a mouth, and swallowed her whole. From within, she had seen that Fareed's legend of silver cages was indeed true. Between the slender bars had stood sheets of palest amber, and she had watched the witches sing, though she'd heard nothing. She had seen Alembord give in and Selim shudder and Hyam struggle. She had wanted to shriek a warning, but the power of speech was as distant as her ability to breathe. She could not even feel her heart's beating, as though the column possessed the ability to trap her somewhere beyond time's reach, out where she would remain a living component of this magical realm for all the eons yet to spin.

She watched Fareed and Meda closely those first two days back with the caravan, almost as carefully as she scouted behind them, ever fearful the witches would swoop down and ensnare her again. But the yellow realm remained empty, and her fellow prisoners showed no foul remnants from their lost hours.

Selim led them steadily onward, pushing them hard. At sunset on the third day they arrived at a well. There was no marking to announce its presence. In fact, the stone circle was hidden behind a sand hillock. The first indication Shona had was when her animal snorted and accelerated. As they halted and watered beasts and men alike, Shona wondered how Selim had led them here across this featureless plain.

That night, after a stew of rice and dates and dried vegetables spiced with desert sorrel, after they had drunk cup after endless cup of mint tea, Selim spoke of his past. He addressed his words to Hyam but spoke in the human tongue so they all could hear and understand.

"Elves are great ones for tales from the distant past. But they are not much for the counting of years. I have no idea how long ago it happened. I only know it was a number of generations before the Milantians invaded. An Elven forebear of mine was of royal blood. The king of Ethrin sent him to Alyss, which supplied the king with all manner of human finery. And there my ancestor fell in love with a commoner.

Their marriage cost him everything, but by all accounts he lived and died a contented man." Selim shrugged. "Legends have a way of growing happy endings."

"It was no legend," Hyam said softly. "Which suggests the ending was real as well."

The two men stared into the magical fire at the center of their gathering. The caravan drovers clustered about their own mage-light, which Shona had lit after Hyam suggested they not use their precious oil for what could be supplied for free. Selim's assistant had thanked her with the quiet solemnity that Shona was coming to recognize as the desert way. Passions were kept well hidden, as though the flames within these hearts were so fierce all were best served by extreme politeness.

Selim spoke that way now, addressing the fire with a voice soft as the night. "My forebear established a trading house of his own, one that served the Elves throughout the realm. A generation or so later, my clan were appointed bankers to the Ashanta, and their house grew in wealth and power. But the legacy of their Elven heritage remained alive. Each child was taught the tongue and the history of the green realms. Those with the talent were also taught the Ashanta speech and that of the bird. Whose own forebears have been our allies since those earliest days."

Hyam asked, "Did anyone ever mention the dragons?"

"I have wondered about this ever since you first spoke of the beast. Just in the past few years the bird has spoken of a master, and I feared it might have been ensnared by the crimson foe."

His features and Hyam's now shared a similar cast, of hard-earned wisdom and tragedy and the impact of experiences beyond Shona's reach. She listened as Selim went on, "When the crimson horde invaded, my forebear was off with a trading caravan. He loved the road and the journey, which is most odd for one with Elven blood. Even so, this oddity saved him. He was in Emporis when word arrived of the destruction of Alyss. By the time he returned to his former home, there was nothing but ash and ruin. Soon after, word arrived that Ethrin had suffered the same fate."

Hyam asked, "Where do you live now?"

"Up ahead is a desert oasis where a city has grown. Olom, it's called, which is the ancient word for golem." Selim's smile was utterly without humor. "You will see some strange things there, I assure you."

"Why make that your home?"

"There are riches to be had for one who is cautious. Olom supplies gemstones to all the human realm."

"And you carry them."

"Just so. My clan has fashioned a haven out of a neighboring valley." He made a distinctly desert gesture, right hand to heart and lips and forehead. "You and your company are welcome."

"I thank you for the offer of hospitality," Hyam replied. "What of the scrolls?"

"The scrolls, ah, the scrolls, had I never come across them." Selim rose to his feet. "That is a tale for another night. Sleep well. Dawn comes soon."

28

As the others prepared for sleep, Shona watched Hyam walk toward his belongings piled by the reclining camel. The beast snorted, turned her ponderous neck, and opened her mouth. She possessed an astonishing array of long yellow teeth.

Fareed called over, "Sahib, do not flinch away or show fear."

"I told you not to call me that."

"Indeed, sahib. Now raise your fist as though you are going to swipe at the animal."

Hyam did as Fareed instructed. The camel might have snarled or she might have belched. Whatever the sound, she lowered her head and did not move again as Hyam rummaged through his things.

He returned to the mage-fire holding the sheathed Milantian blade with both hands. Meda must have known what was coming, for she rose to her feet and watched wide-eyed as he approached.

"I should have done this long before now," Hyam said.

"Sire, this is your wife's—"

"Joelle is with the Elves," Hyam said. "And we face danger on all sides."

Meda slipped off her sword and belted Joelle's into place. Gripping the pommel, she bowed tightly and said, "For the lady."

Hyam nodded stiffly and turned around. Meda watched him stagger toward the perimeter, his distress a sunset shroud. She turned to Shona and jerked her chin. "Follow him."

Shona rose and trailed Hyam over to where he stood watching the moonrise. He showed no surprise at her approach. At least he did not send her away. His distress turned his features craven in the dim light. They stood in silence for a time, then he turned and settled a hand on her shoulder before walking back to their mage-fire. Shona followed him, the feel of his hand still with her as she lay down and gave in to sleep.

The next day, Selim pushed the caravan harder still, explaining that the wells between them and Olom were chancy and often dried out during the summer, which was another reason why theirs was the only caravan trekking over the empty wastes. But Shona was growing accustomed to the trek and the heat. Her body no longer complained except in the day's final hours. She rose each morning with renewed excitement over the adventure and the chance to share this quest with Hyam. She felt the old restrictions fading, the bonds between them growing ever stronger. This was a new world. New rules. New opportunities. It was only a matter of time.

Hyam started each day riding with Fareed and made no complaint when she joined them. Fareed spoke of the desert ways, of guiding by starlight, of the sun's transition, of the small signals that a caravan master learned to read for danger and direction both. He showed them how to shift position from time to time, riding with one leg crooked over the pommel. How to study the horizon, searching for signs. He spoke of his own former master, a wretch who took pleasure in the small indignities that created such misery on the trek. He spoke of magic with the quiet fervor of one who had never thought he might find a purpose for this strange burden called life.

When Hyam's attention wandered back to his absent wife, Fareed read the man's mood and steered his camel away. Shona went with the young mage, as though the only reason she had joined them was to learn. She and Fareed then spent many happy hours talking spells.

Fareed disliked speaking about himself. But the empty reaches proved a good place for revealing secrets. Shona learned how he had pulled so far ahead of all the other acolytes that he threatened even some senior wizards. So Fareed had begun to fake mistakes. When Connell had invited him to help establish the Emporis magery, Fareed had leapt at the chance. Fareed liked and admired Connell. What was more, the master mage of Emporis took with them a caravan-load of spell-scrolls and a chest of gold to acquire more.

That was another reason why Edlyn was visiting the realm's

Long Halls, Fareed revealed. So Falmouth could become a repository for copies of spell-scrolls from other Long Halls. Just in case the darkness spread. Fareed spoke those final words with grim awareness. Just in case the darkness spread.

The next night, Fareed and Shona approached their two leaders, Hyam and Selim, and asked permission to practice magery with their new wands. Hyam and Selim responded with a pair of frowns, then asked for time to deliberate.

Eventually Hyam walked over and said, "It's a good idea. But we can't risk revealing our hand."

"Selim has said we're the only caravan out this time of year," Shona pointed out. "If they are searching, we will be found."

Fareed added, "If we don't practice, how can we use them in time of need?"

Hyam nodded slowly. Shona liked how he gave their words such careful consideration, how he treated her and Fareed both as equals. "Look around you. What do you see?"

"Nothing."

"Precisely. It is one thing to light campfires, another thing entirely to use your wands. We would light up the entire yellow realm with your spells. And there is something else to consider. These amulets might actually be hiding us from view." Briefly he described how the orb had masked the crimson mage from both the Elves and the Ashanta. He went on, "We don't know if it's a spell or some innate trait of the orb. Or even if this power transfers to the miniatures."

"But we can't take that risk," Shona agreed.

"Practice every spell you can. But hold off on connecting to the wands. For all our sakes."

217

The next day Shona and Fareed began using their quirts as wands. They spun the spells and weaved the required designs. They created ribbons of power that streaked the dry desert air. But neither Hyam nor Selim objected. Over and over they practiced the spells until Shona knew both the words and the gestures by rote.

Once Shona asked about Fareed's family. He grew very sad at that and spoke a few words about desert bandits who had seared their village with mage-fire when he was five. Then he turned away and rode alone for the rest of that long afternoon.

That evening they came upon another well, the first since Lystra. They cooked another well-water stew. Otherwise they existed upon hard bread, dates, olives, dried beef, shriveled apples, apricots, and tea. Endless cups of tea, poured from tall bronze kettles with delicate stems embossed in silver. These pots were the first items to be unpacked and the last to be lashed into place. Shona thrived on the steamy mint draughts. They erased her weariness and revived her. As did the quiet moments after sunset.

When everyone but the night's watch bedded down, and Hyam stepped beyond the camp's perimeter to stare over the empty vista and watch the moonrise, Shona joined him. It was almost enough to share in these private moments. Even though her yearnings remained unrequited. Even though it was the absence of another woman that drew them together. Almost.

The next afternoon an uncommon wind blew up from the south. The currents ate at Shona with a low moan that drilled into her mind. The sand bit her skin, hot as ash. Selim rode the caravan's entire length, ensuring all his animals were safe and Hyam's company knew to knot kerchiefs over their noses and mouths and ears. Selim assured them the wind was nothing, a mere foretaste of what the late summer would bring. Shona did not speak because her throat was raw from the effort required to breathe. The wind caused a subtle shift to all her discomforts, a gradual invasion of pain. For the first time she understood the drovers' silent stillness around the campfires, the ingrained need for impossible patience and endurance. After a time she actually drifted into sleep, as though her body took the only escape it could.

Then Selim whacked Shona's leg with his quirt, jerking her awake. "Your animal's natural response to the wind is to stop and turn its back to the storm. If you do that, and we lose you, you die." He rode beside her for a time until he was certain she was both awake and aware of the danger. Then he rode on.

The evening tea had never tasted so fine, an elixir she could not get enough of. The camp was blanketed by a grit that worked into everything, including her cup. She ate because Meda ordered her to. Her brain felt stuffed with the same silt. When Hyam rose and walked beyond the camp's perimeter, she almost left him alone. But she forced her aching body to rise and walk over. She could feel herself rocking slightly from side to side as they stood in silence. Every now and then her muscles quivered, a tight spasm that rose from her feet to her forehead. She heard her breath rasp down her over-tight throat. When Hyam turned and thanked her with the customary hand on her shoulder, she was uncertain whether she had the strength to walk back to her pallet.

That night Shona dreamed of the witches.

Shona was back in the Lystra palace keep, only now every shadow held the specter of doom. Her exhaustion was such that she could not force herself awake. She drifted from one pillar to the next, chased by wisps of deadly crimson smoke and women who laughed from the joy of the chase. The sultry vixens mocked her all night, saving the worst for the dawn, when they captured her. But they did not devour her as Shona had feared. Instead, they welcomed her. She realized in a flash of terror that she was one of them.

The dream's horror added to the next day's trek. When the wind rose again that afternoon, Shona heard the witches' laughter drift in every acrid blast.

29

The journey from the red hills to Olom took fourteen days. The wind blew for six. They stopped at three wells, but at the second, the leather-covered wooden lid had not been lashed down properly and the well had filled with sand. Selim roundly cursed the last caravan master who had come this way. Then he led them on, through the night and the next day, until even the most docile of beasts groaned with exhaustion. But they made the next well at dawn on the third day, and the lid was in place. Hyam and Selim and Fareed shifted off the cover. They all watched and waited as Selim dropped the leather bucket. Even the animals seemed to hold their breath. The well was so deep the rope hummed over the stone ledges, on and on it fell, until they heard the faint splash.

The caravan ran the well dry. The final buckets came up almost half full of mud. Selim fed these to the animals, using every drop. He assured them water would seep in and refill the well before the autumn caravans began.

On the tenth day they entered low hills that closed in and blocked a rising wind. That evening they observed a sunset veiled by whistling ochre streaks far overhead. Now and then the silt drifted down like a mockery of rain.

The next day the hills rose to become yellow mountains. They trekked down a long, narrow valley between two steep ridgelines. The ground remained flat and the ridges trapped the heat. Shona felt fire in her throat with each breath. But Selim pressed on, grimly impatient.

Then the first of the beasts came into view.

A monster identical to the one that had attacked them in the empty vale appeared on the southern ridge. Shona was the first to cry a warning, though making the sound hurt her throat.

Meda drew the Milantian sword and sprang from the camel's back. The behemoth was even larger than the one that had attacked them in Ellismere. Shona pulled her wand from its makeshift sheath beside the saddle and slipped down to stand alongside Meda. In the space of two heartbeats they were joined by Alembord and Fareed. Hyam stabbed the earth with his dagger, spoke the Milantian spell, and began drawing a shield circle large enough to encompass the entire caravan.

"Hold!" Selim steered his mount around them, staring down in genuine consternation. "The beast is not your foe!"

"Not yours, perhaps." Meda's words emerged in a tight snarl. "But we know better."

Fareed pointed and croaked, "There is another."

And there was. Then the two were joined by a third. The monsters slipped from giant tunnels and waved their horrid snouts in the desert sunlight. They seemed to pay the caravan no mind. Men swarmed about them while others entered the circular caves and emerged with great loads on their backs.

"But . . ." Selim waved his quirt at the high ridge. "Those are golems! They harm no one!"

Hyam slowly straightened. "Those beasts are twins of the fiend that attacked us in Ellismere."

Selim gaped down at them. "This is true?"

Hyam sheathed his blade, walked over, and unslung the leather waterskin from his saddle. His hands shook as he drank, then he passed the skin and asked Selim, "Why does this surprise you?"

Selim slid from his saddle, clearly needing to inspect Hyam more closely. "Because not once in centuries has a golem ever attacked a man. Not ever!"

Meda said doubtfully, "I see no sign of aggression."

"Because there is none!" Selim gestured at the empty valley ahead. "The name of this city, Olom, is the name of these beasts. They are why we are here! They mine, we profit."

Up high on the ridge, the first golem approached a stone-lined corral built into the plateau. The great head with its petal-like mouth dipped down and emerged holding an entire live sheep. The animal's bleats pierced the dry air as the golem bit, squeezed, killed, and swallowed whole. The two other beasts shouldered up alongside and took their own animals. Three times the heads dipped and captured and raised and swallowed.

Selim let them watch for a while longer, then insisted that they remount and continue. Hyam and his company cast nervous glances at the monsters on the ridgeline, but did as Selim said. As the caravan started forward, Shona and the others watched first one and then the other golems turn and lumber back into their circular tunnels.

The steep hills to either side were lined with numerous tunnels now, so many they could not have been counted. Two hours later they rounded a bend and faced Olom. The city's wall was a primitive structure of yellow mud brick and fire-hardened cane spears. It filled the valley from side to side, punctured by massive gates. A tinny trumpet-blast greeted their appearance. Faces and spears appeared along the ramparts. Selim gave them no notice whatsoever. He halted Hyam and his company by the central gates and directed his assistant drover with a series of swift hand gestures.

As the caravan plodded past, Selim pointed north and said, "My holdings lie in a hidden valley beyond the city."

Hyam clearly understood the trader's thinking, for he spoke so that Selim did not need to. "If the golems attack, we don't want to put you and your clan at risk."

"But I offered you my clan's hospitality."

"And we will hopefully have an opportunity to enjoy it. But not now."

Selim exhaled his worry. "The city will offer you greater security." He turned to Fareed and asked, "You know the Oasis Inn?"

"Very well, sahib. It was where Kasim stayed."

"Go there, say I ask that you be given the best rooms." To Hyam he went on, "It is a good enough place, one my family secretly owns."

"We need to press on," Hyam replied.

Selim swept his quirt to halt further argument. "The route ahead will make the journey from Emporis appear a garden stroll. Take one night. Rest and eat and prepare."

❈

The Oasis Inn was far grander than Shona had dared hope. Crude exterior walls opened into a vast courtyard filled with sparkling fountains and the singing of caged birds. Countless servants in ballooning trousers and colorful vests salaamed a welcome and ushered them into a private alcove where six rooms opened off a garden all their own. But the greatest astonishment were the baths and three underground pools, one each for men and women and families.

The rock walls were painted with idyllic scenes of an easier life than this desert city had ever known. It was Shona's first proper bath in almost three weeks. Her hair was cemented into a roan helmet and resisted her fingers. Shona scrubbed and rinsed and scrubbed again, then slipped into the perfumed water heated to one degree off painful.

Meda joined her a few minutes later and sighed her way into the pool. "I have dreamed of this for days."

"My muscles have forgotten what it means to relax," Shona said.

"Such pleasures almost make the road worthwhile." Meda

lolled with closed eyes. "My sweetest dreams are often of such places."

Shona had a rare opportunity to inspect Meda. The woman's arms and shoulders and neck all bore scars. "What a life you have known."

"I chose my fate. I stand by my decision. It was right for me. The cost is simply part of the life." Meda rolled her head so as to fasten Shona with a hard gaze. "There are few actions that bring greater satisfaction than knowing the right choice and taking it."

Shona knew there was a hidden message. She knew Meda would not say more. But the heat and the muted lighting and the solitude made this a chamber for secrets. "You don't think I know what I want?"

"Oh, you know all right." Meda closed her eyes once more. "It's the cost I'm wondering about."

She wanted to deny it. Deflect the conversation. But she was drawn forward. "Does everyone else know?"

"Selim, definitely. Alembord, most likely, though he would like to deny it. Fareed, hard to say. He hides his thoughts well."

"And Hyam?"

"Hyam. There is the question. My guess is, he is just now learning to look beyond his distress."

Shona hesitated, then said, "Tell me of the cost."

Meda was long in replying. "When I was a young conscript, my count used a badly wounded veteran to teach us squires how to handle a blade. We were barely in our teens, full of vinegar and certain we would live forever. The count never said anything, nor did our instructor. But we saw the cost and the risk. And when the banquet fires were lit and the goblets raised in fiery toasts, the count made sure our table included several hard-bitten veterans. They spoke of battles, and the loss of friends, and the horrible spectacle of holding an ally while they bled out and breathed their last."

Shona felt her breath constrict in her throat, as though she had been transported to that very table, looking down its length and watching as Meda played the role of that battle-hardened expert. Shona knew this woman, this friend, spoke with her best interests at heart.

Meda went on, "I can't say whether the worst fate awaits you. But in such times, when the blood sings and you hear glory's call, you can become blind to the risk. You might only see the prize. What you long for. The success and the glory. It's important to understand that the coin of life holds two faces. Examine the risk. Then choose wisely how to spend the coin."

30

Selim joined them for dinner, which they took in the small courtyard. Beyond the guard ensuring their privacy, a few patrons gathered at a table by the fountain. Otherwise the inn was silent.

Meda asked, "Your inn is always so empty?"

"Not like this," Selim replied. "Not in generations."

"What has changed?"

"That is part of the mystery we must discuss." Selim gestured to servants who hovered beyond his guard. They rushed in, cleared away the remnants of a very fine meal, and departed. "The history of Olom is the history of our bond with the golems. There are other places where desert gemstones can be found. But only here is there an oasis, with underground springs that have never gone dry. Enough water to fill our baths and turn our fields green. And the fields must grow, because we must raise sheep."

"The golems," Hyam said.

"They have an appetite unlike anything you can imagine," Selim said. "They eat and they mine. They carve the tunnels, so long as they are fed. And thus has it been for a thousand years."

Meda recalled, "Lorekeepers of the badlands speak of how the crimson horde attacked with these monsters at their fore."

"All that is confirmed by our earliest tales," Selim agreed. "When the Milantians were defeated, desert traders found these golems wandering in the desert. They ate whatever was in reach. They swallowed whole camels, along with all the wares piled upon their backs. Spears and arrows did not dent their hide. But once they had eaten their fill, the golems became docile as sheep. There are arguments over who thought to set them to mining. But for ten centuries that is what they have done. They do not mate, they do not sire, and they do not die. They mine and they eat."

"One died," Meda corrected. "And turned instantly to dust."

"Which confirms our suspicions that they never truly have lived at all, but rather are magical constructs."

"Milantian magic," Meda added.

Selim shrugged. "I have long suspected you are right. But until recently, there has been no reason to worry over their origins. For it is upon them that Olom has grown rich."

As the sky overhead turned a sunset gold, servants walked through the empty courtyard, lighting metal bowls holding scented wood. The oily kindling drove away the night insects and perfumed the air.

Hyam asked, "And now?"

"They are vanishing," Selim said. "A year ago, there were almost two hundred golems. They were known by the name of the clan whose sector they mined. Now there are just forty-seven. The others have simply wandered off. Nothing can hold nor stop them."

"Where do . . ." Meda's eyes opened wide. "Alyss."

Selim nodded. "Naturally the beasts have been tracked. The clans who lose their golems face ruin. The entire society of Olom is being demolished. Of course we have followed them."

"And none of those who take the Alyss road have returned," Hyam said. "Which was why you told the dragon that the road was perilous. This was not some missing caravan from sometime in the distant past. This is now."

"Many of Olom's warriors went in search of the beasts," Selim confirmed. "Those who tracked the golems vanished. And still the golems depart."

Fareed said, "And yet you will travel with us to Alyss?"

"I gave my word to a beast who only exists in fable." Selim rose to his feet. "I am a man of my word."

Meda asked a final question. "Who is Jaffar?"

"My grandfather. He led this caravan for sixty-two years. And raised me in the process, for my father died from a fever that swept through Olom when I was nine." Selim offered a salaam of farewell. "He leads me still and speaks to me of danger and dry wells. And right now he is saying that dawn will come too soon, and we must all sleep."

Hyam climbed the stairs and walked the torch-lit corridor. Behind him the company murmured their weary good nights, but he heard nothing.

That afternoon, alone in the men's bath, Hyam had dozed off. And dreamed of Joelle.

She had reached across the impossible distance and re-opened the crippling wound. If she had screamed or begged or called frantically, he could have remained strong. But she had come to him as only Joelle knew how, in loving antici-pation of love.

Now as he walked the empty corridor, Hyam sensed the eye drawing him forward. What he felt was no mere invita-tion. The eye *summoned* him.

It whispered a dread command to look. And drown in memories of that which was no more.

He stopped in the hall and listened. When he was certain the others were still downstairs, Hyam slipped into Meda's room. He rummaged through her pack and took the box holding the eye.

As soon as Hyam entered his bedchamber, the eye captured every iota of his being. He crossed the room as unsteady as a sleepwalker. His last chance to know the joy of Joelle's unique treasures was hidden inside. And just then, he could not recall the reason why he had forbidden himself from ever looking at the eye again.

He opened the box and peered inside.

31

Shona stood in the center of her room, staring into a mirror larger than the veranda's double doors. Behind her, the bed was illuminated by tall candles in bronze stands. Shona inspected herself with a distant passion. She had known of her beauty since childhood. She realized for most men it served as a powerful lure.

Shona slowly undressed, inspecting herself through the process. She had so much to offer a man. Even enough, she hoped, to draw Hyam back from the ashes of loss.

While she had been in the baths, maids had washed her road-weary garments. Now they lay upon her bed, and alongside them was a silken nightgown. Shona slipped the garment over her head. It drifted down, slow as hands, soft as clouds. She blushed at her audacity, for the gown was almost transparent.

She turned from the mirror, determined now. She was

so intent upon the prize she could almost ignore Meda's warnings.

She crossed the room, opened her door, and stopped to listen. Hyam's door was directly opposite hers. From where she stood, it appeared that it had been left open a crack. Her heart leapt at the thought that he too anticipated her arrival. A few steps, a soft knock, and bliss.

Then she heard it. The softest hint drifted down the empty corridor. A tinkle of women's laughter. She tried to tell herself it had come from some distant chamber, where the inn's few guests lingered. But Shona knew better.

The witches called to her. They welcomed her as one of their own. Using her lures to draw in the unsuspecting, the defenseless.

She fought the realization with a furious vigor. She had never wanted anything so much as this.

But the reality was too strong. Meda's cautions and the witches' laughter worked at her like a vise.

Shona closed her door and sank to the hard tiled floor. She wept, defeated by all the reasons not to cross the hall.

Then she heard Hyam call out in an anguish worse than her own.

32

The eye was just a ceramic bauble, almost crudely formed. But this night it drew in the candle's light and gleamed. Inviting. Greedy.

Hyam leaned in closer. And sank into memories. He managed one fractured thought, that none of these memories were entirely real. But just then the truth did not matter. All he wanted was the chance to be with his beloved again. Even if the act was fashioned from a lie.

Once again Hyam rode the cliffs with Joelle. He did not recall the experience. He *lived* it. Only this time the event was better, refined, *perfect*.

They stopped and watched the sea surge and crash. They shared cold tea from a leather skin, the honeyed draught sweet as nectar. Joelle smiled at him in that special way. They fashioned a bed from the wiry grass lining the cliff top. They added their music to that of the sea and the wind.

Then he felt it, a faintly surging cry from deeper within the eye.

Hyam realized that he was not alone.

Farther down inside the cavernous depths, someone else was there. Caught by the same ruse that now ensnared Hyam.

The shock caused him to draw back. Or at least try to. But he was held in place by hands that before had pretended to belong to Joelle.

Then he felt the teeth. Sharp as tiny razors, gnawing at the edge of his soul. Eating away. Drawing a delighted pleasure from his helpless state. There was no rush to the meal. He was trapped. Lost. The flavor of his life was too sublime to hurry through. The teeth would gnaw at him for centuries before he was fully consumed.

From deep below, the lost soul resigned to the dark cage cried a second warning. This time Hyam cried out in agreement.

Too late. Too late.

33

Shona jerked the silk over her head and flung on her trousers and blouse. Her fingers made a mess of the buttons. She cried in her frustration and flung open her door. Meda raced down the corridor, looking even more disheveled. Shona reached Hyam's door first. She entered and cried a second time at the sight of him sprawled across the floor, one fist clenching an oddly painted ceramic bauble.

She knelt and cradled his head and called his name. "Hyam!"

He moaned.

There was a bitter paradox to her position. Holding his head, stroking his face, while alarm grew all about them. She called his name again, wishing with all her heart they knew a private intimacy instead of fear and woe.

But the bond was strong just the same. Shona knew this

because the next step came to her in a whispered flash. She said to Meda, "The eye!"

"What?"

"The bauble he holds! It consumes him!"

Meda used all her strength to pry back his fingers. She stood and demanded, "What now?"

"Destroy it!" Shona had no idea why she was so certain. Only that she was. She wrapped her arms around Hyam's head and called, "Stay with us!"

Meda searched frantically, but the room's only fire was a bedside candle. She held the eye over the tiny flame.

Hyam shrieked in agony.

Meda yelled, "Fareed!"

The young mage rushed in, gripped the eye with both hands, clenched his eyes shut, and spoke.

The eye burst into flames and exploded.

Hyam yelped, gasped, choked, and cried again, more softly this time.

But their attention was no longer solely upon Hyam. For there beside Fareed, another being appeared.

The figure revealed an Elven king, or so it seemed to Shona. A man with a diadem upon his forehead, similar to the one Darwain had given Hyam. He was rimmed by fires that did not burn. The flames held a greenish tint, as though bound to forest shades. The ruler's eyes were brilliant and alight as they studied the room. He gazed upon them with the satisfaction of centuries, smiling with sorrow and joy both. He raised a hand, a silent benediction. Then he lifted both his arms above his head. The ceiling opened, a swirling vortex of light and welcome. The flames encasing the king grew brighter still, consuming him and drawing him up.

The room grew dim, the image gone, and all that was left were tiny ceramic shards covering the floor.

Hyam opened his eyes, looked up at Shona, and whispered, "You were strong for me."

34

Hyam felt roundly abused when they set off from Olom the hour before dawn. After the crisis, he had managed a few hours' troubled rest. Meda and Fareed had both slept on the floor at the foot of his bed. Shona had stayed there beside him, cradling his head in her arms. Now she rode slightly slumped, her shoulders bowed, her young face creased with exhaustion.

They rode a motley assortment of desert ponies. Hyam's head pounded such that each clop of a hoof was matched by another pulse of pain. His sense of guilt fashioned a pain worse than his head. His weakness had wreaked havoc on his closest remaining friends.

He listened as Meda related the night's experience to Selim. Meda made it sound as though the entire experience centered upon the release of the eye's other prisoner. Twice Hyam started to correct her. Confess the temptation that had snared him. Apologize again.

239

But his admission would only focus their attention on a threat that had passed. Hyam lifted his gaze to the unseen road beyond the reach of their mage-lights. Out where the shadows waited and new dangers lurked. He remained silent.

When Meda finished her telling, Selim said, "I wonder who the prisoner might have been."

This much Hyam retained from his ordeal. "His name was Dyamid. More I cannot say. But the name was the last clear thought I had."

"The name is enough," Selim declared. "I will explain when we have left the city well behind."

Olom still slept, yet they could see testimony of the recent crisis all about them. From the road, the dwellings revealed long, dusty brick walls with guard parapets anchoring each corner. But the doors to many hung like wooden flags of defeat, revealing interiors void of life.

As they arrived at the city's eastern gates, the rising sun offered a rose-tinted glow to their departure. The road passed between two springs feeding streams that ran like sparkling veins through vast fields of green. The cultivated valley was rich and verdant and lined by blooming fruit trees. The pastures held thousands of bleating sheep.

Meda asked, "How many animals can one city need?"

"Not us, but the golems," Selim replied. "They eat more than a dozen each day. Rather, they did. Now it is as you see. The shepherds keep raising flocks in hopes that the golems will return, and for the few who still remain. When our last golems depart, the city perishes."

The green farmlands and bleating sheep stayed with them

for several more miles. Eventually they gave way to empty meadows starved of moisture. The buildings became little more than hovels. Most revealed gaping doors and empty corrals.

Hyam waited until they passed the last gnarled olive grove. Ahead of them now was only the empty yellow desert. Then he asked, "Who was Dyamid?"

"Elven rulers take names that are permitted to no other," Selim replied. "The name is used once and buried with their king or queen."

The sun was climbing overhead, the heat swiftly building. Hyam found the intensity helped clear his head. "I did not know that."

"Nor is there any reason that you should. Dyamid was Ethrin's last ruler. The tales of my clan's early days include stories about him. The year before Ethrin fell to the Milantian hordes, Dyamid's wife and only child perished. Some say it was due to a sudden fever, others to poison. Then two months before the hordes invaded, a wandering mage offered Dyamid an amulet or mirror or some such thing that granted him access to the other world."

The gorge rose in Hyam's throat as he recalled the needle-sharp teeth gnawing at his life. From his other side, Meda said, "He was given the eye."

"No," Shona said, her voice a full octave lower than normal. "The eye was made for him."

"That is my thinking as well," Selim agreed. "For the legend states that Dyamid perished while his body still lived. He became a puppet that breathed. And the last command

Dyamid gave was for his warriors to open the hidden portal and allow the Milantian horde to invade the Elven kingdom."

Hyam heard the rush of voices surround him. But the words no longer mattered. He rode convicted by Selim's tale. It was not the loss of his own life that assaulted him. Rather, how he had almost shared Dyamid's fate. Failing in his responsibilities to all those who had placed their trust in him.

Hyam found it helpful to focus upon the empty realm. Gradually the road became erased by the sweep of yellow dust. Up ahead there was no trail, no hint of what awaited them beyond the veil of shimmering heat. He swallowed the guilt with a determined strength. He would not fail his company or his lover again.

They needed him to be strong. They needed him to live.

35

Midafternoon they crested the tall ridgeline marking the end of Olom's reach. Selim said, "From here to Alyss we eat and drink only what we carry."

They journeyed through the remainder of the day and into the sunset and nothing changed. Their horses were sturdy beasts with a light step and delicate hooves. Selim claimed there was nothing on two legs or four able to match them for speed, even when scaling a desert ridge. And whatever else one might say about camels, they were not climbers. Tethered to each mount were two donkeys, four of which carried only water. The sloshing liquid formed a constant backdrop to their otherwise silent passage.

They halted as the light failed, and Hyam drew an encircling shield as others prepared camp and hobbled the horses. He was so fatigued he stumbled over the spell and twice had to restart. But no one seemed to notice, for they all remained stained by the previous night. They ate a cold meal and drank their fill of tea in silence. The stars formed a silver sea overhead. Nothing moved. Of the bird there was no sign.

That night Hyam slept deeply and did not dream until near sunrise. He knew the time because he was drawn from his body. He hovered there above the camp in the clear pale wash of a new day. Then turned to face a king rimmed by green fire. A silver diadem encircled Dyamid's head, one holding a small gleaming orb.

Hyam spoke the first words that came to mind. "Should I kneel?"

"You are the one who saved me," the king replied.

"I saved no one. I almost joined you."

"I am well aware of the debt I owe your entire group." Dyamid looked down to where Shona still slept. "You will thank them for me?"

"I will." Hyam asked because he had to. "Do you have news of Joelle?"

"Your wife is still among the living. Barely." Dyamid did not actually speak. Rather, his words were planted in Hyam's mind. But they still carried a ruler's dread authority. "The Elven healers are doing all they can to keep her there. Now your attention must turn away from her. You understand?"

"I need to focus upon what lies ahead."

"Correct. Far more than your wife's fate hangs in the balance. Use my own tragic tale as your last warning."

"What awaits us?"

Dyamid nodded approval to the question. "This was why I was permitted to return, that I might serve as messenger.

Heed my words, Emissary. Your only hope of survival lies in accepting what you have spent your entire life fleeing."

The Elven king's warning carried Hyam through much of the next day. He did not share the dream with anyone, not yet. He knew exactly what Dyamid had meant by the words. As Hyam rode through the arid plains east of Olom, he felt as though everything about this journey, the mysteries and the threats and the losses, all had combined to draw him here. To the moment he faced the challenge of his own past.

Gradually the hills took form up ahead. Their craggy peaks and razor edges were no higher than the hills that formed Lystra, yet these ran from horizon to horizon. When it became clear that Selim intended for them to scale the ridge that afternoon, Meda pointed to a well far ahead and asked, "Why not camp here and climb fresh?"

"You are not the first to think this way," Selim replied. "Remember my warning. Eat and drink only what we carry."

In past eons, the well might have been lovely, with a domed canopy supported by sculpted columns. A leather bucket lay by the well's base, linked to new rope. Even so, none felt tempted to top up their supplies. For as they approached they saw the trail between the well and the slopes was littered with bodies. Bones of men and animals had been picked clean. They passed helmets and swords and shields and saddles and ragged remnants of clothing that flapped in the hot wind.

Meda asked Selim, "You have come this way before?"

"Once. To the valley beyond this first ridge and no farther."

"Do you know what awaits us after that?"

"Four ridges in all, or so the legends claim. Then a day's hard trek, then Alyss, then the sea. But none have seen this in eons, and legends have a way of being reshaped by time."

The hills were a brilliant red, the color of blood dried to a brittle finish. An ancient trail snaked up the steep rise, but it was blocked in places by slides. Hyam and the others took a newer course, one formed by the golems. Their massive limbs had pounded a broad path straight up the hill. At Selim's direction they dismounted and led their horses. By the time they arrived at the top they were all breathing hard. Their horses balked at the steep descent, but once they were led over the edge the company had to leap aside, for there was no halting their tumble.

Two of the reins snapped in their madcap descent. All but one of the animals arrived at the hill's base before the company. Even so, none of the animals took a single step forward. Soon as his boots touched the valley floor, Hyam sensed the same doom-laden force as in the dread vale before Emporis's front gates.

A very subdued company replaced the broken reins and retied their mounts and mules. But as they were preparing for the next climb, Hyam declared, "We camp here."

A union of horrified gazes met his. Selim said, "This place is full of death."

"Even so," Hyam said. "We go no farther today."

Selim clearly struggled with the need to argue against the only order Hyam had given since leaving Olom. The caravan master pointed to the next ascent. The hills were slightly lower than the ones they had just crossed, but just as steep. The golems had hammered the same straight-line trail up this slope, aimed directly for the unseen harbor city of Alyss. But this slope was punctuated by dozens of caves, all the same round shape as those the golems had carved into the hills of Olom. "That is where I found the scrolls."

Hyam had suspected as much. "Your family's legacy."

"As I said, the Elves are great ones for keeping the past alive," Selim agreed. "The scrolls' location was part of my clan's most ancient bequest. A dreaded treasure, full of warnings and death."

Hyam added, "Hidden away for a moment when the clan's survival is threatened."

Selim nodded. "I knew I would make this trip the day Olom began to die, because their golems went to Alyss."

"Even when the young warriors who tracked the monsters failed to return to Olom," Hyam said. "You had no choice. It was either search for the hidden treasure or watch your clan perish."

The high sun tightened the slant to Selim's features and revealed a hint of color within his dark gaze, the legacy of forests lost to battle and treachery. "We arrived, and we searched, and we found the stash exactly where the clan's lore said we would."

"Are there more amphorae?"

"Hundreds." Selim waved that aside as unimportant. "When we emerged from the cavern, the ridge was lined by ghostly warriors. They started down toward us, and we fled. They followed us as far as the well. When we looked back, there they stood. Guarding the way." When Hyam did not respond, Selim stepped closer and hissed, "Do you not hear me, Emissary? We are in the realm of the undead. We must flee before they awaken once more."

Hyam shook his head. "You've missed the point."

Selim's mouth opened, but more words did not emerge.

"Think back to when you first arrived in Emporis with the amphorae. You claimed you were chased all the way across the yellow realm."

"I do not *claim*. It *happened*."

"And I accept this as truth. How did you know of your pursuers?"

"I am a caravan master of Olom." But the heat was gone from Selim's reply, replaced now by open curiosity. "I know to read the signs of hunters."

Meda asked, "And the bird?"

"It came to me in the valley near Olom that we call home." Selim kept his gaze upon Hyam as he replied. "It warned of pursuers, and of their desire to find the small scroll."

Hyam said, "So you were tracked across open desert by . . ."

"I sensed a dread force. More than that I cannot say, for I saw no one."

Meda said to Hyam, "You're telling us the enemy is up ahead."

"That is not the issue. We've always assumed Alyss is their lair." Hyam gave them a moment, but when the others stared back in blank confusion, he asked Selim, "Why didn't the enemy stalk you as soon as you took the scrolls?

Why didn't they snare you here and take what they wanted before you escaped?"

Selim's gaze widened. "I . . ."

"Because *the enemy can't see*. These hills and valleys are drenched in magic. There are centuries of mage-force at work here." Hyam pointed at the perfectly round tunnels gaping like scores of shadowed mouths overhead. "The Milantians came and they overran Alyss. Then they crossed the yellow realm and they defeated the Elves at Ethrin. Before that, I think they created the golems. Here. In this vale."

"They're preparing another attack," Shona said. "Against the human realm."

"Of course they are. And that's not the point either."

Meda said, "So the witch who stole Joelle's breath . . ."

"Was a scout," Selim suggested.

Hyam looked from one face to the next and saw they were unable to glimpse beyond the obvious. This, he realized, was why Dyamid had come to him. So that he might lift his gaze and *see*.

"We are stopping," Hyam said, "because this is our last chance to prepare."

Selim waved at the empty ridgeline. "What of the warriors who guard this vale?"

Hyam opened his shirt, gripped the silver chain, and pulled out the crystal pipe. "It is time to call upon allies of our own."

36

Hyam blew the silent note, then waited, but not for long. Tendrils of mist rose from the baked desert and drifted like smoke from unseen fires. Dozens of them. Hundreds. They took form. And became the El-lismere army.

When Selim started to back away, Meda assured him, "These are allies, as Hyam said."

The leader held to a shimmering translucence in their mage-torches. He approached Hyam and drew his sword and offered a spectral salute. Hyam touched his forehead in acknowledgment. He started to point at the next ridge when Shona cried, "I can hear them!"

Hyam sighed with genuine relief. "Tell me."

"H-he says you were right to summon them."

"Tell me why."

"Ahead lies danger from beyond time's reach," Shona related. "Beings from the realm of hopeless night guard the approach to Alyss. He says, 'We will serve as guardians against what you cannot see.'"

"Can he also stop these guardians of Alyss from raising the alarm?"

The ghost responded with a warrior's grim humor. Shona replied, "It will be his pleasure."

When the general turned away, Hyam called after him, "I asked before, can I release you from your bonds?"

"He thanks you for your question and the desire to assist them." The phantom general saluted him a second time. Shona translated, "The Milantian threat that overran them at Ellismere has returned. They are content to serve those who defy the tide of evil. For now, it is enough."

❖

The afternoon grew stifling. The valley where they camped was less than thirty paces wide. The steep hills to either side trapped the heat. The desert silence suited Shona's mood. She watched as Hyam spent hours crouched upon a rock, pondering the unseen. She continued her lessons with Fareed, but in a halfhearted fashion. Every time she shut her eyes, she again saw herself cradling Hyam through that long and broken night. Here in the heat and the dust, knowing she had done the right thing mattered little. And ever since Olom, her dreams had been pierced by the distant laughter of witches.

When the sun's descent lengthened the shadows and turned the caverns into leering skulls, Hyam rose from his stone bench and waved for the others to gather. "Come the next dawn or the one after, we are going on the attack. If our spectral allies can keep word from reaching Alyss, we may be able to use the element of surprise." Hyam turned to Fareed and Shona and said, "Now is the time to test your wands."

Fareed showed a rare delight. "Truly, sahib, I have dreamed of this."

"Did you learn how to recharge the Falmouth orb?"

Fareed nodded. "I have read the scroll."

"Then walk the vales until you find a spot where the miniature orbs begin to glow. We have to hope there is an underground source of power. If not here, then in the valley behind us. Find it. Practice your magery. Concentrate on spells of attack. Especially those using fire. When they become depleted, recharge your wands."

Selim demanded, "And if the valleys do not mask their use of magic?"

"Then all is lost," Hyam replied calmly. "But the fact that the amphorae have remained hidden for so long offers a very strong assurance. Because I sensed the scrolls' power from halfway across Falmouth."

Shona could see the change in Hyam. It was as though he had used the sweltering afternoon to endure his own metamorphosis. Gone was the hollow stare, the mourning, the pain. In its place was a fierce intensity. To her, Hyam had never been more alluring. The man was coming into his own.

Hyam turned to the desert trader. "There is only one explanation for how you could claim there are more amphorae containing the spells. Because we can be fairly certain the Milantians have followed your tracks and searched the tunnel your forebear used to hide them away."

Selim did not respond.

"It's because the scrolls are not there, are they."

Selim remained silent.

"Your clan split the treasure apart and buried it in many tunnels," Hyam went on. "And then covered the openings. Didn't they."

Shona realized, "You're going to use a Milantian battle spell against them."

"The protective shield does not require either an orb or a mage," Hyam said. "Which means the same could be true for a spell of war. I'm going to try. If Selim will take me to another trove."

The renegade Elf was already climbing the next ridge. "Are you coming or not?"

37

As they started up the slope, Selim shared his clan's most secret legacy. His voice took on a gentle sing-song cadence, the words stilted and old-fashioned. He described his forebear's headlong dash for Alyss, crossing the yellow realm in just ten days, only to find the city in ruins and every other member of his household perished. The lone survivor went in search of vengeance but found none, for the Milantian horde had already headed east. Toward Ethrin, the badland clans, and the human realm beyond.

But as Selim's ancestor prepared to track his foes back across the desert, he came upon the Milantians' underground library. And took the revenge he sought. By stealing their entire collection of scrolls.

The library had been too vast to carry far. So he stuffed his new cargo into amphorae designed to transport perfumed oils, sealed them, and hid the scrolls in the red hills. He had filled tunnel after tunnel, then buried the entrances. And so the amphorae remained, lost to time and the race of mages. Their hiding places had been passed down to each new generation of outcast half-breeds. But with the declining fortunes of Olom, Selim's own survival depended upon proving the legacy true. And awakening the Milantians' wrath in the process.

Fareed interrupted Selim's telling with a shout. "Sahib!"

"I see them," Hyam replied. "Go on with your story."

But the caravan master had stopped cold. For up ahead the ridgeline held a host of translucent warriors. When Hyam kept walking, Selim called after him, "What if they are not our allies?"

"Then our every step is futile," Hyam replied impatiently. "Come on!"

When Shona crested the rise, the warrior spoke, and she passed on, "Sire, I mean Hyam, their general says that the ghosts enslaved by your foes have been contained."

"For how long?"

"He says again, they are contained."

"Please thank him for us."

"He understands you."

"Of course." Hyam peered down into the next valley, even narrower than where they were camped. Another two ridgelines separated them from the empty yellow plain. He asked, "Can he place scouts on the route to Alyss and warn us of any approach?"

Shona replied, "He says his watchers are already on duty."

"Excellent." He returned the general's salute. When the spectral force turned back into mist and vanished, Hyam searched the sky in all directions. "What has happened to our bird?"

Selim replied, "Perhaps your quarrel before we entered Lystra offended him."

"So much he would disobey commands from the one he calls his master? I doubt that very much." Hyam waved it aside. "Nothing has changed. Where is the next cache?"

"Follow the trail north by northwest a hundred and seventeen paces, each step the width of a man's shoulders," Selim recited. "At the third turning, continue straight ahead ten paces. Where the slope becomes a cliff without handholds—"

"We must ignore that one," Hyam said. He pointed down and to their left, where the hint of an ancient trail was halted by a pair of rock slides that had refashioned the entire slope. "Where is the one after that?"

"Two dozen paces to the north of the trail's base, search the opposite slope for the hint of an ancient spring," Selim recited.

"I see it!" Meda cried.

"There has been no water in this place for centuries," Shona said.

"Meda is correct," Hyam said, already heading down. "See, there is a lone patch of grass with darker soil. There must still be some moisture below the surface."

But Shona did not join them in the downward rush. For the leader of the unreal force reappeared and bade her remain. His words carried a dread music, like the low moan of wind through a crypt's portal.

The general said, "Another hunts you."

"An enemy?"

"Only if you allow him to become one." He pointed down to where Alembord walked with the others. "Him."

Shona said slowly, "If I *allow.*"

"Correct."

Shona nodded. "Thank you for this warning."

But the general was not done. "Your choice in the night's dark hour is commended."

"You observed me there in Olom?"

"Not I. The forces who command us. And they approve."

The unhealed wound caused her to weep once more. "But I love him."

"In life's harshest moments, the only correct action is often the impossible one. Such as not to give in to the freezing cold and the knifelike wind and the exhaustion from standing watch on watch. You understand?"

"I . . . Yes."

"This is what it means to rule. When you are granted authority over others, you are also handed . . ."

She spoke the word aloud. "Responsibility."

"There is no harmony in this moment. There is no easy path. The clutch of lives you hold will shout a multitude of conflicting needs, and your own heart will be the loudest voice of all. And yet if you search beyond the cries and the pleas, you will find the right choice. Waiting. In the impossible silence lies the only proper course." The soldier with no name saluted her with his ghostly blade. "Highness."

Hyam watched with the others as Selim searched for the hidden cave. Shona joined them as the desert merchant marched and muttered and counted his paces. Her exchange with the general had deeply impacted the young woman. But whatever they had discussed would have to wait. Hyam turned back as Selim counted off the final paces, pointed to the cliff face, and declared, "It is here."

There was nothing to see except more of the blood-red stone. No hint of an opening showed where Selim indicated.

Hyam turned to Meda and said, "See if the Milantian sword pierces stone like it does metal."

Meda stepped across the rubble, drew the milky-white blade, and stabbed the rock. The rapier sliced easily. She carved a wide swath two paces long, then drew it up to head height, across, and down. She sheathed the blade and they all pressed in hard. The wall fell in a clattering cloud of rubble and dust.

Hyam stepped away from the swirling debris and said, "Before I enter, there's something you need to know." He recounted his dream and his contact with the last king of Ethrin.

The normally silent Alembord was the first to speak. "So what does this mean?"

"I carry Milantian blood," Hyam said. "It was suspected by the mages who raised me, but they only told me as I came into my powers." He pointed into the dark cave. "The spell I seek is not the end. It is only the next step."

Meda unstopped her canteen, drank deep, then poured more on her kerchief and washed the grime from her face. "Tell me you have a plan."

"The faintest glimmer of one," Hyam said.

She handed her canteen to Alembord and said, "I for one don't need to know more."

Selim muttered, "Milantian blood."

"You've had your chance to take the emissary's measure," Meda replied. "Hyam will lead us. He will do his best to keep us safe. Our task is to be ready."

Selim struggled with some internal discord, then asked, "Ready for what, exactly?"

The guards captain gave an easy shrug. "To fight. To win."

"The six of us against a Milantian horde?"

Meda's teeth sparkled astonishingly white in her sun-darkened face. "Exactly."

38

The cave was an almost perfect circle, the rocks gnawed into furrows deep as the golems' teeth. Hyam heard someone call for a mage-light. But he did not require it. He heard Selim complain that the tunnel was completely empty and knew the caravan master was mistaken, but did not bother to reply. A hunger guided him forward, into the pitch-black. When the light appeared, it merely clarified what he already knew lay ahead. Onward he continued, deep into the round tunnel. What had been a faint hint of power back at the mouth was as brilliant now as the desert heat. Then he rounded yet another curve and knew he had arrived.

The cave's floor was blanketed with a deep layer of silt. The thick dust served as a nest for the amphorae. Their narrow ends were planted down, the mouths rising up to his ribs. Dozens of the stone eggs. Hyam walked slowly forward, his hands outstretched to either side. He graced the surface of each seal in turn. Until one sparked. A quick flash of mage-flame, invisible to all but him. He stopped and said, "This one."

Selim asked, "How can you be certain?"

There was no way to explain without further troubling this renegade Elf. "Help me break it open."

Meda unsheathed her sword, then held it up so all could see how the milky surface sparked and flickered.

"Careful, now." Hyam pointed to the upper section, where the amphora narrowed like a vase. "Cut here."

The blade sliced smoothly through the ancient clay. Hyam lifted up scroll after scroll, unfurling them far enough to read the first few words. He handed Shona one document after another, checked all the documents in that amphora, then stepped back and surveyed their armloads. "We can go."

Selim demanded, "You're certain you have what you need?"

"Yes. Let me help." He cradled two of the fragile scrolls and felt the energy surge. Here in this moment, in this act, he accepted what he could now see had been his destination since casting his first spell. From battling the king's relative in the oval field, Hyam had been aiming for this point. Where he would forge a bond. Not to any scroll or half-finished spell. To his heritage. The portion of himself he had always denied.

No longer.

They retraced their steps to the tunnel mouth and gathered around him, his meager company, as he unfurled one scroll after another. There were four in all. Hyam allowed them to peer as long as they liked. Shona stood to his left, Fareed on his right.

Shona asked, "Do you see anything?"

"Nothing but the crumbling parchment," Fareed replied.

Meda drank from her waterskin, handed it to Alembord, and said, "There's something that's bothered me." She surveyed the cliffs and their myriad of circular caves. "Why did the Milantians come here at all?"

"I have an idea," Hyam said. He heard himself as from a great distance. Separated from these people who had trusted him with their futures. Isolated by who he was. "I think these hills were once another city."

Shona said, "Like Lystra."

"Exactly. I also think this place is far older than Alyss. The harbor city was built as a human settlement beside a Milantian metropolis."

Selim stared at him. "Humans and Milantians—friends?"

"Perhaps." Hyam hoped desperately this had indeed once been true. He hefted the two scrolls. "Remember what the Lystran queen told us?"

Selim nodded slowly. "There were two strands to the Milantian mages."

"Right. The mages of Lystra lived in peace. I think these hills were originally a place of Milantian learning and power. For eons Alyss served as the human gateway to the Milantian empire. Theirs was a privileged position, and they became incredibly rich as a result." Hyam turned to the unseen east. "But the other Milantians lusted after the ability to unleash death and destruction. Gradually their power grew, and the city we see here waned. Something happened, some event lost to time and Milantian lore. The city died. But by this point, Alyss had grown in strength and stature and for a period served as the human empire's eastern port. Even after their Milantian allies vanished, Alyss continued to thrive."

Meda said, "So the golems . . ."

"The golems are not the issue," Hyam chided, but gently. "The question you need to ask is, why did the dark lords return to Alyss a thousand years ago? Why did the attack on the human empire begin here?"

Fareed breathed, "These scrolls, and the spells they contain."

"It is the only logical answer," Hyam agreed. "The dark lords' power was on the rise. They sought what they did not have—the ability to transform normal Milantians, those with no supernatural abilities, into mage warriors. So ten centuries ago, they attacked and destroyed Alyss."

Selim's nods had become a gentle rocking that took in his entire upper body. "Then they created the golems. And they searched."

"They found the scrolls," Meda said. "And they attacked the realm."

"But we survived," Shona said.

"Barely," Hyam said. He pointed to the tunnel and asked Fareed, "Can you seal it?"

Fareed showed genuine relish as he drew the wand from his belt. He gestured to Shona, who hesitated before joining him.

"The lightning spell." Fareed pointed with his wand to a stone outcrop twenty paces above the tunnel entrance. "You strike the left side, I'll take the right. On three, yes? One, two . . ."

39

When they returned to camp, Selim and Meda prepared a meal. They ate in silence and watched as Hyam stretched the scrolls out and crawled along their length, reading silently. Hyam finally ate because Shona walked over and ordered him. At first he did not respond, but Shona stood where she blocked his path. He looked up and did not seem to recognize her. There was a chilling edge to his gaze. Then he blinked and smiled, and the frigid fear she had known was gone.

All afternoon Shona and Fareed practiced with the wands. Fareed had trained with the Falmouth orb, and now he walked her carefully through the stages of binding to the wand and extending out. There was a unique thrill to each act, drawing the power, connecting with the wand, shooting fire at hillsides that were soon scored with their strikes, then recharging the miniature orbs and starting over. The desert-born lad was a natural teacher and was as delighted as Shona when her spells succeeded.

Hyam kept himself isolated farther down the valley, practicing his spell casting. He weaved his arms in complex patterns and droned in a voice too low for her to catch. Time after time he halted in what seemed to be mid-flow, stepping back from whatever forces he had almost unleashed. Standing and breathing and thinking for a time. Then starting over.

They kept at it until the only light in their valley was the mage-fire. They stopped and drank more tea and spoke a few idle words. Twice Meda asked what the plan was, but Hyam merely shook his head and replied, "Not yet." When they unfurled their pallets, he bade them a good night and climbed the eastern ridge. Up to where he could gaze out over the yellow plain.

Shona sat upon her pallet and stared at Hyam's silhouette against the wash of desert stars. Meda said sleepily, "Just like a general." She then rolled over and sighed into slumber.

A movement at the camp's perimeter caused Shona to glance over. Tired as she was, she knew one further task needed seeing to that night. She walked to where Alembord sat on a stone shaped like a narrow bench. The mage-light cast his features in stark vigor. He watched her approach with unblinking intensity. Up close Shona thought she glimpsed a furtive hint of animosity, the sour hostility of unrequited desire. She was glad she had not put this off.

She asked, "Can we talk?"

Alembord responded by shifting over and making room for her. Shona seated herself and said, "None of us knows what is going to happen tomorrow. But I would like to think that Hyam is preparing a way for us to survive."

"Shona . . ."

"Please, Alembord. This is hard for me. Allow me to finish. Please."

She could feel the heat in his gaze, the longing. She went on, "If we survive, what comes next? That is a question I have carried with me since Lystra." She pretended to think for a moment, then asked, "Do you remember the witches' song that night? How they drew you away from yourself?"

Alembord wanted to deny it. She could see the flickering gaze, the desire to focus upon her and the promises he wanted to offer. But in the end he said, "I remember."

"So do I. I was trapped inside a pillar, just like Meda and Fareed. But unlike them, I remember everything. I saw you struggle against the witches' lure. And I saw you give in." She held up a hand, halting his protest. "It was on our return to the caravan that this idea of mine began taking shape. What I want to speak with you about. Because you have seen the power of magic up close. You know as only one can who has stared into the cauldron and survived."

"I . . . don't understand."

"I am not explaining myself well. Forgive me. This is the first time I have tried to put this into words." She pretended to wipe away confusion from her forehead. "Alembord, if I survive, I am to become Bayard's heir. Before, this was a childish notion. Now I see it as reality. And I know that moving forward, if I am to succeed, I need allies."

"I want to be that and—"

"Wait—before you speak, please, hear me out. It is vital you understand fully what this means." Her words carried enough force to halt his entreaty. "The instant I accept that position, I will be consigned to death. Think on this, Alembord, I beg you. I break a thousand years of law by accepting this position. I will become the countess mage."

For the first time that night, Alembord pried apart his raging desire. And saw her. Fully.

"This role is *strictly forbidden*. What I am to become *cannot be*. And yet we know that these laws are already cast aside. The darkness is not just ahead of us in Alyss. It is *everywhere*. If the realm is to survive, we must accept this as fact. And we must prepare."

Alembord licked dry lips. "You want me . . ."

"I want you to become the leader of my private guards. This warrior troop must accept me for who I truly am. They must guard me against those who would seek my destruction." She could see the rank bitterness cloud his vision once again. And knew she had to stop it before the fury was able to take hold.

Shona did what was required. She formed a shield. "My first challenge as an acolyte, put to me by Fareed and Connell, was to create a shield and pick up a candle's flame. Then I was required to apply the force in a controlled manner. Do you hear what I am saying, Alembord? Control is everything."

His features were taut with an ire so bitter it seemed he could scarcely hear her, much less fashion a response. Shona rose to her feet so she could tower over the warrior and repeated, "Control, Alembord. Control is *everything*." As she spoke, she turned and reached out one hand, the fingers that had first known the power.

Shona drew a slender thread of golden flame from the campfire. She wove it about her, binding the force to her shield. The heat built, and with it the illumination, until Shona was rimmed by fire.

Still she strengthened it, adding to it her own frustration, her own desires, her own rage, building and tightening until the light she cast was so fierce Alembord was forced to cover his face. And then the skin of his hand began to blister, and he cried aloud as he stumbled from the rock and fell into the sand. His ire was lost now to the shock of what he beheld.

And still she drew upon the flame and her own internal cauldron. "Observe and remember, Alembord. I want you to see fully. I need you to *understand*. I need an ally who has glimpsed inside the deadly force, seen the true peril of magic in the hands of the despised. How our foes can wreak havoc with a song. Because there is a difference here, one that many soldiers would prefer to ignore. They will see my power, and they will fear me, and they will want to count me as an enemy. I need you to be my spokesman. Do you understand what I am asking?"

Alembord had no choice but to crawl crab-like backwards, scrambling away on three limbs while his blistered hand continued to guard his eyes. She tracked him, but slowly. Bathing him in a heat that would have killed the man had he not moved away.

"Only an officer who has faced the *true* enemy can serve

as my ally here. Only one who knows the real difference. Who can look at me and see me as a protector of our realm."

Shona stopped. She cast aside the shield and the force both. And stood there before him. Cloaked in the night. "I ask that you think on this, Alembord. I understand if you are unwilling to accept the challenge. But I ask that you at least consider being my champion."

She turned and walked back over to her pallet. Only when she lay down and drew her covers up to her chin did she realize Meda was watching her.

The guards captain murmured softly, "Truly, you have the makings of a queen."

40

Hyam climbed away from the camp, drawn by the same wisps of an idea that had flittered about his brain for much of the past two days. Trying to knit them together had proven enormously taxing. His strategy relied on so many assumptions. The unknown swarmed like a dark cloud, consuming every idea as soon as it was forged. So he left the company and climbed toward the stars. Determined to put his fears and his doubts behind him.

A flash of some brilliant light rose from the valley floor below. Hyam assumed Shona or Fareed still practiced and did not look back down. He reached the summit and focused upon the eastern plains. The dark desert floor was flecked in places by the moon's pewter reflections. One worry after another rose before his gaze. He examined each, worked out a solution, set it aside, and barred it from reentry. Moving on to the next one. And the one after that.

There were three key issues.

The first was, what form would the Milantians' assault take? Hyam had one chance. Just one. To see around the bend of time, anticipate, and prepare.

The second, how could he turn their meager numbers into a shock wave of such force to clear a route to the dragon and the sea? Because this was not about winning or defeating every Milantian foe. This was about survival. And rescuing Joelle. And readying for the battle beyond this one.

The third issue was the most troublesome of all.

Where was the bird? Hyam had dismissed this issue when Selim had raised it because there was nothing he could do or say to change things. But this night was made for examining such doubts. What did the eagle's absence signify? Even if they made it to the port, would the dragon know to come for them?

Finally fatigue fashioned weights to his thoughts. Hyam lay on the ground and slept. The ridge was covered by centuries of loam and dust. He was comfortable enough. He dreamed of Joelle, her gentle gaze, and the way she spoke his name.

Hyam woke to the full light of day. He sat for a long moment, pushing aside his hunger and thirst. He examined the decisions he had made the previous night, one by one. Then he pulled the crystal pipe from beneath his shirt, blew, and waited. He would not understand what the ghostly warrior would say. But hopefully that would not matter.

When the general appeared, Hyam explained what he had in mind. As he made his request to the translucent ally, his plans finally crystallized. That in itself made this contact a success.

When he was done, the general stood and studied him. Hyam waited through long minutes, feeling the sweat gather and trickle. Finally the warrior nodded, once. And allowed the smoke of his form to drift away.

Hyam did not realize he had been holding his breath until he was alone again. He turned and stared eastward, trying to pierce the shimmering heat and study the unseen foe.

Then he started down into the valley. Where his companions waited.

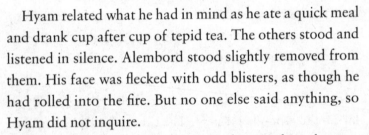

Hyam related what he had in mind as he ate a quick meal and drank cup after cup of tepid tea. The others stood and listened in silence. Alembord stood slightly removed from them. His face was flecked with odd blisters, as though he had rolled into the fire. But no one else said anything, so Hyam did not inquire.

When he was finished speaking, Meda started to ask something, then focused beyond him and said, "We have company."

The general had elected to walk toward them down the valley's length. As though he wanted them to come to terms with what they saw. Which was a good thing, Hyam decided. Because the ghostly officer brought a horde with him.

He was joined by seven other leaders. Five were men, two women. Six wore crowns. The former rulers were flanked by soldiers from a multitude of armies and epochs. Hyam walked toward them, motioning for Shona to join him. To the young woman's credit, she did not hesitate, not even when three of the men drew translucent swords. Instantly a trio of skirmishes formed opaque confusion to either side. Hyam knew the forces gathered here represented a thousand years and more of enmity.

Hyam lifted his empty hands and shouted, "Fighting old battles between yourselves will gain you nothing!"

Perhaps it was the fact that he spoke the words in Milantian that halted most of them. He yelled the same words in Elven, then in the human tongue. By the time the echo of his voice faded, the threat of conflict had subsided. All watched him.

Hyam pitched his voice to carry and spoke each sentence in all three tongues. "I am Milantian. I am also human. My wife is half Ashanta. We represent a future that the foes in Alyss want to deny us. Not just of peace. But of joining."

The forces had multiplied to where the narrow vale could no longer hold their numbers. The ghosts of past wars stretched back as far as he could see. Their numbers climbed the ridges and lined the high reaches to either side. All stood and listened. Waiting.

"The forces gathered against us are not just our enemy. They are yours. They have bound you for so long you have forgotten there was ever an alternative to your prison. But heed my words. *I am Milantian.* If it is in their power to bind you, it must be in mine to free you. I do not know how. But I pledge to you this. Fight with us, and I will spend the rest of my life searching for the key to your release."

He waited with them now. One breath, another. Relishing the simple act of doing what they could not. Feeling his heart thunder. Tasting the fresh salt of sweat from a new day. One where he would fight. And win. Perhaps. With their help.

He repeated a third time, "I am Milantian. If you are required to follow orders from this race, then will you do so now? With us? I do not command. I ask. Will you pledge loyalty to our cause, and in return accept my pledge of seeking your release?"

This time he let the silence linger. Willing to stand all day if necessary. But the sun had scarcely moved a handbreadth before Shona said, "Sire, they are yours to command."

41

They ate a final hot meal and once more drank their fill of tea. Then they hobbled the horses by the narrow patch of green and used a stone with a hollow like a natural trench as a watering trough. They piled oats on another stone, then set off.

They crossed the final ridges and entered the yellow plains. Hyam listened to their rasping breaths and knew their deaths probably awaited them beyond the shimmering horizon. Unless he was right in his planning. Unless he could look beyond his doubts and fears. Unless . . .

They stopped at a series of regular shapes rising from the sands. Selim reckoned they had arrived at the first caravansary, and suggested they make camp. He explained how a city the size of Alyss would have several journeymen camps, and the farthest removed would be for the corralling and butchering of livestock.

The sun was a molten orb on the western horizon. They did

not risk fire or mage-heat, which meant they ate a cold meal washed down with water. The unseen city held them now. As Hyam reviewed their plans for the next day, he felt the vast emptiness swallow his words as soon as they were formed.

He was about to suggest they turn in early when Meda said softly, "Ho, the bird."

A faint speck appeared in the northern sky, drifted down, and became a bird with wings broader than a man's reach. The desert eagle held a bundle in its claws, which it dropped at Hyam's feet before landing.

Hyam ignored the bundle, stomped over, and demanded, "Where have you been?"

The bird chattered swiftly, "Your foes watch the skies. The master bade me hide."

"He promised you would guide us!"

"And that is why I have come."

Hyam planted fists on hips, ready to condemn, but in the end thought better of quarreling with a bird whose help was desperately needed. He translated for the others, who now clustered about him. His relief was so great he had to concede, "It is very good to see you."

The bird preened, clearly pleased. "The master says the enemy suspects you are coming. They do not see you, but they sense your arrival. Which is bad. But they also fear you. Which is very good indeed."

Hyam nodded. It was to be expected, but still the news left him quaking. "Can the dragon see them?"

"My master senses what he cannot see."

"Can we go around Alyss?"

"The surrounding coast is under their control. The seas as well. To meet my master, you must journey from the city harbor. It is the one point of contact ever permitted between your race and his."

Which meant they had to meet the foe. If only Hyam could make it on his terms. "Understood."

"The master asks, do you intend to confront the evil head-on?"

"I see no alternative."

"The master agrees." The bird pointed with its beak at the bundle. "He says this should help you make the required transition."

Hyam glanced down at the bundle. The cloth covering was the color of fresh blood. He realized what he saw and halted his objection before it was uttered. There was nothing to be gained from arguing with the messenger. He said to the bird, "For our plan to work, we need two hills. Set well apart from each other. And from which we can observe each other as well as the enemy's approach."

The bird flapped its wings once, twice, rising up three times Hyam's height. Then it settled, facing east. Its head cocked back and forth. Then, "A mound marks what were the northern corrals."

"How far?"

"On foot . . ." The bird partly extended its wings, almost a shrug. "Just beyond the horizon."

Call it two hours' walk. "And the second?"

"Straight ahead are the remnants of the main gates. To the south rises the last tower of Alyss."

"Excellent."

The bird leapt skyward. "Farewell, Emissary. My master bids you success and awaits you beyond the harbor!"

❖

They rested through the first part of the night, though Hyam did not sleep. There was no moon, and the absence of a fire left Hyam feeling as though the night and the desert fought over who would swallow them.

In the dark hour before daybreak they rose in silence, ate a few bites, drank more water, then stood awkwardly. Hyam was searching for a way to thank them properly when the normally silent Alembord said, "My lady, I have a request to make."

Shona replied, "There is no need to address me in this manner."

"My lady," he repeated. "I would ask that you allow me to offer fealty."

Shona was so shocked, Alembord had already knelt in the dust before she managed, "I hold no title."

"Yet," Meda said softly. "But you will. Soon."

"My lady, I ask to be the first to pledge you his loyalty and his life," Alembord said. He stumbled a bit but struggled gamely on, and neither the night nor their paltry numbers could halt the flow. "I ask the privilege of serving whatever cause you declare your own. With all that I am and all that I have, to the utmost of my abilities, to the giving of my life's last breath if it is required of me. So do I pledge."

278

Meda stepped forward, unsheathed the Milantian sword, and turned it so that she held it balanced upon her forearm, the hilt facing toward Shona. "Do you accept his gift?"

"I . . . Yes."

"Then tap him on both shoulders, and thank him, and speak his name, and invite him to rise."

As Shona did so, the memory of having done the same for Joelle caused Hyam's eyes to burn.

But the pre-dawn hour held more surprises still, for when Shona tried to return the sword, Meda said, "I want you to keep it."

"But . . . Hyam . . ."

"The blade is neither Hyam's nor mine. It belongs to Joelle. And I saw the havoc she wreaked during the Emporis battle. You heard of this."

"Many times," Shona said quietly. "But I don't know how to use it."

Hyam replied, "Neither did she." He nodded to Meda. "It is a good idea. I wish I had thought of it."

Meda offered what Hyam suspected would be the day's only smile. "Good thing you have me here, then."

"It is indeed," Hyam agreed. To Shona, he went on, "Whatever spell you build with the orb, direct it through the sword. That's my advice."

They stood there a moment, united by bonds strong enough to defy the city's oppressive force. Finally Selim said, "Dawn comes."

Hyam embraced them one by one. Then he stepped back and said, "Until we meet at the harbor."

Selim carried his bow and a full quiver as they crossed the darkened plain. "What do your warriors speak of on their way to battle?"

"I have no idea. My only experience with war was Emporis. And the day before that fight, I wed Joelle." Hyam stared into the vague wash of an unborn day. "That morning we spoke of love."

They trudged on for a time, then Selim asked, "You have seen the great forest?"

"I was raised on its borders."

"Some other time, you must tell me of this place."

"With pleasure." The renegade Elf remained a silhouette against the night's final stars. Hyam said, "You're a professional traveler. Why have you never gone?"

"I went to Ethrin once. Nowadays it is nothing but a sweep of desert pines. I breathed the taint of ancient wounds. The lure was still strong for me, and I feared . . ."

"You were concerned you might enter the forest and never leave, and thus lose what you now have," Hyam said. "The desert and the caravan and the life you've built for yourself."

"And my beloved family," Selim added. "My grandfather filled our hidden valley with a grove of eucalyptus and cottonwood and fruit trees. I brought back seedlings from Ethrin. When I am home, I go out at the full moon and sing to them the Elven welcome. I taught my daughters the melody. I have named my valley Ethrin. It is enough."

"I would love to see your valley and walk among those trees."

"And so you shall," Selim vowed. "Soon."

The tower rose from the gloom, a sullen thumb carved into the pale wash. They hustled, then trotted, then raced the gathering dawn. They puffed hard as they scaled the outer wall, the surface so pitted it was almost like climbing a broken staircase.

When they arrived at the top, they scanned the ruined city. There was little left of Alyss save the faint shadows of straight lines and square foundations, the symbols of man's grandeur, now lost to time and sand. Still, it made for an awesome vista, for the ruins stretched out in unbroken silence, so vast they could see no hint of the sea beyond.

When Selim had caught his breath, he said, "I spy no enemy."

"I think Milantians live underground," Hyam replied. "Lystra was not a city that the passing eons turned into hills. The Milantians chose hills as a base and built into them. Same with the red ridges we passed. Perhaps the golems were first created in some distant epoch, intended to carve homes in mountains that are no more."

"So you think they are here."

"I am certain of it. Our job is to draw them out." Hyam inspected the renegade Elf. "Does your clan hold to any tales about Alyss from before the fall?"

"Our family's legacy describes this city as a haven for many races, a carnival for the senses, where even a half-wit could build a fortune and establish both a name and a reason for his days. That was how my forefather referred to himself. A half-wit who fell in love with an innkeeper's daughter."

"And became a man of wealth with a reason for his days." Hyam knelt on the tower's dusty stones and unwrapped the bundle brought to him by the desert bird. "Who could ask for more?"

Selim studied him for a time, then said, "My wife told me I must make this journey. The night of my return from Emporis, she said I had changed, and for the better. I told her of you and of the quest. I then tried to speak of Lystra but could not."

"The dragon told the queen he would seal our lips," Hyam recalled.

"I told my wife of our destination. I wanted her to know the risks. Do you know what she said?"

Hyam held a crimson robe out at arm's length for them both to inspect. "I have no idea."

"She said something had been awakened in me. Something she had loved from our first meeting but never seen fully revealed until now. She said I must see this quest through to the end, then come home to her with my heart intact. At long last." Selim watched Hyam slip the robe over his head. "Why do you suppose the dragon wants you to wear the cloak of a Milantian mage?"

"To confuse our enemy," Hyam replied. "And to confirm my heritage."

"Let us hope it works." Selim pointed to the hill becoming ever clearer in the gathering light. "They signal us. It is time to begin."

42

As they watched Hyam and Selim depart, Meda said, "Remember our aims."

"Diversion, patience, surprise," Alembord replied, his voice hard as the desert light.

"And the vial," Meda added. "We have given Hyam our word. Whoever survives must help the ghost army search the Milantian realm, find Joelle's breath, and deliver the container to the Elves."

"It will be done," Fareed replied solemnly. "Our oath upon it."

Shona walked with the others across a dusty plain toward a hill they could not see. Guided by a bird who was nowhere to be found. The Milantian sword was strapped to her back and bounced uncomfortably as she marched. The sword-belt was bound beneath her ribs and the buckle gnawed at her middle. The wand hung from a loop in the cloth belt holding up her trousers and patted her thigh with each step. She could feel a new blister growing under her sandal strap. Her legs ached and her skin was caked with grit and dried sweat. There was every chance she would not survive the coming day.

She had never been happier.

Alembord observed, "Shona's sword is not riding properly."

"So I see." Meda adjusted the scabbard. "How is that?"

"Much better, thank you."

They walked for a time, until the hill appeared as a vague lump directly ahead. They paused to drink, passing the skin from hand to hand. The land remained as empty as the sky. The hill was a lone mound, a hundred paces high, and not steep. But the surface was ankle-deep sand, fine as milled flour. They scaled the slope on all fours. When they crested the hill, the light had strengthened to where they could see the city clearly. There was little left except vague hints of past triumphs and wealth. There was no sound save the soft rasp of their own breathing. But the dawn light had competition now, for both Shona's and Fareed's wands had started glowing.

Meda watched as Fareed held his wand aloft. "What does this mean?"

"There must be a current of power running through the earth below us," Shona said.

Fareed said, "The legends claim mages lived in all the ancient cities. Practicing magic in the open."

Meda gestured to the long straight-line indentation that ran horizon to horizon, between them and the ruins. "Why not build the city wall to include such a place of power?"

"Perhaps all the city has such veins of force," Fareed suggested.

"Or they kept magic outside the walls," Shona said.

Meda clearly disliked starting their attack in the face of such mysteries. But all she said was, "Signal Hyam that we are in position."

❖

Hyam thought the light shining upon the distant hilltop held an uncommon brilliance. He stood for a moment and relished the silver-violet illumination. Its aura took him back to the last time he had held his orb. The morning of the Emporis attack, he had given it to Trace, who had wielded it until Hyam had extended his power across the desert valley and shot the orb like a crystal bomb at the red mage. And like a bomb it had exploded, turning both orbs and their crimson foe into dust. But Hyam's usage of mage-force without his own orb as a conduit had burned him so badly he had lost his abilities. Victory for the realm, defeat for him.

Hyam refocused on the battle at hand. Selim's bow was triple curved and not large by hunting standards. What was more, the two ends of Selim's bow slanted away from the archer, while the middle was so thick it looked deformed. A handhold was carved into this broad center. Time and sweat had oiled the wood and turned it slick as a black mirror.

Hyam watched Selim string it and said, "I have never seen such a bow."

"It is a desert weapon, made for shooting from the back of a galloping animal. The tips are enameled antler horn. The wood I carved from the heartwood of a felled tree within the Ethrin grove."

Hyam flicked the string and listened to the hum of a death harp. "It was made for this very day."

"So I am thinking also." Selim selected an arrow. "Make your spell."

Hyam turned to the ruined city. He touched the center of his forehead and shouted in Elven, "Reveal!"

Instantly his own earthbound star defied the morning, the desert, and the unseen foe.

In some respects, Hyam was more frightened than when he had entered the Emporis battle. Then he had been guided through Elven tunnels, while an army of allies had surrounded him on all sides. But this morning his meager company had been guided into position by a bird that had now vanished. Even so, Hyam's fear could not touch some deeper part of him. Down at the level of bone and sinew and spell casting, Hyam was gripped by an uncommon calm, a stillness strong as the grave.

As he began weaving his spell, Hyam wondered if this was what it meant to embrace his Milantian blood. Perhaps fear, that most human of emotions, did not touch them.

Hyam finished the spell. He then drew his dagger and touched the arrow fit into Selim's bow. "Now we will see."

Selim hesitated. "I sense no power at work."

Neither did Hyam. He had the momentary sense of leading his company off the edge of a cliff. Onto the rocks far below. Lost to the shadows of a morning they would never witness. But it was too late now. They were committed.

"Loose your arrow!"

"All right, that's enough." Meda gestured for Fareed to extinguish his wand.

The absence of Fareed's light left Shona feeling both isolated and vulnerable. The ruined city stretched out before her, silent and deadly. Suddenly she felt as though every spell she had studied was lost to her, brief wisps of a life that she would not have a chance to claim.

Meda squinted at the tower and asked, "What's holding them up?"

Fareed said, "Patience, mistress."

Shona could not fully hold back her terror. "Show me the spell to recharge the wand."

"You did it in the valley," Fareed pointed out. "Several times."

"Remind me again."

Fareed was clearly reluctant to look away from the silent tower, but he lifted his wand and said, "Pay attention."

She repeated the words, as much from memory as his instruction, and felt her own confidence return as the wands became traced by lingering ribbons of power.

Then Alembord pointed to the north and cried, "There!"

Hyam watched the arrow fly from Selim's bow and create a thin river of fire across the dawn. The scrolls he had found in the cave had contained segments of several spells. Hyam had built his plan upon the hope that he might rework them into one. Join them all, and in so doing compound their force.

It all came down to this. Doing the unexpected. Surprising the enemy right out of their safe little holes.

But as Hyam watched the arrow fly through its golden arc, all his logic and plans and hopes seemed paltry indeed. The light seemed a trivial force, blazing merrily against the backdrop of another hostile day.

"Is that it?" Selim demanded.

❖

All four pairs of eyes atop the hill squinted against the sunrise and watched the fire arrow rise.

Alembord muttered, "Did his spell fail?"

Shona felt her own heart sink in agreement. The arrow's trailing flames were a trifling, of no importance whatsoever.

Beside her, Fareed said, "Patience."

Meda asked, "You know what Hyam is doing?"

"No, mistress. But I am coming to know the sahib."

And at that moment, the dawn erupted.

❖

The remaining spell came much easier, which was good, because Hyam had little time to cast it. Just the space between the arrow's fiery zenith and striking the earth. Call it three heartbeats. Hyam shouted the words in a fluid rush, weaving his hands so fast that the magic's lingering trace formed a ribbon, then a knot, in the air before his face.

His hopes proved correct in a quite spectacular fashion.

To Shona's mind, it seemed as though the arrow suddenly became a fist. One fashioned from flame and fury, and a force great enough to dim the desert sun.

WHUMP!

The fist slammed into the earth.

The earth shuddered such that Shona might have toppled from the summit had Alembord not gripped her arm.

The impact threw up a dust cloud that caught fire. A circular wave of flame swept over the entire city of Alyss. The blaze lapped against the tower and hill both. Shona felt the heat scald her face and hands. Then it vanished.

The silence that followed was as deafening as the blast.

Meda spoke in a conversational tone. "Well, I never."

Fareed laughed out loud and pointed north. "The sahib, he is just warming up."

From the ruined tower came a faint cry, but Shona could not make out the words. "What is he saying?"

"I expect," Fareed replied, "the sahib is introducing himself."

"My name is Hyam," he shouted. "I am human. I am Milantian. I serve as emissary to the Ashanta. I am crowned by the last Elven king. You have stolen something precious from me. I want it back."

He turned to the grinning Selim. "Loose another arrow."

"With pleasure." Selim lifted his bow and aimed to the right of his first shot.

Hyam cast his series of partial spells, the words coming now with swift ease.

WHUMP!

He waited until the tidal force had broken against the tower's base. Into the silence he shouted, "Return to me the vial holding my mate's life-breath. Grant my company safe passage to and from the harbor. Vow never to set foot in any human or Elven or Ashanta settlement. And I will let you beg me for your lives."

WHUMP!

"Respond or perish!"

WHUMP!

Selim loosed another arrow when the first enemy appeared. The arrow became a fiery fist that pounded the earth a hundred paces from an opening where warriors climbed forth. Hyam cast the spell and sent out a further circular flame. When the wave subsided, it appeared to him that the impact had not affected the warriors. He could see where several more openings had appeared, where before there had been nothing except yellow dust and ruins.

"Here they come!" Selim notched another arrow.

"Hold," Hyam said, waving the caravan master to lower his weapon. "We may need those."

"What are we to do?"

Hyam was wondering the same thing. For the dozens of warriors had become hundreds, and still more climbed out and formed into ranks and marched with weapons drawn. All of them headed straight for their tower. Hyam doubted they were actually Milantians. If so many real foes existed, then all was lost. For him, his company, and the entire realm.

"Hyam?"

"I'm thinking."

As if in response, the two mages atop the distant hill struck.

43

Shona watched as the warrior horde rose from the parched earth. They were all dressed exactly the same, in white robes with a crimson belt and tall boots of polished red leather. They carried a round shield in one hand and curved scimitars in the other. They marched in silent unison. Every step struck the earth precisely in time with the soldiers to either side. Thousands of warriors advancing in deadly synch.

Meda declared softly, "They are not human."

Shona glanced over. Meda's face had tightened into hard angles and fierce determination. She studied their foes with an unblinking gaze. Shona found an odd sense of comfort, two women and two men against thousands, but knowing she was in the company of such a fighter.

Meda sniffed as though searching for a scent upon the heat-drenched breeze. "My guess is these are golems in human form."

"Look at their precision," Alembord said. "They march like machines."

"How do we . . ." Shona's question went unformed, because a cry rose upon the wind, this one coming from somewhere deep inside the city.

A charge ran over the horde, a flickering wave of force that blocked the army from view. When the marchers reappeared, the horde had grown. Not in number, but in size.

Another cry, and another flickering shroud passed over the soldiers. It came and went in two frantic breaths.

The horde had grown larger still.

Shona now watched an army of giants on the move.

They roared with one voice, a single unified blast that caused Shona's chest to quaver.

Fareed stepped up close, where Shona was forced to look at him. Gone was the young acolyte eager to help train her. Gone too the former desert waif who had helped her adapt to the yellow realm. In their place was a young wizard whose mage-force was etched into his features. "We must strike."

"But so many, how . . ."

He lifted his wand so that its gleaming tip was directly before her eyes. "The sahib needs us. Remember the fire-blade spell?"

Shona drew her own wand. "I . . . Yes."

"You strike right, I shall go left. Avoid the tower! Ready? One, two . . ."

As she chanted the words, Shona felt a change. Power surged through her as though her entire body was merging into the wand. The force rose through her feet and up, up, passing through her frantically beating heart, along her arm, through the wand, and . . .

She did not speak the final word. She screamed it.

The flames shot out in blinding ferocity, thousands of sickle-shaped blades that spun outward. They sliced through the army. The giants blasted apart into dust the color of dried blood. Their remnants spun in the soft wind, then vanished.

"Golems," Meda repeated.

Alembord lifted his blade over his head and shouted a war cry all his very own.

The sound seemed to galvanize the giants. The entire horde wheeled about, taking aim directly at them.

They shot out another spell. Fareed screamed with her. They cut down dozens of the giants. Hundreds. But still more of the blank-faced warriors poured from the holes in the earth and were caught up in another of the magical veils, became giants, and filled the ranks. In half a dozen breaths, Shona could not even see where their force had struck.

Steel snickered as Meda drew her sword. She stepped midway down the hillside, took a two-handed grip upon the hilt, and crouched. Ready. "Alembord! By me!"

Then Shona remembered the sword.

The giants seemed to take the two warriors as a challenge, for they spurred to greater speed. Shona drew the Milantian blade from its shoulder holster, reached out, and cast the spell a third time.

When she reached the final phrase, she touched her wand to the milky blade.

The effect was blinding. Shona had to wait through several

breaths to even see what had happened. When her vision finally cleared, she saw that a broad channel had been cut through the golem force, fifty paces wide and stretching all the way back to the city's distant border.

The army faltered, a single moment of hesitation. But it was enough for Fareed and Meda and Alembord all to shout their exultation to the midday sun.

In response, the giants regrouped, tightened their ranks, gave a unified bellow, and surged forward. The hilltop trembled at their stomping progress. They even ran in unison.

Shona started to cast another spell, only to realize the orb at her wand's point had gone dark.

"Here, here, take mine!" Fareed snatched away her wand, gave Shona his, and began casting the recharging spell.

Shona turned back to the army, lifted her arms, and fired off another round.

Hyam and Selim stared in astonished delight as the spell-waves tore through the giants. Each strike resulted in spumes of dust that filtered up and vanished. Hyam assumed Fareed recharged a wand while Shona applied the other to the Milantian sword. It was a brilliant idea, one he should have thought of himself. Part of him fretted over what else he might have neglected. But mostly he knew a biting satisfaction. Things were holding to his strategy. Hyam was afraid to name what he felt as hope. But he hoped just the same.

His plan, his company's survival, relied on him having solved one key mystery.

The Milantians were few in number.

There was no other reason Hyam could find for why a lone enemy would have attacked his home. Or why the next assault came from a golem guarding a deserted valley. Or why a single witch hunted Selim all the way to Emporis, then lingered in solitude and attacked the Ashanta banker's residence, then stole Joelle's breath.

The answer he had hoped for was now clear as the desert light. The Milantians sought to weaken Hyam because they themselves were weak.

The master's pet, the Emporis witch had said to Shona. *The master commands*. Which led Hyam to the most crucial element of his mystery. Where was the one they called their master, this senior Milantian mage?

The only answer that Hyam could see, the only solution that worked, was this:

Not here.

Hyam watched the giants' dust settle and the silence grip Alyss once more. The only sign the giants had ever existed were the holes that dotted the ruins.

Selim asked, "Is it over?"

Hyam remained too caught up in his internal dialogue to respond. These meager remnants of the great Milantian army had returned here. Once again they gathered the golems. Hidden behind battalions of enslaved ghosts, they built a new force of giants. They had hoped for enough time to uncover the missing scrolls and rise up to their full power.

But Selim had come and disturbed their secret strategy.

As a result, the Milantians chased him, both for the scroll

to create the miniature orbs and to keep their secret from reaching human ears.

Up to then, no citizen of Olom had tracked the golems to Alyss. No word of the Milantians' return had reached the realm. Until Selim arrived in Emporis. Then the enemy had been forced to reveal itself. Hyam stood by the tower's ruined outer wall and realized this was why they had come after him in Falmouth. The unseen master had assumed Hyam would be alerted. The enemy had sought to destroy him before he realized the foe had returned.

But their attacks had failed. And now Hyam stood at the border of their hidden lair. With powers they assumed were theirs and theirs alone.

Selim handed him a full waterskin. Hyam drank greedily. As he handed back the skin, the earth gave a cautious shudder, as though the entire city vibrated.

Selim exclaimed, "What is happening?"

The thunder accelerated, and Hyam knew it could only mean one thing. He replied, "Monsters."

44

The golems scrambled from the same holes that had released the giants. Their trunk-like limbs had difficulty finding purchase on the crumbling ledges. Their bellowed frustration shook the tower.

A beast far larger than all the others lumbered into view. Atop its back rode a glittering palanquin. Pillars of spun silver supported a golden canopy that shimmered in the sunlight. A Milantian mage gripped the front banister, riding the golem like a pasha on parade. At his command the beast halted.

A blast came from Hyam's allies on the hilltop, the same streaking flames that had destroyed the giants. But the mage had already shielded them. Shona's mage-fire spun and wove in brilliant currents, great streamers that flashed over and around the golems. When the flames dissolved, the golems and the mage remained untouched.

A command rose from the distant canopy, and Selim

groaned as the golems all turned as one. Taking aim at the four standing upon the hill.

The golems marched in the same military unison as the giants, but their bellows carried an unhinged frenzy. Hyam felt the same frantic dismay he had known in the Ellismere Vale, where they had almost been defeated by just one of the beasts. Shona responded with another blinding flash from her sword-wand combination. But the mage's shields held, and the golems accelerated.

Hyam understood the Milantian strategy now. One assault after another rose from unseen depths. Each wave learning from the one before. Each more deadly.

Selim cried, "Call the ghouls!"

Hyam did not waste breath on a reply. By this point the golems' roars were so fierce he doubted Selim could hear him. Hyam had already seen how futile the spectral army had proven against just one such monster. These golems numbered perhaps two hundred—he had to assume they included all those missing from Olom. But they threw up so much dust it was impossible to see more than the first dozen or so.

He drew his dagger and began the shield incantation. The same spell had saved them the last time a golem had attacked. But Hyam did not drag the blade in the earth as the scroll dictated. Instead, he drew in the air before his face. The distant hill became a bull's-eye at the center of a glowing circle. Hyam spoke as quickly as he could manage and completed the final swirling flourish just as the first line of golems reached the hill. He cast the spell forward, flinging it like a giant invisible loop, spinning it with his mind and his empty arms, attempting to shift it by will alone. He did not allow himself to think what might happen if his effort failed.

The Milantian mage rose from his embroidered cushions so as to better observe the assault.

Then Selim shouted in utter glee.

The first golems slammed into an invisible wall. Those behind either could not stop in time or were unable to break the magical commands. They piled on, more and more, until the hill's base became a churning, bellowing mass of gigantic bodies. The dust rose until it consumed the beasts, curving around the shield wall, higher and higher, until it seemed as though the four humans stood atop a golden cloud.

Even before he turned away from the hill, Hyam knew the mage's attention had refocused upon the tower. The Milantian's languid air was gone now. Even from this distance Hyam could detect the fury and the speed with which the mage cast his new spell.

Hyam lifted his dagger, fearing he had left it too late. He only knew the attack spells he had combined in the arrow. He only knew the one shield spell. No doubt the mage had learned from Hyam's previous successes and was ready to deflect both.

So Hyam sprang what he hoped was yet another surprise.

Hyam pointed the dagger and sent the shield spell out. To surround the mage.

Only this time he cast the spell in reverse.

The circular enclosure surrounding the wizard and his golem would become a cage.

If it worked.

He completed the shield and willed it forward, just as he had to protect his companions. The shield scrolls had warned against mage-force. Anything applied to the shield would be shot back as an amplified destructive force.

The Milantian's arms wove a ribbon of light that grew into a searing ball shot through with crimson flashes. The mage gripped the ball with both hands, drew it over his head, leaned back, then heaved it straight at Hyam's tower. The globe seared the air over the golem's head. The flames became refashioned into a monster's face whose gaping maw revealed crimson fangs.

Then the mage beast struck the shield Hyam had fashioned. And exploded in a truly spectacular fashion.

The blast was so enormous the shield's interior became a pillar of fire. The circular flames rose far into the heavens, for a moment outshining the sun.

Slowly, gradually, the blinding flash died away. When the fire dissipated, the shield Hyam had fashioned was empty. Of the mage or his golem, there was no sign. Not even dust remained.

45

By the time Hyam and Selim arrived at the hill's base, the golems milled about in lowing confusion. Most of the dust had settled. Hyam thought the beasts now resembled mammoth cows. Except, of course, for the petal-like mouths filled with teeth longer than his arm.

Hyam said to Selim, "Speak to them. See if they'll obey."

"And tell them to do what?" But Selim did not wait for a response. Instead, he climbed far enough up the hill to look over their weaving heads and called, "Heed my voice! There are sheep waiting for you in Olom. And clans needing you to dig more tunnels!" He pointed back toward the long red hills. "Go! Now!"

Hyam climbed up beside Selim and repeated the words in Milantian.

To their vast relief, the golems departed.

Meda descended the hill as the beasts trundled away. "Nice to see them behave."

Hyam asked, "Is everyone okay?"

"We are indeed. But it was a close-run thing." Meda grinned a welcome to Selim. "Your arrows carry quite a punch."

Selim's reply was cut off by a cry from the hilltop. Hyam looked up to find Fareed, Shona, and Alembord all pointing in the direction blocked by the hill's curvature.

When Hyam and Selim scampered up the steep slope, they discovered three crimson-robed Milantians standing beside a trio of holes. They were positioned so that four or five hundred paces separated them. Then a fourth mage emerged from the hill upon which they stood.

Shona gasped, "That's her!"

"Who?" Selim asked.

"The witch who stole Joelle's breath," Meda snarled. "She's mine."

"There you are, my lovelies! The master will be ever so pleased." The witch clapped her hands, which apparently was the signal for her companions to begin casting their spells. "Now come down off the roof of my house this instant!"

Shona was already preparing her own response, fueled by the revulsion that creased her voice and features both. Hyam admired her spirit, though he was filled with the sinking certainty that her attack would come to nothing. The Milantians had waited for this moment. All the earlier attacks had been the mages' way of taking their measure.

Shona completed her spell and touched her wand to the sword. Her fire shot forth, a huge blast of fury. But in swift response, the mages simply melted away.

The Milantian wizards dissolved. All four of them, in the span of a single heartbeat. Gone.

Four crimson dust clouds rose up, swirling in deadly intent. The arid crimson mist flowed like desiccated blood.

Swiftly Hyam encircled them with a shield. But the four clouds joined together, swept down, and entered the portal through which the witch had emerged. Too late Hyam realized what was happening. The mages were attacking from beneath, through the unshielded earth.

The mist emerged in a hundred tight streams from the hill where they stood. They wrapped around all of Hyam's company. Chaining them with the relentless pressure of forces that yearned for nothing more than another chance to kill.

Hyam knew he had lost. He could not even cry a final apology to the company who had trusted him. His breath was already stolen, for the tendrils clenched his chest with impossible strength. The pain was so intense he could scarcely even think the final word. The one person whose trust he had most forsaken.

Joelle.

The air around his head was thick with the dust. So much, so fast, there was no air at all. Hyam was as blinded as he was choked.

His final panic was a breathless cry. His lungs burned, his open mouth was packed full with the crimson dust. Every shred of his being shrieked that all was lost.

Unless . . .

Hyam had a lightning image of Shona relating the witch's

attack in the Emporis tent, how the mage had sucked in the power that had ensnared them, growing larger and larger . . .

But Hyam could not breathe.

Even so, he sucked in. Not with his lungs. They were locked tight. With his entire Milantian being.

He could feel the mist filling him. And as it did, three impressions shot through him with the intensity of a departing life.

First, he could feel some inner portion of himself growing steadily larger, a balloon-like component that spread and swelled and took in ever more of the putrid killing dust.

Second, he felt the scar tissue of all his lost abilities, the remnant of his last battle against crimson foes, crack and break apart.

Third, he knew he was dying. The physical component of his being still could not breathe. He no longer had the ability to force his body to do anything. Even as he sensed the hilltop becoming free of dust. Even as his company gasped and cried and breathed and survived. Hyam felt his own body drift down, down, to collapse upon the dry and dusty hilltop.

He gave in to the darkness and knew no more.

46

The first impression Hyam had upon awakening was that someone breathed for him.

He felt his chest pump up, then he felt hands press down. He heard the sigh of his own breath.

As his awareness continued to return, he felt a mouth fit over his and push more air in. He tasted a salty tang and realized the warm lips belonged to Shona, and that she wept as she gave him air.

Hyam felt a surge of surreal clarity. He was alive! What was more, his company had survived as well. Though his eyes remained shut, he sensed their presence and heard vague murmurs he could not yet fit into words. Alembord, Meda, Fareed, Selim, all there, and then Shona's lips fit over his again and helped him breathe. Alive!

Hyam coughed weakly and was rewarded with exclamations on all sides. Only Shona did not celebrate. She sobbed and breathed with difficulty and fitted her lips once more over his.

With each of Shona's breaths came her mage-force. Hyam could feel it surging through his veins. He knew this was why he lived. She had given him far more than air. She shared everything.

And finally, at long last, Hyam understood. Another lungful, another surge of her force, and Hyam knew this was no childish infatuation. Shona *loved* him. She was *bound* to him.

And after this day, he was bound to her as well.

Her sorrow over being forced to accept he would never be hers pierced Hyam with shared agony. Somehow the situation had to be remedied. Yet this quandary had no ready answer.

Then it hit him. Joelle would know what to do.

Hyam opened his eyes.

❖

Hyam sat up with Shona's and Meda's help. The sight that greeted him proved well worth the effort. He was seated upon a long central bench, wide as a bed, that ran the length of their ship. The vessel was perhaps thirty paces long and eight or nine wide. Two further broad benches ran down the gunnels. Selim snored on one, Alembord on the other. Fareed was perched in the distant bow. He turned and waved and called something that was lost to the salty wind.

The boat was curious indeed. At first glance it appeared to be made from the sea itself. Hyam leaned over for a closer look and spotted bits of seaweed and a fan coral embedded in the bench where he sat. There was also no means of power or steering, neither mast nor tiller nor wheel. Even so, they sped across the sea. The water chuckled and rushed beneath the vessel, and spray bathed his face. The taste was exquisite, a salty assurance that he lived.

Hyam had a thousand questions. But there was one thing that must come first. He turned to Shona and used his hands to sweep away her tears. The woman was no longer young. The effort required to save him had aged Shona a century and more. He would not speak of her love. Not until he knew what should be said. But he wanted her to know that he acknowledged her, and her gift, and would respect it. Forever.

Something in his gaze caused her to weep harder still. Hyam allowed her to melt to his chest. He stroked the fine hair, he felt her warmth, he listened to the music of one who cried because she cared.

When she quieted, he said, "I live because you breathed your mage-force into me."

"I . . . tried."

"You succeeded."

Meda asked, "Is that even possible?"

Hyam held up one finger, silencing the guards captain. "I will not say there is a debt between us. Such vows exist between allies. Our relationship is far deeper. The first thing I noticed upon awakening was the flavor of your life."

Shona drew back, her breathing unsteady, but she was clearly determined to hear him with far more than just her ears.

Hyam went on, "I acknowledge the gift you have given me. I am able to speak these words because of your bequest."

Gradually the young woman settled, steadied. "I tasted your life as well."

Hyam nodded. "It is only fitting."

The emotions carried by the words not yet spoken caused her face to crimp up tight. But all she said was, "We have to rescue Joelle."

Hyam embraced her again, a silent thanks, then said, "You should rest."

"I'm fine."

"You look exhausted," he replied. "There is no telling what lies beyond the horizon. Sleep. We will talk more later."

In reply, she stretched out on the bench beside him. Meda slipped off her travel cloak, folded it, and settled it beneath Shona's head. Hyam touched the point where her hair bordered her temple. Shona reached up and captured his fingers.

Meda handed him a small leather pouch and said, "We had enough supplies for one meal. We saved your share."

Hyam ate with ravenous appetite. When he was done, he felt more hungry than when he had started. "Tell me what happened."

"The mage dust was killing us all," Meda said. "And blinding us in the process. The first thing I saw when my eyes cleared was a whirlwind above your head. You sucked it all in. Four mages. I waited for you to explode. No one could have held all that evil and survived."

Hyam resisted the urge to say that he had not, for he knew Shona still heard them. She stirred, sighed, and slipped into slumber.

Meda went on, "Shona was the first to reach you. She clamped down on your mouth and breathed in, then coughed out a putrid mass. With every breath she expelled, a miniature mage took form at our feet. Never have I felt such an utter repulsion. Fareed came up beside her and blasted away at the remnants before they could attack. Then Shona fastened herself to you and drew out more.

"Fareed's wand gave out, so he used hers. When that one went dark, I used the Milantian sword. They scampered like frantic Milantian rats, trying to strike us. On and on it went. My arms grew so weary I couldn't lift the sword. Alembord took over. Then Selim. Fareed blasted all he could manage. We were beyond spent. And this one, this child mage they tried to leave behind . . ." Meda shook her head. "Twice now she has rescued us."

Hyam studied the course they followed. The sea before and behind their vessel was crystal calm. The only wind was that caused by their swift passage. They traversed a valley in the middle of the sea. Liquid walls rose to either side. Hyam saw a lone fish swim up alongside their craft, long as his leg and striped like a tiger's back. The creature kept pace with their craft for a time, then flicked its tail and vanished. Otherwise the sea cliffs remained empty, clear, mysterious as their journey.

Hyam asked, "How did we come to be here?"

"When we were certain your heart still beat, we carried you down to the harbor. We had no idea whether the mages had yet another attack in store. But for the moment our only threat came from the Milantian dust-rats that continued to reform. As the amount Shona drew from you lessened, the beasts grew smaller, but they remained deadly, growing fangs and going straight on the attack soon as they landed. Fareed fashioned mage-lights for Alembord to hold, because by then it was pitch-black. Dark as ever I had seen it, not a moon, not a star. Night as close and tight as death.

"Selim carried you, then Alembord. Shona breathed for you the entire way across Alyss. Fareed and I kept the rat creatures at bay. We had one bad moment when we almost spilled into one of the holes, but Fareed caught sight at the last moment. We rested there on the shore, wondering if dawn would ever come. But it did, and at first light we found the boat there waiting for us. We climbed on board, and off we went. These walls grew up soon as we passed the harbor mouth."

Hyam studied the sun's position through the transparent western cliff. "We've traveled all day?"

"No, Hyam. A day and a night and now much of the second day."

He asked because he had to. But the answer was there in Meda's tight gaze. "The ghost warriors were to hunt for . . ."

"The vial holding Joelle's breath." Meda sighed around her shared pain as she lifted a chain and crystal pipe from her pocket. "I blew. The general came alone. He might have given her a message, Shona hasn't said. Her every breath was used to keep you alive. Once we arrived portside we debated whether one should go back. But with the dark and the threat . . ."

"And search where?" The sorrow was so intense he could scarcely form the words. Because he knew he had failed. He turned and stared back behind him, back to the unseen city and the foe that had, in fact, defeated him.

Hyam waited until Meda slipped away, then wept with the pain of breathing while another could not.

47

In the late afternoon, the lone fish returned. Hyam recognized the tiger stripes as it sprang from the sea cliff and landed in their vessel. Alembord shouted with delight and pounced, pinning the madly flapping beast to the gunnels.

Meda sat beside Hyam and watched Alembord skin and dress the fish. "Kind of the dragon to remember we need to eat."

Hyam shook his head. "You're missing the point."

"Which is?"

"How many other fish have you seen?"

Meda frowned at the sunset-streaked water rising to either side of their vessel. Her response was cut off by Fareed calling, "Sahib, dare we risk a mage-fire?"

"Set it alight," Hyam replied.

Alembord looked up from slicing hand-sized filets. "How can you be certain?"

"A fire-breathing dragon would not shape a vessel that

melts from such small flames," he replied, and pressed on Shona's shoulder. When she opened her eyes, the years had begun to fall away, and she even managed a smile. Hyam said, "Dinnertime."

They did not eat their fill, but at least their hunger was abated. The sun melted at an angle into the right cliff, confirming that they still traveled north by east. As twilight gathered, a lone cloud appeared overhead and drenched the stern of the boat without touching them at all. A basin extended from the point where the tiller should have been, and as soon as it was filled the cloud vanished.

One by one they all drifted off, until Hyam was left alone with the night, or so he thought. He walked to the bow and settled on the central bench's front ledge. Soon after, Shona came to sit beside him. She kept her distance, however. And Hyam knew why.

He checked to ensure all the others were asleep, then said softly, "Tell me what the general said."

The starlight was strong enough for Hyam to see her nod. This was, he knew, why she had come forward. "He reported that the vial containing Joelle's life-breath was not in the city. He and his new allies would try to hunt farther afield. He said he thought you would survive. He commended me for trying."

"And so even though you could feel the crimson dust eating away at your own life, you kept at it. Drawing out their poison and breathing in your life."

She dragged a hand across her eyes. "I was so scared."

Hyam asked, "Our allies tracked the vial?"

"They tried to. The general returned the first night we journeyed on the sea, while the others slept. He said to tell you there was a fifth Milantian mage in Alyss. This one held back from the final attack. He fled across the desert. Toward Emporis. And he took the vial with him."

Hyam nodded. He had dreaded it, and expected it as well. "Into the realm."

"The general said to tell you that this mage traveled with uncommon swiftness. And left no footprint. Something blocked them from tracking the mage beyond the realm's borders."

Which could only mean one thing. "There is another crimson mage, this one carrying a miniature orb."

She shivered, all the confirmation Hyam needed. "Then why . . ."

"Why did their master not join in the attack at Alyss?" Hyam said. "I can think of only one reason. There is another battle elsewhere. One that has reached a critical juncture."

"Which means," Shona said quietly, "we were fortunate in a way."

Hyam felt the aching bitterness bloom. "It simply means my quest is not over."

"Our quest," she corrected.

He would not argue with her that night. "The vial exists. I will find it."

"*Our* quest, Hyam." More sharply this time.

He did not point out how such a decision lay in hands other than theirs. For this night, he was grateful for the young woman's strength. "Our quest."

314

She rose and looked down at him. She whispered, "Could you ever love me?"

Hyam had no idea how to respond.

"I know you don't love me as I do you. But if I can accept this, what does it matter?"

Hyam stared into the star-flecked valley and did not speak.

Finally she turned and sang a soft "Good night, Hyam."

He did not turn around. "Sleep well, Highness."

48

Hyam woke to the full light of day. The sun bathed him with a manner that, for once, was not overly harsh. He lay there for a time, savoring the salt air. His entire being felt both exultant and hollow. He rolled over and groaned from having laid in one position too long. He pushed himself off the bench to discover he was alone and the vessel moored. The sea cliffs were gone.

His company stood about an otherwise empty beach. Beyond the shore stretched an emerald-green island whose central spine rose to lofty peaks. Hyam dropped from the vessel's side into water warm as life itself. As soon as his feet touched bottom, the ship dissolved in a soft splash.

Meda greeted him with, "Do you recognize this place?"

"Sort of." Hyam took a long look around. "Always before I saw it from the air."

Selim waved at the vast plain leading up to the central hills. The pasture was dotted with mounds the color of autumn stones. "There are dragons everywhere! But they don't wake up, not even when we shout."

"That's because they're not asleep," Hyam replied. "They're dying."

A shout from Alembord turned them around. As the dragon emerged from the sea, Hyam recognized him from the autumn-gold stripes about his wings and head. The beast gripped another of the tiger-striped fish in his mouth, only this one was larger than Hyam. He dropped it flapping on the sand and used one talon to keep it from dancing back into the water. The dragon chattered, "You are hungry. Eat."

"Your mate is hungrier than us," Hyam replied. "Feed her."

"My mate receives the first of everything. There are others in far worse condition." The dragon inspected Hyam gravely, then scooped up the fish. The dripping wings extended to offer balance as it crossed the beach and entered the meadow.

Hyam followed at what he hoped was a respectful distance. The dragon set the fish by an inert form. He nudged the mound, which was only slightly smaller than the Alyss tower Hyam had scaled. When the animal did not respond, the dragon tore off a strip of flesh, nudged the mound once more, and chattered, "For the little one."

The hillock shifted, a neck uncurled, and a skeletal head lifted, but only slightly. The skin had stretched so tight Hyam could see the bones shift as she replied weakly, "What does it matter?"

"Two lives are at stake," the dragon urged. "You must eat."

The female's chatter was slow as a funeral march. "I depart

today or tomorrow, and the one asleep in her egg will soon follow."

"I do not bring just fish," the dragon replied. "But hope."

At this, several of the other mounds shifted. Weak-eyed behemoths studied Hyam and the male dragon. But none made a move toward the fish.

Hyam called, "I will bring food."

The female's eye was almost as tall as Hyam, palest yellow and very dim. "What can a puny mortal do for the likes of me, and for what purpose?"

Hyam heard her reluctance to return to the realm of life and of hope. So he replied at length, pausing now and then to translate for his company, who had now joined him in the meadow. "The Milantians called together an army of beasts known as golems." There was no term in dragon speech for the monsters, so he used the human word. "Some are almost as large as you and eat constantly. The enemy then raised another army of the nonliving, in the human shape, but giants. They too ate."

"They stole our fish," the male dragon rumbled to Hyam, steam emerging with the words. "And our lives. For this is my race's only breeding ground. One male comes to hunt for all those resting upon the nests. Our treaty governing this island holds this limit. One male to tend the mothers and eggs. Until this breeding season, there has never been need for more."

"The Milantian monsters were bred for war, and while their masters prepared, the golems cleared the seas of fish," Hyam said, casting his voice loud enough for all the nearby dragons to hear. "They used magic to sweep the ocean. But the Milantians have been defeated, and Alyss is home to nothing save dust and heat."

"But the seas remain empty," the nearest female replied.

"We will not bring you fish," Hyam replied. "But sheep."

There was a word in dragon speech for the wooly beasts. Hyam hoped this meant the animals would make a tasty meal. This was confirmed by how his news turned the male dragon entirely around. The movement revealed an ungainly awkwardness. The wings extended partway and he shifted like a beached cormorant, the body leaning heavily from side to side. When he was fully facing Hyam, he chattered, "Truly, this is so?"

"Hundreds of them. Spread the news. Tell your friends not to lose hope." Hyam trotted toward the meadow's perimeter, calling back, "Selim!"

"I come!"

49

Hyam walked to where a clutch of windswept pines formed a living canopy. They were angled against ocean storms that did not blow this day. Hyam's shirt buttons were encrusted with salt and old grime and opened reluctantly. He drew out the chain, gripped the crystal pipe, and blew.

The shadows between the wizened trunks solidified and became a portal that opened into a tunnel of living green. Elven guards stepped out, saluted Hyam, and signaled him to wait. Moments later they were joined by Darwain and his queen.

The Elven ruler demanded, "What news?"

"Sire, the Milantian foes of Alyss have been vanquished. More than that must wait. How is Joelle?"

"She lives." Darwain's gaze widened as the dragon poked his head through the branches overhead. "Legends upon legends!"

"These are our allies, and they are dying," Hyam said,

320

pushing his own heartache aside. "And this too is the Milantians' work."

Darwain was nodding agreement before Hyam finished explaining. "This we can do. Who will speak to the shepherds of Olom?"

Hyam gestured to his friend. But Selim did not step forward. Hyam turned to discover him staring at the newcomers in genuine fear. He stepped back, gripped Selim's arm, and said, "These are friends."

Selim remained planted in the earth, rigid as iron.

Hyam explained to the Elves, "Majesty, this is Selim, merchant of Olom. His family was formerly traders of Alyss. He is the last of Ethrin's line, and the man responsible for our having survived the yellow realm."

Darwain offered a regal salute. "Then we welcome you as the ally you are."

Selim did not move. "Forbidden," he croaked. "Banished. Forsaken."

"Already a thousand years of edicts have been demolished," Darwain replied. "Swept away by the return of our foes."

When Selim stayed where he was, Darwain's wife stepped forward and offered Selim her hand. "Would you refuse a queen's entreaty?"

Slowly, tearfully, Selim reached forward. "No, Majesty. I will not."

"Welcome, Selim of Ethrin and Olom. I, queen of the hidden realm, invite you to enter your new home."

Sheep spilled from the portal, a torrent of white wool and delicate hooves and frantic bleats. Far back along the green avenue, Fareed and Shona used their wands to spur the animals along.

Over a hundred dragons dotted the surrounding pastures. Many had needed to be supported, some managed to crawl over on their own. The first sheep to arrive were taken in one gulp. Most of the dragons rested now, observing in bemused contentment as the wooly animals continued to flood out, decorating the meadows.

Selim returned through the portal, surveyed the scene, and nervously cleared his throat. "I am required to raise an indelicate topic."

"The shepherds and merchants of Olom want payment," Hyam interpreted.

"I asked them to wait," Selim said. "But their needs are great as well."

"Give me the reckoning and I will—" Hyam stopped because the dragon demanded to know what concerned Selim. He explained, "My friend is asking for payment. I can arrange this through the Ashanta bankers. The Earl of Falmouth will also help."

"There is no need."

"The Milantians have harmed Selim's city," Hyam continued. "Not so severe as your clan, but bad enough. They need payment now."

"They will be paid in full, and in gold, and by me," the dragon replied. "Take hold of my right leg, and use the talons as support."

Hyam doubtfully eyed the massive leg as the dragon extended his wings. "Can I not ride on your back?"

"Not without a harness, and there is no time to fashion one."

Hyam stepped in close and gripped the leathery skin as he would a tree trunk. "I am ready. I think."

"Hold fast!"

They did not journey far, which was good, as Hyam's perch was not secure. The dragon flew in a series of rapid ascents and descents, as though he cast a new spell with every few beats of his wings. As a result, he flew like a snake swam, writhing through the air and almost losing his passenger a dozen times and more. When the dragon finally settled upon the island's loftiest peak, Hyam staggered about on unsteady legs and said, "Perhaps I should walk back."

The dragon coughed, or laughed, or both. Then, "Enter the cave behind you."

The cave's entrance was larger than Falmouth's main gates, which was good, for the dragon lumbered along behind him. When his bulk blocked the sun, the dragon fashioned a mage-light. The way wound downward at a gentle slope and finally opened into a chamber so vast the ceiling was lost to the gloom.

The dragon's chatter echoed off distant walls. "One legend about our race is true enough. We have always been drawn to gold and gemstone. Why, I cannot say, for we do not spend, only hoard."

The chamber opened into another that to Hyam appeared even larger, and then a third, and perhaps a fourth, but the distances were so great he could not be sure of anything save they were all filled with treasure.

On display were vast seas of gold and jewels. They lay in piles ten times Hyam's height and spilled from chests scarred by coral and fire both. What appeared to be an entire bank vault lay gaping in the far corner, with gold bars spilling out its portal like a glowing tongue.

The dragon touched one chest bound by rusting iron bars and filled with coins milled in some ancient age. "Will this do?"

"It is twenty times too much," Hyam replied. "Fifty."

"Take it, take more. For all that you see here is yours."

The unemotional drumbeat carried such finality, Hyam found himself unable to keep his sorrow in check. "I have failed my beloved."

"Your quest has faced a setback, nothing more. And know this, human. The bonds between us are not ended simply because my own needs have been met. Whenever you require assistance, in whatever form, it is yours."

Hyam cuffed away tears and said, "I do not know where to go, or if I have the strength to continue."

"I and my kind will help in the search. As for strength . . ." The beast extended his wings fully, lifted his head, and roared flame and power. A pillar of fire rose and spilled across the distant ceiling, transforming the dragon into a beast of lore and majesty. "To know a dragon's name is to bind him for life. But I am already bound to you."

"And I to you," Hyam managed.

"My name is Tragan, king of the northern reaches." He blasted the chamber with fire a second time. "We dwell in the land of ice and storm at the earth's pinnacle. Once in three of your brief generations, we return to our breeding ground. The island was granted to us by the same treaty that bound us to remain beyond the reach of man. Elf and Ashanta and Milantian all built their realms and forgot us in the process. In truth it pleased us to become mere legend and myth, for in our secret tongue, our race is called the Unknown."

Hyam forced himself to focus beyond the ache that threatened to consume him, sure as the ceramic eye. "The queen of Lystra called you the covert one," he recalled.

"Those witches hold to the old ways, but poorly. Their city's secrets are known to the dark ones of their race, who threaten to expose and destroy them if they do not do their bidding. But they did not pass on news of your visit and our meeting, which is to their credit. Even so, you should not trust them unless you must. If you do, be prepared, for they will demand payment of a sort. In the case of our meeting, the witches demanded magic."

Hyam pushed aside his grief. "There is much you can teach us."

"Again, you need ask and it is yours. We are the last holders of the ancient ways. Some among us claim the Ancients came to us to learn spell casting." He gave a ponderous shrug. "Some of my kind show an arrogance to match their size."

Now that this chapter of his quest was coming to a close, Hyam felt overwhelmed by the misery of fatigue. But he did not want to respond to the dragon's gift with sorrow, so he turned and pretended to survey the treasure. "So much wealth."

"This is nothing. We males sent to feed the nesting mothers compete to see who can draw up the most gold from the Ancients' cities, those now scattered about the ocean floor. Our northern lair would swallow this in one small corner. You must come and see for yourself."

Hyam cuffed his eyes a second time. "I would like that."

The dragon saw the motion and pointed with his giant head. "Atop that pile to your left is a golden vial. Bring it here."

Hyam climbed the hill of treasure and returned with a king's goblet, twice the size of his joined fists and topped by an ornate cap that was held in place with a pair of gold catches carved like swans. The goblet and cap were heavily engraved with a flowing script that Hyam did not recognize, and rimmed by rubies the size of acorns.

"Remove the cap and hold it aloft." Tragan lowered his head such that one cheek grazed against Hyam's hand. When he spoke, he exposed teeth the length of Hyam's thigh. "The Ancients held us in high regard for one thing above all else. They claimed that a dragon's tears healed all wounds. But I suspect it will not bring back your beloved, bondsman."

"I understand," Hyam said. And he did. For Joelle was not ill.

"Even so, perhaps it will sustain her." He leaned closer still. "You will now behold a mystery that few have ever understood."

"Why is that?"

"Because a dragon cannot cry." Tragan tilted his head slightly so that the lower lid of one massive eye touched the cup's rim. "Hold very still."

Tragan blinked and released a drop of blood the size of Hyam's hand. Again. A third time, and the cup was full.

50

The four Elves guarding the portal's entry watched the dragon land. Hyam found the return journey as unsettling as the first. As he stood in the meadow and waited for strength to return to his legs, Tragan opened his jaws and deposited the chest of gold at his feet.

"It is a hundred times too much," Hyam protested again. "You could buy most of Olom with that."

The dragon turned his back on the Elves with their bows and spears. "You have a place of safekeeping?"

"With the Ashanta bankers," Hyam said.

"Hold it for what comes next. Who knows what our quest will require."

Hyam felt an uncommon urge to hug the dragon, which of course was absurd. "*Our* quest."

"I must determine a means for you to contact me that will not break the treaty. I have no idea how. But I will find a way."

He was struck by a thought. "Can you help free the ghostly army?"

"I am aware of your vow to assist your new allies." The dragon extended one wing partway, a vague salute. "It speaks well of you, bondsman."

Hyam had started to take his leave when Tragan began a series of motions that could only be described as awkward. He ducked and weaved his head and massive frame, almost like the nervous desert eagle.

"What is it?" Hyam asked.

"The elixir you hold—most likely it will not heal your mate."

Which the dragon had already said up in the cave. "I do not hold you accountable for my failure." Hyam lifted the covered goblet with both hands. "I thank you for this gift, as I do for the honor of knowing your name."

"You misunderstand me, bondsman." The dance grew more frenetic. "The gift of tears, they are *intended to heal*."

Hyam froze.

"A dragon's life cannot be counted in your years. Our memories are shared and thus stretch farther still. But never have I heard of a mage who burned away his magical abilities. Even so, I would call this a wound."

"But if I . . . Joelle . . ."

"There is more than enough for you both. Give her a spoonful, take another for yourself. No more, lest you do harm with the unleashed potency. Hold the remainder in safekeeping." The dragon's tail whipped about, sending one of the trees crashing to earth. The Elves cried in protest, but it seemed that Tragan neither noticed nor heard. "Each tear is a vital portion of my life's energy, bondsman. I will sleep now for several months of your time. My wife will give me her place upon the egg and she will tend to me as I have for her."

The dragon started away, saying as he departed, "Never before has there been this shift, a male guardian of the island taking his place upon the unborn. Nor has a human ever set foot in our breeding ground. Nor a dragon risked breaking the treaty by entering the human realm through dreams. Nor has one of our kind shared tears with anyone save the Ancients. Or given one of your race our true name. So many components of our primeval ways have been broken. And yet I count myself fortunate to know you, bondsman, and to call you my friend."

51

The Elves were still watching Tragan's departure when Hyam asked, "Where is my company?"

The Elf who had accompanied Hyam into the Emporis battle replied, "The head mage of Falmouth, the one who summoned our king with fire and havoc . . ."

"Trace," Hyam replied.

"That one summoned Meda, Alembord, and Fareed to a council gathering. Bayard ordered Shona to meet with her king."

"And Selim?"

"He wished to show his mate that he had succeeded in the quest she set out for him." The Elf shrugged. "He said you would understand."

"I do indeed."

"Selim also said he awaits your call to resume the quest."

Hyam found it very good indeed to have such friends. He said, "Take me to my wife."

✦

The Elves had given Joelle her own palace. The haven was formed from a single tree. Living pillars covered an area larger than the Emporis citadel. The branches wove together into floors and ceilings and even a circular staircase that Hyam climbed to the balcony where Joelle lay. Two female attendants greeted Hyam with a sorrow that turned their greetings into a shared lament.

The healer was summoned, and he assured Hyam that Joelle took water and an occasional mouthful of soup, enough to sustain her. The Elf exclaimed over the goblet of dragon's tears. He and Darwain and the Elven queen all fretted and argued over dosage and such, for none could say whether Hyam should use a dragon-sized spoon. Tragan had, after all, referred to the goblet as a vial.

When the moment finally came, Hyam found himself unable to administer the dose. So the queen knelt by Joelle's side, dipped the spoon into the ruby liquid, and administered the dose herself.

When the liquid touched Joelle's lips, she swallowed. Again. And then went still. The queen refilled the spoon and held it out. Four times she touched Joelle's lips, but Hyam's lady would take no more.

Finally the queen stood and said, "Now we wait."

Hyam struggled for some way to show the depth of his gratitude, but the words did not come, or perhaps did not exist at all. But the queen must have sensed his effort, for she said, "Such are the times when true friends are counted." She turned to her mate. "Darwain, I feel this is the moment."

In reply, the king waved the healer and Joelle's attendants from the room. When they were alone, he said, "When a new ruler takes the Elven throne, their spouse accepts two names. One is the Elven title of consort, which is used by all those who seek her favor as ruler. The other is hers and hers alone."

"To be used once and buried with her, never to be taken by another," Hyam remembered.

"Just so. The consort's name holds a special purpose. The name is intended to represent his or her hidden treasure, the portion that keeps the ruler from being consumed by the power they wield. Their deepest talent, their heart's gift."

"The flavor of love," Hyam said, for once not ashamed of his tears.

"My wife's name is Ainya. It comes from old Elven and signifies a heart that shines with a unique brilliance and splendor."

He bowed in gratitude at yet another priceless gift and said, "Highness, it suits you."

A voice faint as a sunset breeze whispered, "Hyam?"

He did not kneel so much as collapse at the side of her bed. "Joelle, my darling."

"Is it really you? I've been so . . ." And then she was gone once more.

"Joelle, my treasure, my heart, please . . ." But she had already resumed her half state, lost to him.

Hyam fitted his face into the shadows where her hair spilled across her neck and wept for his failure and for all the empty hours. He felt hands settle upon his shoulders and sensed the caring strength of friends. But they could not respond to the accusations that wracked him. If only he had not failed. If only he had retrieved the vial. If only he had been wiser. If only he had been enough.

※

Over the next four days, Hyam scarcely released Joelle's hand. He slept on the floor by her pallet. The maidservants worked around him. The healer came regularly and made him eat. When they were alone, Hyam talked with her. He dwelt little on the past, for what could he say that mattered, save how he had returned without her breath? So he spoke of the days to come. He gave voice to his hopes for them both, and he formulated his plans. Now and then he knew a faint hint of peace, as though Joelle had managed to reach across the divide and share her love.

Bryna came daily, sometimes accompanied by an Ashanta elder, more often alone. Twice Hyam woke in the night to find her gazing down at them both. He found considerable comfort in her silent sorrow.

Trace came once every day, accompanied by either Darwain or his queen. Each time, Hyam shared the component of his plans that was ready, for there were things that needed to be put in motion. He must leave Joelle in order to help her return. He knew this. Sitting with her in this tree haven granted him the clarity to piece together the next stage.

When Hyam explained his plans to his allies, he was prepared for objections or doubts. For he spoke with people who had vast experience at forming strategy. But neither Trace nor the Elven rulers found it necessary to say more than, "It will be done as you say." Hyam assumed they were being kind, and took this with the same broken gratitude as he accepted most things these days.

On the fifth day, Trace was escorted into the balcony by Ainya. The Elven queen was flanked by two guards who carried bundles. There was a certain formality to how the senior mage of Falmouth and the ruler of the hidden kingdom stood and punctuated the moment with their silence. Telling Hyam with utter solemnity that it was time.

Trace asked, "Has she taken more of the dragon's elixir?"

"Not since the first day. When I offer, she tightens her lips."

"Has she awoken again?"

"From time to time she sighs. I think I hear my name. She has squeezed my hand. Occasionally she stirs, as though she tries to waken." Hyam stroked her arm. "Most of the time, she is as you see."

Ainya asked softly, "Have you drunk the elixir?"

Hyam did not respond.

The queen motioned to her guards, who deposited their bundles and departed. When only Trace remained with them, Ainya seated herself on the floor beside Hyam. She took hold of his free hand. And waited.

Eventually Hyam did as she wished, which was to turn from his beloved. And meet her gaze.

Ainya's complexion was more blond than green, like

sunlight seen through a minty veil. Her cheekbones were pronounced in the manner of her race, which slanted her eyes up at an angle that on her was beautiful. Her golden eyes held a combination of authority, wisdom, and compassion. As did her voice, even when she whispered, "Joelle needs for you to continue your quest."

Hyam found both comfort and dismay in hearing what he knew to be true.

"For you to succeed, you must take the next step."

Hyam wanted to speak. He tried to fashion the words, here in this haven where time was not made welcome. He wanted to explain how his desperate longing to drink the elixir felt like treachery. How could he even *want* to be healed when he had failed to restore Joelle? How could he know the exquisite joy of regaining his mage powers when her own breath was lost? But the words did not come.

Ainya went on, "Everything you suggested has been put in place."

Trace added, "Bayard has done as you requested. Not because you asked. Because it is right for the kingdom. But the Earl of Falmouth is not a patient man. You have kept him waiting as long as you possibly can."

Ainya said, "Your company is ready. Ashanta and Elf, human and ghost, even the dragon king's mate has made contact through the general of shadows."

Trace said, "My liege, my oath requires me to offer you counsel. Hard as this step must be for you, it must be taken, and now."

Ainya continued, "I understand your reluctance. You are

alive while your beloved's breath is held by fiends. You are wracked by the guilt of living. Of knowing hope. You fear being made whole."

At a gesture from Ainya, Trace unlatched the top to the golden cup. "Highness."

The Elven queen filled the spoon and held it before Hyam's face. The dragon's gift gleamed in the forest light. "I will not belittle your burdens with arguments. But you must drink. For Joelle. And for us all."

52

For Shona, returning home was disturbing on many levels. Traveling the Elven road back from the dragon island, she worried that her father might see her as the child she was no longer. She feared her mother's criticism. She could almost hear her brothers' mocking laughter.

When she arrived home, Shona found everything she had dreaded, and more besides.

Her family's response to her journey was clear within the first hour. Her mother exclaimed in horror over her clothes, her filthy state, her unkempt hair, her sun-blasted complexion. Shona found it oddly unsettling to bathe and have her hair trimmed and put on a dress. The woman in the silver-backed mirror showed both a stricken gaze and a wealth of stories her family did not wish to hear.

Timmins then insisted she help him work through a scroll he had recently acquired. Shona spoke hardly a word, but rather sat and listened as her two brothers and her father argued over how the information fit into Falmouth's history. It began to rain while she sat in Timmins's study. Shona watched the storm and felt herself struggling to draw a decent breath.

For dinner that evening, her mother invited a young man from one of Falmouth's most powerful clans. Everyone chatted gaily except Shona. No one asked about her adventures. Her absence was treated like a temporary inconvenience that held no lasting importance.

Shona slept little that night. When she arose the next morning, her mind was made up.

She found the clothes she had worn home in a pile of refuse waiting to be burned. The salt and the grime scratched her skin. The smell could only be described as ripe. The cotton trousers and blouse were more grey now than white. By the time she finished packing, her doubts were all but vanquished.

When her parents came downstairs an hour later, they found Shona seated at the kitchen table. They stared in outrage at the two satchels by her feet.

Timmins demanded, "What on earth—"

Shona did not allow him to complete his question. One by one she used her mage-light to fire the candles in the kitchen. There were fourteen in all, counting the candelabra stored on a shelf and used only for formal meals. Then she lit the four lamps. Then the two fireplaces.

Her mother's features turned stricken. Shona almost gave in then, but her father chose that moment to shout, "I *demand* you halt this nonsense *this instant!*"

It was all the affirmation Shona required.

She shielded herself, then plucked the flames from their sources. She drew them slowly across the room, gathering them one by one above her head. When all the flames were extinguished save that one, she began the strengthening process. She fed into the flaming ball all her bitter regret, all her determination, all her frustration . . .

All her love.

"Turn that off!"

In reply, Shona made the light grow stronger still.

"Child, did you not hear—"

She added heat to the light. She built it to such an intensity that her parents, whom she did not shield, cried aloud in shock. They had no choice but to retreat from the room.

"Shona!"

She extinguished the light and waited. They returned to the kitchen, hesitant, uncertain. It hurt her to see the confusion on their faces. But Shona knew she had done the right thing. Her parents watched in despair as Shona lit the lanterns and the fires once more. She did nothing with the candles, for the heat she had created had turned them into puddles.

When her parents looked at her, truly *looked*, she said quietly, "We must talk."

Shona moved into the dorm for female acolytes, a windowless chamber deep in the castle's rock-lined cellars. She was assigned to the beginners' class, where she was the oldest student by seven years.

She found herself unable to contact any of Hyam's company. Bayard refused her request for a meeting. Trace and Fareed actually turned away from her. The one time she found Meda on the practice grounds, the guards captain rebuffed Shona's attempt to give back the Milantian sword, telling her instead to take it up with Hyam. Which Shona would have been happy to do. Except that she had not seen him once since their return.

By the fourth day, Shona was convinced they intended to send her home again. She readied a multitude of arguments, but she knew Bayard's command would leave her no choice. Frustration mounted in lockstep with her helplessness and her fears.

On the fifth morning, Trace entered the classroom and spoke softly with Shona's teacher, a pompous greybeard who treated the acolytes as his personal serfs. The teacher's protests ended when the Earl of Oberon stepped into the doorway. Bayard gestured for Shona to join them. As she passed the mage, the old man muttered, "Good riddance."

They climbed the main stairs leading into the palace proper. As they entered the central vestibule, Meda and Alembord stepped to either side of Shona, flanking her as they would a prisoner. She started to ask what she had done, but their expressions were almost warlike, their gazes sharing a fierce glow. Shona walked on between them, following the earl and his master wizard, feeling very small indeed.

When they entered the grand council chamber, Shona saw her parents standing at the far wall, along with the earl's entire inner cabinet. Then she spotted Hyam. He was seated directly across from the earl's throne-like chair, the position normally taken by the lord chancellor, the earl's chief of staff. Hyam was surrounded by a faint ethereal glow. It reminded her of Dyamid, the Elven king, in that slim moment between his release from the ceramic eye and his departure. Hyam looked scarcely more attached to earth than his wife.

Shona asked, "Are you all right?"

Hyam smiled a gentle welcome and waited until she had seated herself to reply, "I'm not sure."

Up close Hyam's glow was even more pronounced. "Do the Elves not understand that you must eat and sleep?"

Hyam pointed across the table. "Your uncle has something to tell you."

Shona glanced across the table and was surprised to find Bayard and Trace watching her with genuine satisfaction. As though they mightily approved of this conversation. She was about to demand an explanation when Bayard said, "Everyone please take your places."

Shona's gaze was captured by her parents as they seated themselves on her other side. The gazes of Timmins and his wife mirrored a shock so deep they moved as if asleep. Shona then realized that Meda and Alembord had taken up position behind her chair. Just as two honor guards did for Bayard during formal ceremonies.

She asked no one in particular, "What is happening?"

Hyam took hold of her hand and said, "Pay attention."

Bayard began, "After considerable deliberation, I and the

council have come to feel that Hyam is correct in his thinking. I cannot ask you to become my heir."

Hyam's grip tightened slightly, and in that instant Shona realized Hyam had drunk the dragon's tears. The force carried with it an otherworldly potency.

Then she realized what Bayard was asking her to do.

53

The word was *investiture*, and it meant the bestowing of a title.

In her younger years, the lone candle in Shona's bedchamber had often become a dozen golden chandeliers, a parade of light that burnished the trumpets playing her fanfare. She had dreamed of a golden tiara with an emerald the size of a goose egg. Then Bayard had led her onto a balcony overlooking the main square, and all the people cheered.

This reality was very different indeed.

For one thing, everything took place in a frantic rush. The morning of her investiture came just two days later. Bayard had never been a patient man. But now his haste was shared by all of Falmouth. When she protested to Trace, he said simply that certain events have a life and a speed all their very own, as she would soon discover.

Shona's investiture most resembled a council of war. Bayard was flanked by his council and senior officers. To their numbers were added two dozen badland chieftains. The two Calebs accompanied the Rothmore leaders. Connell and the earl's representative came from Emporis. At dawn that same day, Selim, the newly appointed governor of Olom, offered Bayard fealty. All this was possible because Darwain had opened the Elven portals and sent messengers throughout the fiefdom, inviting all who wished to join them.

Wonder upon wonder was how Shona heard the day described. She watched from the palace balcony as Darwain and his queen marched with his Elven guard down the long road leading to the Falmouth gates. Joining them were the elders of the Ashanta empire, the seldom-seen folk who never stepped beyond their white boundary stones. Yet here they were, the green warrior race not seen for a thousand years, entering Falmouth with the same people who had stood aside and let the Milantian hordes destroy their civilization. By the time the newcomers reached the palace gates, the entire city of Falmouth was rendered silent by the spectacle.

Bayard and his elders had told her what was to take place, of course. In fact, they had spoken of these events as if asking her permission. Shona knew her role, and she also knew what her actions would represent. Word of this day would soon filter throughout the realm. What she said would matter little. In fact, Shona had every intention of saying nothing at all. Instead, she wanted her actions to make a statement. She wanted people to remember who she was, not by what she said, but by how she met this challenge.

She worked in secret with Bayard's wife, a regal woman whose good nature had remained intact despite her only child's illness and her husband's fief being erased from all maps of the realm. Tamara brought in a trusted seamstress who worked night and day to give form to Shona's plans.

When it came time for Shona to appear, she left her chamber dressed in a formal gown modeled after a penitent's robe. The cloth was pearl grey, a fabric so soft it drifted cloud-like about her. Her hair was woven into a long braid with nothing save a grey ribbon for adornment. She wore no jewelry.

In her right hand she carried the wand with its glowing miniature orb.

The company who greeted her were dressed in royal finery, which only highlighted her humble state. Shona stood with them in the stone antechamber leading to the palace's main hall, studying each in turn. Fareed looked mightily uncomfortable in tailored mage robes, which Shona knew were from Connell's own wardrobe. Trace wore the blue-striped robe of master wizard and greeted her with a smile intended to gentle her nerves. Alembord and Meda wore the golden breastplates that Shona knew had last seen the light of day when Bayard's forebears were kings of Oberon. The Milantian sword hilt rose above Alembord's left shoulder. Selim wore desert robes laced in silver. Even Hyam was adorned in the golden overmantle of a king's adviser.

There was no fanfare as Shona entered the banquet hall. Nor was there crown, nor diadem, nor any other element of gold or gemstone. On this she had been most firm. Bayard wore his formal robes, as did his wife. But he also wore his broadsword, and beside his throne rested his shield. He and all the others rose as she entered the chamber. They stood in silence as she marched down the length of the hall, up the stairs, and took her place upon the throne.

Bayard turned to the gathered company and declared, "I gave my oath never to seek the crown for myself. And I for one keep my oaths. But we all bear witness to what has happened in our beloved realm. Darkness spreads its cloak once more. The capital has become a haven for the fiends who once sought to enslave us all. They have returned and been received by our so-called rulers with open arms." The Earl of Falmouth unsheathed his sword and lifted it high overhead. "I for one will not stand for this!"

The entire gathering rose and responded with one voice, so loud and so long it seemed to Shona as if the stones of Falmouth trembled in agreement.

Bayard continued, "We are gathered here because we are at war! We have not sought this. It has been brought to us. All men and women of good spirit, of all races, are left with no choice but to take up arms against the blight that threatens our peace and our way of life. We have been forced to take this step, and we now accept the challenge. The enemy will be destroyed and the realm will be restored!"

When the roars subsided, Bayard turned and gestured for her to rise. "I give you Shona, forty-seventh in the Oberon line. Queen of the realm!"

54

Over the days following the investiture, Joelle visited Hyam from time to time. Though she never actually woke from her breathless slumber, still she came to him in dreams. Also Hyam occasionally felt her peace invade his lonely hours. She remained with him for one silent heartbeat, and she departed. Hyam knew it was her way of reminding him that time passed, the world awaited, and he had tasks still undone.

His departure was far harder this time, for Hyam had no idea where his journey would take him, nor how long he would be gone. Even so, he left his forest haven ten days later. Hyam was accompanied by four trusted friends. Meda and Fareed had accepted his invitation with such joy it seemed as though they longed for nothing else. Shona was traveling with them only as far as Emporis. These days the newly crowned regent was always accompanied by Alembord, head of the palace guards. The fact that Shona wore no crown and had no palace of her own was of no importance to anyone.

Elven guards escorted them down the avenue of woven green. They emerged in the glade of desert pines across from the Emporis gates. Hyam stepped to the ledge and discovered a vast horde of spectral warriors filling the vale from end to end. He saluted their leaders and called out words in Milantian and Elven and the human tongue. "You failed at nothing. You held to your vows. You did all I asked and more. If it is in my power to release you from your unseen bonds, I do so now!"

Shona carried herself differently these days. She still wore the simplest of dresses. She refused all manner of adornment and carried nothing save the wand with its miniature orb. But more striking still was her solemnity. She seemed draped in a veil of all she could not yet behold, the threats and the danger and the challenges yet to come. It granted her a timeless grace.

Shona said, "The general replies as before. He says that for the moment, your desire is enough."

The sun and the heat drenched them all. Hyam asked, "You will hunt the mage that the wizards of Alyss called master?"

"Already our scouts are searching for this one and the one who carried your mate's breath," Shona replied for them. "But they remain hidden."

"Which suggests they possess an orb," Hyam said.

"That is our thinking as well," Shona said.

Hyam saluted the half-seen horde. "My vow still stands. I count it as a lifetime quest to free you all."

The soldiers returned his salute, then drifted away, carried by winds none felt. When the vale was empty, Hyam turned back and said, "Emporis is not ready to greet you, Highness."

Shona replied, "I wish you would not call me that."

"Highness," he repeated, "when you first arrive in this city, it must be formally announced, and it must have purpose."

"More than saying farewell to the leader of my company?"

"Far more," Hyam replied.

"Promise you will return as soon as you can."

Hyam bowed in response. "The very hour my quest is complete."

"Our quest," she corrected, then hugged him. Her arms carried an uncommon potency, as though she shared her breath within her embrace.

Hyam started across the empty vale, accompanied only by Meda and Fareed. When they reached the Emporis gates, Hyam glanced back and found her still there, a lovely figure in palest grey, alone even when standing between Alembord and four Elven guards. Hyam bowed once more and turned away.

❖

Selim and his three drovers were ready, and together they left Emporis that same evening. The caravan's only cargos were food and water, for they intended to defy the season and elements both. Meda and Fareed kept well away, granting Hyam the space he had never asked for yet needed desperately. He might as well have traveled alone, for no one respected another's solitude like a desert dweller.

They were slowed by a pair of storms, too minor to halt

progress but most uncomfortable just the same. When the red hills of Lystra finally came into view, it seemed to Hyam as though they had traveled the yellow realm for years.

He approached the solitary hills with Selim, Meda, and Fareed. When they reached the base, Selim fretted, "You are determined to do this alone?"

"I must," Hyam replied.

Fareed asked, "Sahib, forgive me, but have you tested to see whether your powers have returned?"

Hyam slipped from the camel and handed the reins to Meda. "You know I haven't."

Selim showed shock. "You don't know whether the dragon's potion healed you?"

"Not yet," Hyam replied. "But soon."

"Hyam, the witches will know this," Meda said.

Fareed added, "And the dragon is not here, and the witches are no longer bound by its commands."

Hyam started away. "I will be safe."

When he was halfway up the hillside, he turned back long enough to wave his assurance. The dragon had asked Hyam not to mention how he was recuperating, or how they visited almost daily. Tragan appeared in a mirror's surface, or a sword's blade, or the sunlit reflection of standing water. They spoke briefly, in the manner of friends who knew what the other would say before the words were even formed. And the dragon agreed that this trek was important.

As he climbed, Hyam recalled another solitary walk, taken after laying his mother to rest. He had traversed the great forest to the Three Valleys Long Hall, where he had been informed of his secret heritage. Now Hyam scaled the arid peak and wondered at the meandering route that had taken him so far, only to deliver him here, alone upon a lifeless hilltop, staring into empty shadows. Filled with a determination so fierce he felt nothing save the force that yearned to be unleashed.

The hand moved on, writing the next line of the quest he now shared with a multitude of allies and friends. All he could see of the journey was the next step. From here they traveled on to Alyss, where Hyam would read all the remaining scrolls and commit the war-spells to memory. But before that, he had a solitary task that he knew must be fulfilled here. Alone.

The witches of Lystra had gone against the commands of their own kin. They had done so with the twisted motives of their kind, demanding payment, trying to entrap Hyam's company, fearful and defiant and fierce. And yet they had helped him. And so he came here now, because their powers were going to prove invaluable. How, Hyam did not know. But he and Tragan were now convinced the time was coming. Hyam would soon call upon them and needed to be certain they would obey his command.

And so he stood, isolated by far more than the desert heat. There was no more fitting a place, Hyam knew, to reveal his new powers.

The dragon's gift was now joined to Hyam's despised heritage. What was to grow from this combination, Hyam had no idea. Only that it began here.

The forbidden tongue was made for this hill, for this moment. The Milantian language had been forged in the furnace of magic. Ages past, it had been intended to crystallize those abilities, when joined in the heart of Milantian mage.

His heart.

Hyam touched the center of his forehead and spoke the Elven word *reveal*. For the first time in over a thousand years, the language of a race destroyed by Milantians was spoken here. The light burned with a defiant supremacy.

Then he raised his hands and drew upon the sun.

The power surged and soared. He knew an instant of human guilt over his exultation and his raw joy. Then Hyam granted the Milantian component of his being full rein.

His outstretched arms melded the desert sun into a blinding arc, a river of light that he shot down the long central valley. The power illuminated every nook and shadow and fold.

Hyam saw the men caged in the central pillars shifting in their blissful sleep. He saw every witch cast awestruck looks his way. He saw the queen of Lystra fear for her crown and her domain.

Hyam lifted his gaze and stared into the ribbon of flame that joined him to the sun and the futility of time. Binding him to the quest and all the unknowns his days would soon reveal.

He looked back down the hidden realm. He knew the witches and their queen now understood that he held their future in his grasp. When he sensed they were truly terrified by his potential to destroy them, he released his bond to the sun.

The shadows returned, the hill resumed its timeless pose.

Then Hyam spoke a single word, one that carried the force of the power he now wielded. He caused the mountain and all its occupants to resonate in time to the future they shared. They had no choice. That was why Hyam had come. So they would understand that he had taken up the Ancients' mantle. And claimed it as his own.

Hyam shouted, "Treaty!"

Thomas Locke is a pseudonym for Davis Bunn, an award-winning novelist whose work has been published in twenty languages. He has sales in excess of seven million copies and has appeared on numerous national bestseller lists. His titles have been main or featured selections for every major US book club.

Davis serves as Writer-in-Residence at Regent's Park College, Oxford University, and has served as lecturer in Oxford's creative writing program. In 2011 his novel *Lion of Babylon* was named a Best Book of the Year by *Library Journal*. The sequel, *Rare Earth*, won Davis his fourth Christy Award for excellence in fiction in 2013. In 2014 he was granted the Lifetime Achievement Award by the Christy board of judges.

A film based upon *Emissary*, the first novel in the Legends of the Realm series, is now in development.

EXPLORE THE
LEGENDS OF THE REALM
BOOK 1

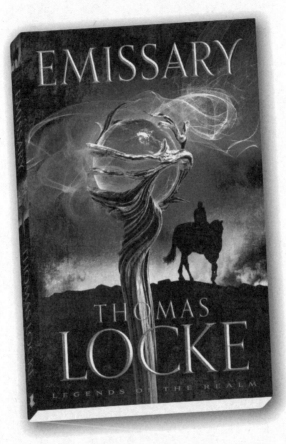

As a growing menace threatens the hard-won peace of the realm, one young man could stem the ominous tide . . . but only by turning away from everyone and everything he has ever known.
And facing dangers he cannot fathom.